I0679304

Economic Hitman

The Stopper Files, Volume 2

Eugene Lloyd MacRae

Published by CreateSpace, 2017.

This is a work of fiction. Similarities to real people, places, or events are entirely coincidental.

ECONOMIC HITMAN

First edition. September 5, 2017.

Copyright © 2017 Eugene Lloyd MacRae.

Written by Eugene Lloyd MacRae.

Chapter 1

MERLIN ARTHUR DRAGON never felt like a square peg in a round hole. He felt more like the square peg who never quite found the right square hole. But he had to admit being The Stopper was starting to cut a few edges. All he had to do was–

"So how much do you think my grandmother and I should charge to strip naked at the family reunion?"

Merlin's eyebrows moved close together, "Pardon?

Across the table was his apartment neighbor, Jaimee Hartman. She was a willowy beauty with jet black hair who had her elbows on the table, chin on her hands and her bright blue eyes sparkled, "I mean, we're in good shape. Right? Our bodies aren't gross or anything and we should be able to get–"

"Uh...one hundred dollars for both of you would sound right."

Jaimee wrinkled her nose at him.

"I'm sorry."

Jaimee took her elbows off the table and sat back, "I guess your mind is on your new job. I understand it." She gave him a shrug, "Maybe we should have waited for a month or so before we–"

Merlin shook his head, "No, no. I owed you for taking care of Jigs and I made a deal."

"Is that the only reason?"

Merlin didn't know what to say. He felt uncomfortable. He just wasn't good with people and really bad with women. But he liked Jaimee and was determined to improve. He leaned forward–

The cell phone on his belt vibrated.

And his countenance fell. His special cell phone was connected to Interpol's I-24/7, their secure global police network and he was on call 24/7 as well.

"Go ahead and check it."

"Sorry." He reached down and slipped the phone from the holder.

Jaimee picked up her glass of wine, "I understand. It's your job. That's how it works in a government town." She took a sip as she watched him over the rim of the crystal glass.

As he had suspected, Merlin saw a text message from Director Aubrey Laurent, the man who ran Interpol's National Central Bureau office here in Ottawa and Merlin's boss. It read; *You have a job. Return the message confirming you are in the air.*

"You have to go," Jaimee said, the look on her face showing she was resigned to the fact the dinner was over.

Uh...yeah. But we can finish first–"

Jaimee shook her head and gave him a tight smile as she reached down and picked up her purse from the floor at her feet, "No. I've seen that look on family and friends." She pushed her chair back before standing up and giving him a shrug, "Like I've said before, it's a government town." She put the purse strap over her shoulder, "Can you drop me off or should I take a cab?"

Merlin felt badly as he pulled several bills from his pocket and set them on the table, "No, I can take you back to the apartment."

"Mine or yours? Or would there be enough time for that?"

Blinking as he stood up, Merlin was again at a loss for words.

Jaimee smiled, "I love how you get so tongue tied. You're the epitome of the socially awkward sweetie-pie."

Merlin's brow furrowed as he stepped around the table and started walking towards the exit. He was just a step behind her as he asked, "Is that your way of making me feel better, Hartman?"

Turning and looking over her shoulder, Jaimee said, "No Dragon, it's just a little foreplay." She giggled at his expression and led the way outside to Merlin's car.

The ride back to the Stonecliffe Arms apartments was silent as Merlin's thoughts went back and forth from Jaimee to his task as The Stopper for Interpol. And as he walked with her up to his third-floor apartment and pulled his key out he realized he hadn't said a single thing to her. He stuck his key in the door as he glanced at her, "Sorry. I guess—"

"It's fine, Merlin. I know your thoughts are on your job."

As the lock clicked and turned, Merlin was amazed at how easily she read him. If he could only do the same for her...or for anyone else for that matter. His blue, woolly Chartreux cat was already padding across the floor from his window perch, "Hey, Jigs. Guess who's here?"

Jigs scooted past Merlin and leaped into Jaimee's arms.

She had already taken a half-step back in anticipation but he was still a handful and she laughed at his eagerness, "Hey, Jiggsy. It's me and you and a big chicken dinner tonight."

That comment made Merlin feel uncomfortable.

And Jaimee read him again. She held Jigs in her arms and leaned forward and gave Merlin a kiss on the cheek, "Don't worry so much about it, Merlin. "I'll take a rain-check on the dinner."

"Thanks. I guess I owe you two diners now."

"Yes, you do. And don't forget the musical at the National Arts Center."

"I won't. Thanks again for looking after Jigs." He took a step into the doorway of his apartment.

"Hey, Merlin?"

Merlin turned, "Yeah–?"

Jaimee was right there and leaned in again, taking him by surprise and giving him a light kiss on the lips, "You owed me the good night kiss as well."

As she pulled back, Merlin didn't know what to say.

Turning and walking away, she looked back over her shoulder, shooting him a sly smile, "And I intend to collect fully on *all* of your debts, Mr. Dragon."

Merlin watched her head for her apartment, already cuddling Jigs and talking to him. He realized he had a very good friend in his down-the-hall neighbor. And probably much more if he played his cards right. Merlin shook his head. He didn't even know how to shuffle the cards let alone play them in social settings. He pushed the thoughts away, closed the apartment door behind him and headed for his bedroom and the 'escape and survival kit' he had been working on after his first job.

The first thing Merlin did was take an undercover bracelet from on top of his dresser and put it around his wrist. A black, common-looking 'gummy bracelet' he could claim was given to him by his 'young daughter'. But this rubbery flexible bracelet was actually connected around his wrist by a handcuff key that was permanently built-in to one end of the bracelet.

Next he pulled his 'escape belt' from the top drawer, removed his belt and slipped this one through the loops. It was made of 1.5" nylon webbing, completely non-metallic and was part of the field kit for used by some of Canada's elite forces. The inside of the belt buckle itself held a non-metallic handcuff key and a ceramic razor blade. The inside of the belt webbing had dozens of elasticized compartments, ideal for stashing currency or other small items. When Laurent first gave it to him it had held three items. A non-metallic handcuff key, 4.5 feet of Kevlar survival cord and an American Liberty nickel. You turned the nickel to heads-up, slid a fingernail clockwise along the edge and a small blade of hardened stainless steel rotated out. All you had to do was slip it into your pocket and it was doubtful anyone patting you down would be concerned with a small coin, if they even detected it.

But Merlin had added several new items. There was the Escape Stick by Shomer-Tec that looked like a simple round rubber rod. Only 3 inches long and 3/8" around, it was actually a unique miniature escape tool. It held a rod saw that could cut metal, plastic, wood, and fibrous materials, another integrated handcuff key, and a toothed saw which also functioned as a shim pick for releasing zip-ties.

Breaking and entering had been another task he had needed to improve on. Even though he still had the bump key Laurent had given him that handled most cylinder locks, he decided he needed more. He took lock-picking lessons from a local locksmith who then sold him a 4-piece, titanium lock-picking kit that included Bogota triple, single and shallow hooks along with a basic tensioner. It easily fit inside one of the longer elasticized compartments.

The last item he had added was a fish hook utilizing a unique dual-action hooking mechanism. It was made of stainless steel with a corrosion resistant non-reflective black nickel finish and was only 1.25" long and 0.63" wide. He had no idea if he would ever use it. But he also had no idea where he would be sent to do a job or where he could end up since there were 190 member countries in Interpol.

Slipping his shoes off, Merlin pulled on the dress boots with the shoelaces that had blacked-brass tips. One tip on each lace was actually a boot-lace handcuff key. The design had been created for covert units of the U.S army that had a high possibility of being captured by the enemy during a mission.

Grabbing his Interpol badge, passport, credentials, the special cell phone, and his 9mm carbon fiber Beretta PX4 Storm Subcompact handgun, Merlin was now ready. He walked out of his apartment and downstairs to the limousine he knew would be waiting.

Chapter 2

MERLIN CLIMBED THE AIRSTAIRS and entered the Bombardier Global 8000, the ultra long-range business jet that was on constant standby for his use. He nodded a greeting at the pilot, Captain Charity Sherrell and the co-pilot, Captain Faith Saab, both members of the Canadian military. The two officers gave him nods in return as they set to the task of closing the airstairs and getting ready for take-off.

Sitting in one of the four plush seats, Merlin pulled his cell phone out and quickly composed a return text message.

The airstairs closed in place with a thick whump. As Saab headed for the cabin, she said, "Please buckle in, sir."

Merlin set his cell phone on the seat beside his thigh for a moment without sending the text and put the seat belt in place.

The TechX high bypass turbofan engines came to life in a deep, buzz-saw moan, sending the sense of immense power surging through the cabin.

After a quick and efficient run along the taxiway to the runway, power was applied.

Within a few moments, Merlin was pressed back in his seat and the business jet rose from the tarmac and soared into the sky. Before they even leveled out, Merlin sent the text reply that he was in the air. He put the cell back into the holder on his belt and as soon as the bell dinged and he could remove his seat belt, he was up and heading for the galley that was just through the doorway toward the back. He made a coffee and was headed back to his seat when his cell phone buzzed. The secure text message gave him the day's code for the electronic locker that was in the suite situated further back in the plane. Apparently, the cockpit was receiving their destination and Merlin headed to the suite to find out for himself.

He retrieved a thick envelope, a lightweight 4-wheeled carry-on with a Louis Vuitton logo and a garment bag. Returning to his seat, he set the piece of luggage on the floor, locking the wheels, and draped the garment bag over another seat. The envelope was labeled Economic Hit Man; Case #743312. Merlin pulled on his ear lobe several times, considering the words. He had never heard of an Economic Hit Man.

Opening the envelope and dumping the contents on the table, Merlin picked up a passport atop two sets of papers and flipped it open. There was a folded piece of paper inside and a bank card. He removed them, checking out the information on the passport first. It had his picture and showed he would be going as Kyle Charles Horton, an America born in Los Angeles, California. Unfolding the paper, Merlin saw the PIN number for the bank card. He memorized it and set the paper aside to burn later as he turned his attention to the first set papers. It three sheets of paper stapled together and gave an overview of what an Economic Hit Man did. He could be freelance and take jobs as they were offered. Or he could actually work for a government, a business corporation or a banking structure. Either way, the Economic Hit Man's job was to get developing countries to take out enormous loans, often based on fraudulent studies, to fund government projects such as infrastructure or other economic developments. Those projects would be performed by outside companies who would then have the cash in their pockets. The loans themselves would be so massive the countries could never pay them back. The Economic Hit Man would move in again and work out a deal, often under pressure from other governments to restructure the debt and often have the effected country's natural resources, such as oil auctioned, off to another business to help repay the debt. It was all designed to suck the wealth of a country into someone's greedy pockets and to continue to exert a vice-like grip to maintain that economic pressure and control.

And to top it off; if the leader of the country refused to cooperate or even refused to pay off the debt in order to get his country back on an even keel, the real meaning of the term 'hit man' would come into effect. Actual assassinations were performed if necessary.

Merlin shook his head. This was nearly unbelievable. He set the papers down and picked up the next set. His assignment was to prevent an Economic Hit Man from taking advantage of a newly formed African nation and the latest member of Interpol, the Democratic Republic of Vertrosé. Attached to the top of the first page was the picture of a jovial, middle-aged man with coffee-colored skin, white hair and a white goatee. This was the new President of the country, Adisa Balewa. Apparently, Balewa was in Monte Carlo (I'm going to Monte Carlo?) to meet bankers from the Banque Monégasque de la Finance, one of the largest banks in Monaco, to obtain a loan to develop his country. The ownership, or the board of directors if there was one, was hidden in a maze of interlocking shell companies.

Merlin flipped through the remaining pages, scanning the contents. His problem? There was no indication of *who* the Economic

Hit Man was. Was it one of these bankers? Was there more than one? As in a *team* of Economic Hit Men?

Setting the papers down, he checked inside the Louis Vuitton carry-on. The no-doubt-expensive luggage held a white shirt, a black, formal tie, several pairs of socks and underwear and an envelope containing $10,000 in US currency. Interesting. Next, he pulled the zipper down on the garment bag and looked inside. It was a tuxedo. The absurdity of it all struck him as odd. He was going to Monte Carlo and he would be dressed like a James Bond character. If there was anyone who felt less like James Bond, it was Merlin Arthur Dragon.

Chapter 3

THE BUSINESS JET came to a smooth landing at the Nice Côte d'Azur International Airport. The pilot had kept the Global 8000 at high-speed cruise, Mach 0.90, and had covered the 3,895 miles in just over eight hours. Merlin had grabbed a few hours sleep and was already up, sipping a coffee as he checked his watch. It showed 7 a.m. He adjusted it to the local time, 1 p.m. As the plane taxied to the private area, his cell phone buzzed and he checked the message. It held a link to added information on his assignment and he called it up. Interesting. Interpol had intercepted President Adisa Balewa's itinerary. Apparently, the man loved gambling and his itinerary included a stay and entertainment over the next three nights at the Monégasque Casino de Monte Carlo. Interpol felt that was the only public place where Merlin could get close to the man. The fact the itinerary had been 'intercepted' told Merlin someone besides the President was behind this assignment. The rest of the information outlined a back story that had been created for Kyle Horton by Interpol. His alter ego had served four years of active duty in the U.S. Army and was working for a private security organization, Mallard Security, in Los Angeles, California. The owner was Conrad Mallard and no doubt anyone checking out the company would find someone answering the necessary questions to preserve his cover. Horton's employment consisted of executive security jobs protecting celebrities, CEOs, CFOs and politicians at various functions. A reservation had been set up at the Casino de Monte Carlo under the premise he had just completed a job escorting a movie star and was taking a few days vacation before returning home. In addition, the technicians would be adding phone numbers, a few email addresses and a picture of his dog to his cell phone. The special features below that false information could only be accessed by Merlin as the advanced facial recognition software would recognize only him and unlock it. Everything sounded plausible- except for the dog. Jigs would not be happy.

As the jet stopped, Merlin unbuckled and stood up, getting ready to go.

"You look very sharp, sir."

Merlin saw Captain Saab coming from the front of the plane and he turned and lifted the toe of his right boot, "These don't look out of place, do they?" He had chosen to wear the dress boots with the blacked-brass-tipped shoelaces instead of the black oxford shoes that had come with the tux.

Saab's eyebrows drew together, "No, they look fine...?"

"They're not regular dress shoes. They have a handcuff key on the end of the laces."

"Oh." She shook her head, "I didn't realize...."

"So you're not just *saying* they look okay. Right? There's a method to my madness and I don't want to stick out like a sore thumb."

Saab shrugged, "No, more like a sore foot." When Merlin looked concerned she said, "I'm just kidding, sir. They look fine."

"Okay," Merlin said, still not totally convinced. His hand touched the escape belt. He had decided to wear that as well and...he pushed it from his mind. Since the Casino de Monte Carlo was the only public place where Merlin could get close to this President Balewa, he would just have to do his best. If anyone there noticed how he was dressed, he would easily pass as newly rich and a gambling rube. That last part was definitely true.

The airstairs were lowered and Merlin stepped outside and down to the tarmac with the carry-on in tow. The sun was warm and the air had a fragrance to it, one of limestone soil, piney shrubs, spicy herbs and sweet flowers. A Mercedes Benz was waiting for him, the keys in the ignition and he was soon driving for an exit gate. Director Laurent had told him his Interpol passport was special. That it was tied into the government offices of all 190 countries who were a part of Interpol and it gave him the ability to move freely across virtually every border in the world. This was his first trip outside of North America and he decided to test the theory. Handing it over to the customs guard, he was surprised at how fast it was accepted. After a few keystrokes into a computer, the guard waved him through without a word and he was on his way.

The drive along the coastal road was a brief diversion from his task at hand. Passing through the charming fishing village of Villefranche-Sur-Mer, he was delighted to see people hanging out their windows, talking to their neighbors and giving him a friendly wave as he drove by. The sparkling waters of the Mediterranean off the Saint-Jean-Cap-Ferrat peninsula were breath-taking and he slowed his pace, taking him nearly an hour to reach Monte Carlo. Merlin was hungry by this time and found a place called Chez Edgar where he sat down in the midst of boisterous English tourists who talked about the nearby sights and the shopping. He wasn't one for fancy dishes or seafood and he was delighted to find a hamburger and a local beer on the menu.

AS DARKNESS FELL MERLIN reached the hotel attached to the back of the Monégasque Casino de Monte Carlo. Lavish, expensive cars, with names liked Lamborghini, Ferrari and Bugatti that he had only heard about, lined the outside drop-off area, their deep throated engines punctuating the night air. Feeling out of place, he decided to park his own car and use a side entrance.

But the glittering, opulent décor in the lobby only served to reinforce the fact he was in a world completely foreign to the nondescript one he inhabited every day. He felt like every eye was on him, gauging whether he was worthy to be here as he checked in. Finally making it though the self imposed gauntlet, he dropped the Louis Vuitton carry-on in his room on the third floor. The room itself was decadent and the smell of rich, cut flowers invited him to rest after a long flight. But there was no time to relax and no time to waste. Slipping the envelope with the $10,000 US into an inside pocket of his jacket, he headed back downstairs to start his assignment.

But stepping into the casino itself was another shock to his system.

Chapter 4

TWO FAMOUS ACTORS Merlin recognized were casually walking through the casino crowd. A crowd that didn't pay them the slightest attention. He also spotted several well-known European politicians as well as a number of the glitterati he only recognized from some celebrity shows he had half-watched. Many of them were carrying long stem glasses and guzzling champagne. A number of sheiks in flowing garb were talking in a corner and several professional footballers from the French Ligue 1 and their wives or girlfriends mixed in with people who looked like they had more money than many countries. And not one of them paid the slightest attention to the amazing marble floor, gold pillars, glass chandeliers and high ceilings that were adorned in swirls of ivory and gold. The air itself had a clean linen scent to it and mixed with the scent of perfume or cologne of people passing by where he stood simply feeling so out of place..

Merlin shook his head as he walked to the casino cage where he exchanged some of his cash for casino chips. This 'James Bond' was definitely the square peg in a round hole and he wasn't sure if you could take the edges off fast enough to fit in. He bought just enough casino chips to fill both of his side pockets, deciding he had no interest in carrying around one of the trays. Keeping his hands free was a bigger priority.

Strolling back through the unique environment of sights and sounds of the casino, Merlin watched for his 'assignment'. It took nearly twenty minutes before he spotted President Adisa Balewa trying his luck at a crowded roulette wheel. Merlin watched for a few moments and actually liked the man from this distance. He was a stocky man, jovial and laughing in the midst of the cheers for his gambling wins and the groans following his losses. It didn't matter if he won or lost, he stayed the same. From time to time he talked to a tall woman who stood to his right side. She was in her 20s, extremely beautiful with mocha caramel skin and a tight and edgy corn-row hairstyle. Her red gown flowed over her shapely figure and there was enough cleavage showing for two women. Now he had only one problem. The fact he wasn't here to try and talk to the President out of selling his country down the river meant someone had already tried that. No. He was here to get close to the man in a personal sense to be able to figure out who the Economic Hit Man was and figure out how to intervene. But how could he get close?

Pulling some chips from his pocket to fit in, he moved around to an open spot on the other side of the table. Holding the chips in the fingers of both hands, he played with them as if he was contemplating a bet while he continued watching the President and those around him. As the wheel spun and clicked rapidly and the little ball bounced around, the players all cheered and called out their number.

A breathy, South-African voice spoke teasingly in his ear, "Are you just going to watch? Or will you play?"

Merlin looked to his left to see an ebony-skinned woman with bright cerulean-blue eyes looking at him with some amusement on her lips. The eye color against her dark skin startled him.

The woman cocked her head, "Do you even know how to play?"

Going with the truth, Merlin said, "Not really. I just thought it would be fun."

She gestured to the table, "You can simply choose a number and place a chip on it to bet where the little ball will fall. Do you have a favorite number?"

Merlin shook his head softly, "Not really."

Raising an eyebrow, the woman said, "Why don't you play 36? That's the size of my bust."

Blinking at the comment, Merlin's eyes dropped to that area of her black dress and lingered there for a second. "I think you're underestimating yourself," he said finally.

"Perhaps." She looked at him with a steady gaze, "We can check that out later, you and I. Does that sound like a plan? For now, you can place a bet and see if we win."

Merlin nodded as he considered how the red lipstick she wore emphasized her full lips. Then he turned and placed a chip on the number thirty-six. As the croupier spun the wheel, he glanced at the woman and then watched as people made last minute bets and began cheering the little ball as it began to rattle around. He froze in position as something was pressed against his side.

The woman's lips came closer to his ear, "Who are you?"

Merlin looked down cautiously to see what he expected; the business end of a polished and engraved, Sig Sauer P238 Micro-Compact handgun pressed against his tuxedo.

"Why don't we take a little walk you and I?"

Chapter 5

PUTTING A FIRM HAND on Merlin's arm, the woman urged him to move away from the other players who were still cheering on the little ball as it clinked its way around the spinning roulette wheel.

Merlin obliged her and allowed himself to be led away through the other patrons of the casino, the fingers of both hands still holding onto his poker chips. He had the sense of power in the woman's arms and he lowered his head slightly, his eyes sweeping over her body. She was athletic looking, the black dress hugging her body with no suggestion of an extra ounce of fat beyond the womanly curves. And the way she moved, almost gliding across the floor, told him she was very fit. Her calm manner, despite having a gun in his ribs, also told him she had some type of training. Or maybe she simply used to doing this. Whatever this was.

The woman led him away from the crowds and pressed a shoulder against a swinging door to take him into a hallway and the sounds of gambling muted as it closed behind them. Quickly escorting him part way down, she checked in both directions and then stepped a few feet away, facing Merlin with the gun held discreetly held just in front of the right hip. "Now answer my question. Who are you?"

Merlin looked into her now-flinty blue eyes as he slowly raised the poker chips to chest height, still held in the fingers of both hands. He tried to throw her off with some witty Bond like banter as he prepared to act, "Look. If this is a robbery, take the chips. But please leave my virginity. I've guarded it very carefully over the years and would hate to lose it in a hallway."

The woman's eyes narrowed and then she said firmly, "I wouldn't throw those chips if I were you. I'll just shoot you before they even reach me."

Merlin, kept his hands still, "Okay. I believe you." So much for channeling Bond.

She gestured with the weapon, "Put the chips in your pocket. Do it slowly, just use your fingers and keep your hands *outside* the pocket. Very good. Now turn and place your hands high on the wall. Nice and slow."

Merlin complied.

The woman moved in, holding the gun to the back of his head as she patted his jacket, rattling the clay poker chips in the process. She found his passport and I-24/7 cell phone, slipping both inside a side pocket on her dress before continuing the search. She found his weapon in the conceal holster in the small of his back and lifted his jacket as she pressed the gun against his skull. Pulling it out, she slipped it into her left pocket before continuing the pat down.

As she patted his butt, Merlin said over his shoulder, "Nice and firm, isn't it?"

The woman snaked her hand around and cupped his groin.

Merlin's body twitched lightly at the unexpected move.

The woman brought her lips closer to his ear, "Not firm *or* big enough, unfortunately."

"That hurts."

She quickly checked his legs and then stepped away again as she pulled his passport, flipped it open and glanced at it, "Who exactly are you...Mr. Kyle Charles Horton?"

Merlin took his hands off the wall and turned to face her, shrugging slightly, "Just a tourist, Miss...?"

The sounds of the casino reverberated for a moment as the door swung open behind Merlin and then muted again.

The woman glanced at whoever had come through the door and then gestured with the weapon, "Keep to the wall please, Mr. President."

Merlin was surprised when Adisa Balewa moved past him, trailed by the young woman. Balewa had the young woman stand behind him as he looked at Merlin, "I saw you come in here, Lesedi. Who is he?"

The woman held the passport out to the President, "An American. He was watching you too closely out there."

"I see."

As the passport was taken from her hand, the woman pulled Merlin's 9mm, carbon fiber Beretta PX4 Storm Subcompact handgun from her pocket and held it up as she kept an eye on Merlin, "And not an ordinary American. He had a very high-end, sophisticated weapon on him."

"Really?" Balewa held the passport over his shoulder to the young woman who took it. Balewa then took the Beretta in hand and examined it with curiosity. His eyes flicked to Merlin, "Are you an assassin?" He smiled a row of white teeth, "Or would you tell me that?"

Merlin now had to hope his cover story held up. He took in a deep breath and let it out slowly as if he was talking reluctantly, "I work for Mallard Security in L.A. That's Los Angles, California–"

"We know where that is," the woman said curtly.

"Of course. Anyway, I work as private security for clients who hire us for special functions such as movie premieres or–"

"Who is your client in Monte Carlo?"

Merlin gave her a nice-try-smile, "Sorry, but those kinds of details are confidential. All I can tell you is my celebrity client is headed home on her jet and I'm taking a few days vacation before I head back home." He shrugged again, "It's not every day you get a chance to be in Monte Carlo on somebody else's dime."

"If what you say is true, what would your interest be with me?" Balewa asked.

Merlin held his hands out, "I apologize for that. My boss is always encouraging us to look for new clients. That's one of the reasons he gave me a few days vacation and some cash to do a little gambling when my assignment here was finished. He figures a casino in Monte Carlo is a perfect place to find some high-end clients."

Balewa flashed a skeptical smile as he placed his hands on his chest, "And I look like a high-end client?"

"Well...let's just say you *stood out*. You were laughing and joking, win or lose...."

"Ahh, I understand. I looked like an easy mark to get some easy cash from."

"Something like that." Merlin quickly added, "No offense."

Balewa considered Merlin for a moment, looked again at the Beretta he still held before handing it back to the woman, "This is Lesedi Noxolo. She handles my security. I will leave your fate up to her." He then turned slightly and put a hand on the young woman behind him, saying to her, "We will go back to what we were doing."

The young woman took a few steps, handing the passport back to Noxolo as she eyed Merlin, "What will you do with him, Lesedi?"

"Does it matter?" Lesedi Noxolo asked without taking her eyes from Merlin.

"My father does not need those who are *too* paranoid around him. It is not good."

"Spoken like someone who has no idea what our country has gone through to achieve our independence. Or those who would remove it in a heartbeat."

Balewa put a second hand on his daughter's arm, patting it, "We must let Lesedi do her job, Aziza. She is protecting me, is she not?"

Aziza Balewa grudgingly admitted as much without saying a word and without taking her eyes from Merlin. Her father led her back to the door,

Merlin heard the sounds of the casino again and then it muted once more. He and Lesedi looked at each other. Merlin finally spoke, "We could go back to your room and do a strip search."

There was a sparkle in Lesedi's blue eyes, "And who are you suggestion should strip? Me? Or you?"

"I'm fine either way. A cavity search can be a beautiful thing between friends."

Chapter 6

LESEDI NOXOLO FINALLY LOWERED the Sig Sauer P238 handgun, extended her right foot slightly and the black dress parted half-way up a shapely thigh. She wore a lace thigh-holster and slipped the gun back in place.

"I wondered where you had that hidden. I have to say I love the choice of–"

"Making a comment about my clothing or my body will get you shot between the eyes." Noxolo stacked his passport with his cell phone and weapon, strode forward and held them out.

Merlin took the items and slipped them one by one back in place.

The door opened behind him and the sounds of gambling spilled into the hallway.

Turning, Merlin hustled to catch the door with the flat of his hand before it closed, following the woman back into the hustle and bustle of the casino.

Lesedi Noxolo stopped and looked for Balewa. The President had moved on to a Black jack table with his daughter in tow.

Merlin stood beside her, "Can I just say one thing?" He did it before she got her lips parted, "I was going to bet on number 40. I think that better fits the–"

"Just like a man," Noxolo interjected, "always inflating the actual size. Are you compensating for something, Mr. Horton? If that is your name."

"You doubt it?"

Noxolo smiled without looking at him, "Your accent has a Canadian inflection on certain words."

That deflated Merlin just a tad and he shook his head softly, "Is this where I say something like I'll have to kill you if you tell–"

"No. You could sleep with me."

Merlin felt his eyebrows draw together.

Noxolo turned and looked at him, "Or *threaten* to sleep with me. That would certainly scare me quiet."

Merlin let out a slow, silent breath, "I'm not sure I can keep up with you."

"If we do sleep together, Mr. Horton, you definitely won't be able to keep up with me."

Letting out a laugh, Merlin held his hands up in mock surrender.

For her part, Noxolo stayed silent despite her own amused grin and she turned her attention back to Balewa. He was talking and shaking hands with a middle-aged man who had joined him at the Black Jack table. A younger man, maybe in his late twenties or early thirties, stood just behind them. The daughter stood just behind her father.

Merlin eyed the two men. Both were dressed in tuxedos that looked even more expensive than the ones he had already seen. Both had hairstyles he could only describe as 'slicked back' and the younger one wore sunglasses. Sun glasses inside? He had the impression these two were the types you called high rollers. "Friends of the President?" he asked Noxolo.

Noxolo stayed mum for a moment. Her eye was on the younger man who was now talking with the daughter and eying her ample cleavage. A moment later Noxolo said, "Those men are why we are here, why we came to Monaco. The one talking to the President is Renée Bérubé, President of the Banque Monégasque de la Finance. The other one is James Pleasant. He works for Co-Fusion Consultants Ltd of New York. His title is Senior Development Economist."

Narrowing his eyes, Merlin took the men in again. A *banker* and an *economist* who gave him the impression they were *high rollers* didn't quite sit right. Plus a man around thirty who was in a 'senior' position? He was either brilliant or related to daddy. And brilliant wasn't the vibe he was giving off. A moment later, he realized Noxolo was looking at him again. "What?"

A sly smile crept across Noxolo's lips, "You see the same as I do. Correct?"

Merlin didn't answer. He looked back at the men.

"You are here on vacation, correct?"

"Uh...yeah–"

"You should answer quicker to avoid suspicion."

Merlin glanced at her, "I was just thinking–"

"I know."

"$10,000 a day."

"Pardon?

"U.S. dollars, of course," Noxolo said.

Merlin studied her for a moment.

"You said you are in private security. Yes?"

"Yes, but–"

"There is an old African proverb," she said. "Cross the river in a crowd and the crocodile won't eat you. I need a crowd, Mr. Horton.

You can work for me until we leave in three days." She looked back at the daughter, "I am going to have my hands full taking care of the President *and* the vultures who have already started descending on the daughter. Her mother died when she was young and she has no one to teach her about what men like that really want." She took a step, "Follow me and we can get started–"

"You do realize I work for Mallard Security?" Merlin wasn't sure if she was testing him. "I'll have to talk to my boss–"

Noxolo whirled around, "Screw your boss." She put a hand on his chest and almost purred, "And if you do this, maybe you can screw me as well."

Merlin looked into those blue eyes and said, "Something tells me you would be more woman than I can handle."

"True. But you are a man and you are intrigued by the possibility." She smiled, "Something tells me I can trust you." The smile fell, "And if I find I can't, I will kill you." The smile flashed again, "You will make $30,00 on your *vacation* and you have something to look forward to before we all leave."

"And what would that be?"

Noxolo winked.

Merlin looked over her shoulder, "So you want me to guard the daughter then–"

"O course not. Another African proverb says 'you don't leave the antelope to be cared for by the jackal.'"

Raising an eyebrow, Merlin said, "You just made that up."

"Of course. But it does fit nicely, doesn't it?

Chapter 7

MERLIN FOLLOWED NOXOLO through the crowd to the Black jack table where she leaned over President Balewa's shoulder and said something.

President Balewa looked at Merlin and then asked Noxolo, "Are you sure, Lesedi?"

"Yes." Noxolo set her hand on the daughter's arm, "And since Aziza expressed interest earlier in doing some shopping rather than be here, perhaps I can take her while you talk business?"

"Very, well, Lesedi, I trust you." Balewa looked at Merlin and gave him a nod.

The daughter looked miffed to be pulled away from the young man but Noxolo held firm.

As Noxolo turned to lead the daughter away, Merlin took a stride and put a hand on Noxolo's shoulder, stopping her setting his mouth close to her ear, "Why do I feel there is more to your concerns than just a young man looking to get lucky with Aziza?"

Noxolo considered him for a moment and then her shoulder sagged just slightly. Moving her head closer to his, she said, "You are right, Mr. Horton. Many African countries have a less than stellar reputation for subverting democratic rule. Apparently the new nation of Vertrosé is no different. After we landed, I received some disturbing information from the Under Secretary of the Army. He has learned that the opposition party has a plan to kidnap Aziza in order to force the President to step down and take power themselves. As I said, I am overwhelmed...."

Merlin glanced at the President, keeping his voice low, "I take it he doesn't know?"

Noxolo shook her head, "No, not yet. It is imperative for our young country to begin down the path of growth and prosperity. Whether we are here or back home in Ténemané, the threat will remain the same. For that reason, the Under Secretary and I both agree the President must concentrate on things he *can* do something about."

Aziza pouted and whined as she tried to pull away, "Can we please go?"

Noxolo had a touch of anger in her voice as she held firm, "Yes." Then she looked at Merlin with equal exasperation, "Is that enough of an explanation for you, Mr. Horton?"

Merlin decided not to push it. He was in a position that should have been impossible but here he was. "Do you have a cell phone number if I need to reach you?"

Holding her hand out, palm up, Noxolo said curtly, "Give me yours."

"How is taking mine...? Never mind." Merlin slipped his phone out and slapped it in her palm.

Using her thumb, Noxolo concentrated on entering something and then handed it back to Merlin, "You now have my number. Use it wisely."

Merlin slipped it back under his jacket, "Like arranging a midnight rendezvous with you?"

Aziza's eyebrows rose at the comment and she looked at Noxolo, wondering.

Scoffing, Noxolo pulled the young woman away from the Black jack table and through the crowd.

Merlin smiled as her shapely figure receded from view–

"Mr. Horton?"

Realizing Balewa had been talking to him, Merlin looked at the President, "Pardon?"

Balewa gave him a brief, knowing smile, "I asked if you would come with us."

Merlin's eyes narrowed.

"We are going to the bar to discuss some business. If you are to act as my security, I would presume you would be coming along?"

"Oh, right. Or course." He gestured with his hand for them to head for the bar.

"Shall we, gentlemen?" Balewa said to the two men.

The younger man nodded and he led the way through the crowd, the older man talking with Balewa as they followed.

Merlin brought up the rear, listening to try and pick up some information that might help him but not able to make out their conversation.

The bar itself was an amazing splash of glitz and glamour with sparkling glass and gold trim on mahogany tables and chairs. President Balewa sat down with the other two at a table in the corner.

Merlin took up a spot behind the President and just off his right shoulder, clasping his hands in front and taking the measure of several other people inside the bar.

As a server approached, Balewa glanced over his shoulder at Merlin and flashed him a toothy smile, "You are taking your job very seriously, Mr. Horton."

"I'm just afraid of Noxolo, that's all," Merlin said as he watched the other two men order drinks.

Balewa laughed and then placed his own order as well.

Merlin stood in his place, acting very much like the President's private security while listening very carefully for any tidbit of information he could glean from the conversation.

As the men talked, Pleasant spoke very much like an economist. He brought up various facts, figures, charts and studies on his cell phone from time to time as he discussed a variety of infrastructure development projects. They included developing the oil and gas fields, two dams and a new electrical grid to modernize the country's electrical energy generation, clean water and safe sanitation projects as well as new roads, railways and airports.

Balewa was interested in them all, but was especially interested in an information and communications technology project, hoping to bring his country into the age of the Internet.

Pleasant said he would put that on his list of projects to cost out and do some 'number crunching' for the President.

Bérubé the *banker* enthusiastically backed every project Pleasant discussed but was very interested in pushing the development of the oil and gas fields to the top of the to-do list, citing the need for the country to generate cash and keep the loan solvent. Once they did that, there was the possibility of increasing the loan down the road and speed up the other projects as the country grew richer.

And that's when the talk turned to the size of the loan available. Merlin was surprised to hear the talk of billions...with a B....in U.S. dollars.

An hour later, Pleasant and Bérubé stood up and shook hands with Balewa, making an appointment to meet at the bank at 10 a.m. the next morning and hammer out a final deal.

Balewa headed back to the casino with Merlin beside him. As they walked along the edge of the crowd, Balewa glanced at Merlin, "So what do you think, Mr. Horton?"

"Think about what?"

"About the arrangement Mr. Pleasant and Mr. Bérubé discussed with me to build Vertrosé's infrastructure?"

Merlin's brows knit together, "I don't think I'm the person to be asking about high finance."

"Why not?"

"I have no expertise in the area. Why would you even ask?"

"I was just wondering what your opinion was," Balewa said. He was silent for a moment as they walked and then he said, "There is an old African saying, the fool speaks, the wise man listens. Lesedi is so often my sounding board. I miss not having her here to talk about such an important matter to Vertrosé."

A smile crept across Merlin's lips, "She seems to like those sayings as well."

Balewa stopped walking and considered the roulette table again, watching the action and reaction of the players. His voice was low as he said, "I have a big decision to make, Mr. Horton. And it is said you only gamble with money you can afford to lose."

"Another one of those African sayings?"

"No. One of the Texas Holdem players I read about from your country. Amarillo Slim, maybe?"

Chapter 8

IT WAS NEARING midnight when Merlin made it back to his room. President Balewa had spent time at the roulette wheel and then at a card game called Trent et Quarante. Merlin wasn't a gambler and didn't understand much of the play, maintaining his role to the max and looking out for Balewa's welfare.

A knock came at his door.

Merlin wondered who it was. Maybe it was a mistake. But as he looked through the peephole, he knew it wasn't a mistake. But what it was he wasn't certain. He opened the door, left it open, turned and headed for the mini-bar. The door closed softly behind him as he took a cold bottle Kronenbourg 1664 beer from the lower shelf and popped the cap with the opener on the door, "Help yourself."

Lesedi Noxolo crossed the floor, "Thank you. And don't think this is some type of visit for any sexual purposes."

"Of course not," Merlin said as he sat on the rust-red sofa, "women always show up at my hotel room door at midnight looking for a beer."

Closing the mini-bar door and with a bottle of Paulaner Dunkel, a dark German beer in hand, Noxolo walked across the room, "I needed this but I want more than a drink from you."

She sat down in the large gold colored chair across from the sofa, crossed her legs and took a drink.

"That kind of talk is sending mixed messages." Merlin saw the tired expression on the woman's face, "Long night?"

Noxolo nodded as she pressed the beer against her cheek and closed her eyes for a moment. "Aziza is a fine young woman but she can be a handful. Under normal circumstances...."

"Adding in a plot to kidnap her makes even the slightest desire to let lose and have fun a stressful situation."

"Exactly." Noxolo took another drink and then tilted her head as she looked at Merlin, "And how did the meeting with Mr. Pleasant and Mr. Bérubé go for the President?"

"Okay, I guess. Why don't you ask him?"

Because I'm asking you. You were there, correct?"

"Are you wondering if I was shirking my duties?"

Noxolo gave him a long look, "Aziza is not the only one proving to be a handful."

"I have more than a handful."

Throwing her head back, Noxolo let out a laugh.

Merlin was surprised at how easily he conversed with this woman. Usually he felt awkward at making small talk.

Noxolo shook her head in amusement, "You definitely don't have a handful. I checked, remember, Mr. Horton?"

"That hurts."

"So you said before. And once again you will survive." She grew serious, "Did the President make a tentative deal while you were with him?"

"Why don't you ask him?"

"You already asked that question, Mr. Horton. I don't wish to disturb the President at this hour but I am anxious to know my country's future. So I ask you again, was a deal struck?"

Merlin shook his head, "No. They discussed numbers but they are meeting tomorrow morning at ten to make whatever deal they agree on."

"I see. What were the numbers discussed? How much were they willing to loan–?"

"The big number I remember hearing was $150 billion. That's billion with a capital B."

Noxolo's eyes blinked several times as she looked at him, "Are you sure?"

"Yes."

Looking down, Noxolo's eyes narrowed.

"You look like that's a bad number? I thought it was quite a bit on the high side. But then I'm used to mortgage numbers in the hundreds of *thousands*–"

"While we were preparing to come here, I discussed the matter with Professor Akintola. He is a retired economics professor who is part of the President's financial team. He told me experts on a country's development advocate a benchmark of 5-6 percent of Gross Domestic Product for infrastructure financing. If that country wishes to sustain growth, it should not be higher."

"Okay...?"

Noxolo looked up at him without raising her head, "Our GDP is $347 billion, one of the highest in all of Africa. According to you, our two friends have offered financing that is approaching the range of 50%...nearly *half* of our GDP."

Merlin's finger slid up the side of the beer bottle, the condensation forming a wet drop against his skin.

Her voice low, Noxolo asked, "What do you know, *Mr. Horton*?"

"Pardon?"

Noxolo blew a breath out in frustration, set the beer on the small table beside her and stood up, smoothing the wrinkles of out her black dress, "Can I expect you to accompany the President to the meeting tomorrow morning?"

Merlin looked up at her, giving a nod, "Yes, I can do that–"

Pulling something from the right pocket on her dress, Noxolo took a step and held it out, "Good. You can have this back."

Merlin's eyebrows rose and he remained silent for a few moments before he reached out and took what he knew was his Interpol passport.

Turning and heading for the door, Noxolo said, "I have no idea why you are here but it appears to be fortunate for me. It will allow me to guard Aziza again tomorrow." She opened the door and looked back, "You didn't think I hired you simply because you have an honest face, did you?"

As the door closed behind her, Merlin felt his body deflate. In his rush to get down to the casino and get into the meat of his assignment, he had forgotten to leave the Interpol passport in the safe as he had planned. To make matters worse, Noxolo had pulled both passports from his jacket and he hadn't even noticed. He had totally failed to maintain his undercover identity. Some Stopper he was.

Chapter 9

HIS COVER WAS BLOWN. Well, maybe half-blown. Lesedi Noxolo knew who he was but she had no idea why he was here in Monaco. Or did she? He couldn't afford to underestimate the woman. Also half-wondering if Director Laurent would have him shot, he decided he had to take a few chances to move his assignment along. He left his room and took the back way out to avoid anyone seeing him.

The night air was warm and he could hear the sounds of gambling coming from the casino as he headed for the Mercedes Benz. Once inside, he called up the GPS unit, asking for the address to the Banque Monégasque de la Finance. It appeared to be four blocks away and overlooking the water. A block or so and he would have walked, but he couldn't afford to get turned around like a bumbling tourist and lose valuable time he may not even have. Setting the address into the GPS, he began following the directions.

The streets were busy until he turned onto the street that took him to the bank. He made a slow pass of the address and even in the low street lights he was impressed. This wasn't like any bank he had ever seen. This building was a three-story, caramel colored structure with detailed cornices and a central, triangular staircase leading to an opulent front entrance. There were two sets of windows on either side of the stairs and the second and third-floor windows each had a fancy balcony. The whole thing smelled of money. Lots of it.

Parking just down the street, Merlin made his way back on the other side, watching for anyone nearby. Everything was quiet. There were no lights on in the bank. Discreetly looking back down the street to make sure no one was watching, Merlin then moved silently to the side of the building, squeezing past several trees until he stood under a second-floor balcony. He checked the building behind him. There were no windows that would allow someone to see him. The closest tree had a limb that was close enough to allow him to jump across to the balcony. Or *looked* to be close enough. A broken neck could prove that assumption wrong but it seemed like the best bet to get inside.

He moved along the side of the building until he found a one-foot square box on the wall that had a Téléphone label on it. Accessing one of the inside pockets on his 'escape' belt, he pulled out the American Liberty nickel. Turning the nickel to heads-up, he slid a fingernail clockwise along the edge until a small blade of hardened stainless steel rotated out. Using the blade he undid the two slotted screws holding the cover in place and accessed the internal box that held the phone wire and the Internet connection. He cut both and listened. No alarm sounded and he had to assume it was a silent alarm. Assume because for all he knew they had a wireless alarm. He would find out soon enough.

Putting the coin back inside the belt, he headed to the tree and started to climb. Did James Bond climb in a tuxedo? He couldn't remember him doing that in any of the books or movies. He must have. Reaching the limb, Merlin's heartbeat sped up as he held his arms out to maintain his balance and shuffled his feet sideways along the limb. Bouncing lightly to get some momentum from the branch, Merlin jumped and grab the railing. His momentum caused his body to bang against the lower edge of the balcony but he held firmly and pulled himself up and over the railing.

The balcony door was locked as he expected. He knelt and pulled the bump key from his belt. Sticking it into the cylindrical lock, he tapped the end with the butt of the gun. The door unlocked. Merlin slipped the key into his pocket but held the gun firmly in hand as he opened the door and listened. No sounds meant he was either okay or it was a silent alarm. If it was wireless, he should hear the police coming. He listened for ten minutes. So far, so good.

He slipped inside to find an empty room. Treading lightly, he moved across the carpeted floor to the door and cracked it open. The hallway outside the room was dark and silent. Holding the Beretta at his shoulder, Merlin slipped into the hallway and moved quietly to the next door. Putting his hand on the doorknob, he opened the door slowly and peeked inside. Closing it, he moved to the next door and peeked inside. He did the same at the next door and the next

Merlin felt confusion seep in as he closed the door and stood there for a moment, thinking.

Every room was empty.

No furniture, no paintings on the wall, nothing.

Treading cautiously to the stairs, Merlin looked down and listened.

Silence.

He looked up.

Deciding down would be better, Merlin stayed close to the wall to avoid squeaking any stair as he descended. At the bottom he found an open doorway leading to the main floor of the bank. This looked more like a bank but was a lot fancier than any he had ever been in. A large, open space was lavishly decorated and the marble walls gleamed even under the low light. Two luxurious lounge areas were set off to the sides and a series of gold stands with a red rope funneled the customers to a curved set of wickets.

Making his way across the marble floor he found a number of offices beyond the wickets. He quickly moved to the central one with the nameplate Renée Bérubé - Président on the door and slipped inside. The room was dominated by a large desk on the far side of the room. It sat in front of a window. Crossing the dark room, he made sure the drapes were closed and then moved back to the light switch and turned it on. The sofa, chairs, small tables, liquor cabinet and main desk were opulent and obviously very expensive, no doubt designed to impress anyone who came inside. He checked the desk drawers first. They weren't locked and that told him he wouldn't find much. But he looked anyway. As he closed the bottom drawer he turned his attention to a small, rich looking credenza sitting beside the desk. The double doors were locked. Time to test the lock-picking skills he had picked up from the locksmith back home. He lay the Beretta on the floor, pulled the 4-piece, titanium lock-picking kit from the inside of his belt and went to work. To his surprise the task was easy and he quickly had the credenza open. Inside were a line of thick binders with labels on the spine: l'Afrique du Sud, le Bélize, le Brésil, le Guatamala, la Guinée équatoriale, Haïti, le Libéria, le Pérou, le Sénégal – his hand went right to the last on the right and pulled out the one labeled le Vertrosé.

He flipped it open. Everything was in French but he could tell there was page after page on the country. It appeared to list all the various political figures, government officials, all the statistics on the population including the demographic breakdown of the people, including the tribal chiefs, as well as the details on the existing infrastructure of the county. One of the pages had a series of dollar values associated with various infrastructure programs. Two words were handwritten on the top right corner; 'approuvé Minard'. Merlin pulled his cell phone and made a note on the name before returning his attention to the rest of the binder.

Halfway back he found a number of pages with James Pleasant's name on them. They were in English and outlined the kind of projects he had heard presented to President Balewa. There were also pages from other employees of Co-Fusion Consultants Ltd. Nothing seemed to be a red flag. Although Merlin had to admit that his basic understanding of economics and statistics wouldn't let him see if anything stood out unless it smacked him in the face.

Then a page caught his eye. It was a report on something that hadn't been mentioned in the talk between Pleasant, Bérubé and President Balewa tonight. And something told Merlin it should have been part of the conversation. He wondered why not. Opening the rings, Merlin took the page out and used his cell phone to take images of the front and back of the page. Returning the page to the rings, he snapped them shut and then went back to the page with the handwritten 'approuvé Minard' on the top right corner and took an image of that as well. Setting the binder back in place and closing the doors, Merlin then composed a quick message asking for information on Renée Bérubé, James Pleasant and the reference to the Minard name. Attaching the images to the request, he sent it off to Interpol.

All the way back out and across from the balcony to the tree and down to the ground again, something nagged at the back of Merlin's mind. Just before getting into the Mercedes, he looked back at the building. There was something odd about the 'bank' but he couldn't put a finger on what it was that bothered him.

Chapter 10

A S SOON AS the morning light speared through the gauzy sheers, Merlin showered, donned a fluffy hotel robe and called for a room-service breakfast. Just before he was finished his last buttery croissant his I-24/7 cell phone, sitting on the table, buzzed and rattled.

Merlin grabbed the cell phone, eager to get additional information before he had to accompany President Balewa to the meeting. It held basic reports on the people he had asked about. Renée Bérubé was born in Paris, France and was a graduate of école des Hautes Etudes Commerciales de Paris, a European business school located in the southern suburbs of Paris, France. He had worked for Banque de Baecque Beau and AXA Bank Europe before joining the Banque Monégasque de la Finance. He was not married and there was little other information. There were no red flags.

James Pleasant was born in Ithaca, New York, had attended La-Guardia Community College in New York and graduated with a degree in accounting. There was absolutely no other information in the dossier they held on him.

Merlin felt a bit deflated with the lack of information that could help him until he realized he had some good news.

The name Minard had given Interpol a thread to pull on and they were able to uncover the man behind the Banque Monégasque de la Finance - no, make that *two* men. Davet Minard and Dirk VanDaele were partners and the owners of the bank.

Merlin scrolled through the details; Davet Minard was born in Montpellier, France, he had an MBA from the London School of Business and Finance. His partner Dirk VanDaele was born in some place called Harderwijk in the Netherlands. He also had an MBA from the same London school. That would probably explain how they had met and formed a partnership.

Merlin's thoughts went to the handwritten 'approuvé Minard' on the series of dollar values associated with the various infrastructure programs. They no doubt pertained to the amounts the bank was willing to loan. The fact Minard - indeed, both men - had graduate degrees from a school for business and finance meant they hadn't made an error in offering a loan that Noxolo said was nearly half her country's GDP. It was a loan that could potentially cripple Vertrosé financially and these men would know that.

Since James Pleasant had an accounting degree under his belt, Merlin was now certain he was the Economic Hit Man working on behalf of these two men.

The final message was an explanation of the page he had photographed from the binder. Interpol had reached out behind the scenes to a few members of the Vertrosé government but could find no evidence the report it contained had ever been ordered by them and no indication they even knew about it. The finding was tentative but it was all he had to go on. What did it mean and how could he use it?

When it was time to go, Merlin realized he would have to wear the wrinkled tuxedo again. He shook his head. He had left the clothes he wore on the flight over in the plane's suite when he had changed into the tux. And he had forgotten to get another suit or jacket or something else to wear once he got here. There was no time to do it now. He would just have to stand out as a 'James Bond' security man.

MERLIN FOLLOWED PRESIDENT Balewa (now wearing a standard business suit) up the central staircase and into the Banque Monégasque de la Finance. Inside the atmosphere was hushed and the air smelled of rosemary and peppermint. That wasn't present last night. A number of well dressed people were sitting in the two luxurious lounge areas and a number of customers were lined up along the red rope that led to the curved set of wickets. A woman with a gold purse and wearing sunglasses was at the back of the line and she turned and glanced at him and the President for a brief moment and then went back to waiting her turn. Merlin saw Balewa glance in her direction, his eyes talking in her shapely form. A number of young women were behind the wickets, serving customers, and the other desks had someone sitting behind them, engrossed in whatever banking work they were engaged in.

A very attractive, dark-haired woman in a blue blouse and matching pencil skirt appeared from the area of the offices, "Président Balewa?"

"Yes?"

She held out an elegant hand, "I am Evonne Tremont, Superviseur des Opérations. Welcome to La Banque Monégasque de la Finance."

Balewa shook her hand, a toothy grin crossing his face as he gave her a half bow, "I am very happy to make your acquaintance and I am very happy to be here."

Tremont gave Merlin a quick once over before dismissing him and then extended her hand in the direction of the offices, "Monsieur Bérubé is waiting in his office for you."

As she led the way, the tight pencil dress caused her shoes to almost cross over each other and gave her an exaggerated, slinky walk.

Glancing back at Merlin, Balewa's eyes shone with delight.

Merlin gave him a slight grin of understanding and then glanced toward a pretty young woman in a tight yellow dress at the closest wicket.

Balewa gave her a quick look over as well and then turned his attention back to Tremont's figure as he followed her to Bérubé's office and inside.

Merlin's eyes swept over the staff and the customers again, double-checking to make sure everything was okay before he followed the President inside. Two men were off to the left. They had ear pieces which told Merlin they were security of some sort. And they were in a very serious discussion, gesturing from time to time towards the second floor. One of the men turned and looked at Merlin, giving him a fixed look. Merlin could tell the man would be a tough opponent in a fight. He ignored the attempt at intimidation and entered the office to find Bérubé and Pleasant were already greeting Balewa.

Tremont gave Merlin the once over again and then left, pulling the door closed behind her.

Bérubé went around behind the desk and Pleasant indicated for Balewa to take a seat in one of the two plush chairs on this side of the desk. Pleasant took a seat in the other and the meeting was underway.

To Merlin, everything sounded very much like the night before, with Pleasant once again discussing the various infrastructure projects and Bérubé pushing for his agenda. It became clear how much of the loan would be funneled to associates of the bank. Co-Fusion Consultants Ltd of New York would provide the engineers to do the planning for each project. Spate Construction Group of New Jersey would begin the first project of building the roads and airports that would allow the other projects to move faster. And to Balewa's delight, a project to modernize the communications and Internet capabilities would also begin, handled by IntraCom Technology Corporation out of Florida.

When Balewa suggested he would prefer to tender bids for the projects, Bérubé said the loan was contingent on using the companies Co-Fusion Consultants was working with. There was no way it could be done otherwise. And he insisted the developments of the oil and gas fields were to come next, before clean water and sanitation.

Balewa relented, eager to get everything done and put in place.

Merlin felt uneasy about the page he had seen in the binder. He leaned and said, "President Balewa, excuse me for a moment, I'll be right back."

Balewa gave him a nod but didn't seem too happy to be interrupted.

Merlin stepped out of the office and made a call. And a big decision. He wondered again if the Director would have him shot.

Chapter 11

MERLIN DIALED THE number and listened as the phone on the other end rang. He glanced to the right and saw the two security men further away, talking with a man in a suit. Beside the man in the suit was another man dressed in blue pants, a white shirt with black lettering and a black cap with a red hat band. He was a member of the Direction de la Sûreté Publique - the Monaco police. Merlin had the feeling they were talking about the wires he had cut last night. His mind wandered to the fingerprints he had no doubt left behind. But since there wasn't anything missing or out of place, he doubted they would go to the trouble of processing the entire place to try and figure out–

His thoughts were interrupted as a voice answered on the other end of the call, "Hello?"

Merlin turned away from the police and lowered his voice, "Lesedi Noxolo?"

"Of course. Who else would have my phone? And what do you want?"

"Was I right about the size of the bet I should place?"

"What?"

"Never mind. I need you to trust me. Can you do that?" Merlin asked.

"Is that not a stupid question since I already have you guarding the President of my country?"

"Okay. Fair enough. I'm sending you something." Merlin looked at the phone, ignoring the faint sound of Noxolo's complaining voice as he called up the images he had taken. He sent them to Noxolo's phone and then spoke to her again, interrupting a few choice words on her end, "Take a look at what I sent you."

"What are you talking about–?"

"Just shut up and look at what I sent you."

Noxolo's voice rose an octave, "You tell me to shut up?

"Yes. You can spank me later. Can you read French?"

"Of course," an irritated Noxolo snapped. "My country was a former French colony and everyone learned French in school."

"Then hurry up and take a look at what I sent you. We don't have much time. If I'm right...just look."

There was silence on the other end.

Merlin listened and waited. He turned slightly to look at the security men and the police again. Only one of the security men was there, watching him with a look bordering on suspicion. Merlin wondered just how guilty he looked. This undercover thing was a tough nut to crack–

"Where did you get this? Is this for real?"

Merlin tried to lower his voice more, "Is it what I think it is?"

"*Where* did you get this?"

"Let's just say someone found it in a binder on Vertrosé that Bérubé had under lock and key."

"But how–"

"I asked you to trust me."

Noxolo's voice lowered like she was trying to avoid someone hearing on her end, "Who are you?"

"I think you already know that. Now...the images...?"

There was a long silence. And then Noxolo said, "It appears someone has prepared a report on deposits of high-grade rare-earths in my country."

"I take it you didn't know about this?"

"No. The bottom line says these deposits are worth $129 Billion in American dollars."

"At a minimum," Merlin said. "I looked up some of the symbols and names of the deposits. I'd never heard of them before but I can remember the weird names. Neodymium, Europium, Terbium, Dysprosium, Yttrium...all chemical elements critical to a number of high-tech applications around the world. When you couple the scarcity of these elements with the high demand around the world...."

Noxolo's voice was just above a whisper, "This would make my country very wealthy."

"In yesterday's meeting and the one today, Bérubé only discussed the development of the oil and gas fields. There was never any mention of these deposits. Does President Balewa know about them?"

There was another long silence and then Noxolo said, "Not that I am aware of. I am very close to him. And I'm sure Professor Akintola would have known but he never said anything about it in our discussion. And something this important...."

"Then I would say your country is being set up. I need you to tell your President about this–"

"Me?" There was anger in Noxolo's voice, "You are right there. *You* need to tell him now–"

"No. It has to come from someone he trusts and that's you. Make up what you're going to say because I'm heading back into

Bérubé's office before your President signs a loan you already know will bankrupt your country." Merlin turned and headed for the office door.

"But this doesn't make any sense. And if these deposits are real then out GDP will be much higher–"

"I asked you to trust me. Now make up a story on how you got this if you have to, but I'm going to tell him I just got them from you to show him." He cut her off as he opened the door, "No more talk." Merlin stepped inside to see Bérubé extending a set of papers across the desk.

President Balewa reached out and took them in hand, sitting back in his chair.

Bérubé pulled a gold pen from his shirt pocket, clicking it as he gave Pleasant a sly grin.

Merlin set his hand on Balewa's shoulder and extended his hand with the phone, "You need to take this."

Balewa moved his head back, looking up at Merlin like he was a crazy man. He opened his mouth, an angry expression on his face–

"Believe me, Mr. President, you *need* to take this."

It took a moment before Balewa snatched the phone from his hand and stuck it to his ear, "Who is this?" He blinked and then his countenance turned angry, "Why are you–?"

Merlin heard Noxolo's voice rise several decibels.

Balewa was shocked at her tone but looked up at Merlin, "I am to look at what?"

Taking the phone in hand, Merlin called up the image again, handing the phone back to the President.

"Is there something wrong?" Bérubé asked.

Merlin bent over and used his fingers to zoom in on the image. He could hear Noxolo's voice talking fast and hard, trying to convince the head of her country.

Balewa had a look of disbelief on his face and then out the phone to his ear, "Where did you say you got this?" He listened. "But I must know if I am too – very well." He handed the phone back to Merlin, stood up and buttoned his suit jacket.

Bérubé held his hands out, "Where are you going, Mr. President? We have a deal–"

"I will be back in the morning," Balewa said. "I have a private matter to take care of."

Merlin ignored the back and forth between the three men as he said low into the phone, "We're leaving. Okay, I will."

Balewa turned and headed for the door, hissing to Merlin, "Take me to her. Now!"

"Yes, sir." As Merlin led the angry politician across the floor to the front entrance his eyes swept their surroundings and he saw something odd. And now he knew what else was bothering him last night.

Chapter 12

NOXOLO HAD TOLD Merlin she would meet them back at the hotel and she was pacing in Balewa's suite as they entered. The daughter was nowhere to be seen.

Balewa bellowed as he crossed the room, "Lesedi, what is the meaning of your refusal to tell me who sent you that information?"

"As I told you, Mr. President, it was sent to me by someone who wishes to remain anonymous. He only wanted to–"

"So it is a *he* then. At least you tell me that much," Balewa yelled. "Why would you withhold this information from me? Is it authentic?"

"Yes–"

"And how do you know that?"

Noxolo opened her mouth and closed it.

Merlin realized he had put her in a difficult spot. But he admired how she drew herself up, without so much as a glance toward him.

"Mr. President...Adisa," Noxolo said, "please allow me to–"

"Do *not* use my first name."

Noxolo looked hurt, "But...I've done so before...we have been so close–"

"Apparently too close," Balewa intoned. "I have looked upon you as a friend. But now you feel you are my equal. That you can withhold vital information from *your President*."

"I am sorry you feel that way...Mr. President. But what is done is done and we must deal with this information—"

"We?" Balewa thundered. "There is no *we*. In fact, I think it is imperative that I find another security officer."

The air seemed to flow from Noxolo, the pain evident in her voice, "I understand. I...." Her eyes were downcast as her head nodded faintly several times.

Merlin made another decision. Still wearing the tuxedo he had arrived in, he slipped his hand into his inner pocket and pulled one of his passports. He took several steps across the room to stand beside Balewa and held it out in front of the man.

Balewa looked down and his voice sounded irritated, "What are you doing? And why are you still here? Perhaps you should leave as well since it was Lesedi Noxolo—"

"You wanted answers," Merlin said, "so look at it."

His eyebrows knit together as Balewa looked down at the blue passport. And then his eyes blinked in surprise. He looked at Noxolo.

For her part, Noxolo was surprised as she looked from Balewa to Merlin and back again.

Balewa slowly took the passport in hand and looked at the title written in block letters, "Interpol?" He flipped open the passport and his eyebrows rose and then the brows drew together again, "Merlin Arthur Dragon?" He glanced at Merlin and then at Noxolo again, "You knew about this Lesedi—?"

"Yes," Merlin said. "She found that passport on me when she took me into that hallway. That's why she hired me to help guard you. She knew who I was."

Balewa shook his head softly, "But why didn't you tell me about this as well, Lesedi?"

"Because she knew I was working undercover," Merlin told him.

"Undercover?"

Merlin took the passport back and slipped it into his pocket, his own voice slightly bitter, "Yeah. The truth is I'm not supposed to exist."

"I don't understand."

Merlin let out a slow breath and then walked across the room to the mini-fridge where he pulled out a small bottle of hard liquor. There was silence in the room as the other two watched him pour it into a glass. He screwed the top off a bottle of water and added some to the glass, "Let's just say I handle special assignments for Interpol."

"What do you mean special assignments?" Balewa asked.

Merlin tilted his head back and emptied the glass before setting it down with a heavy clunk, "The kind I'm not supposed to talk about." He turned and looked at Balewa, "I'm the one who asked Lesedi to tell you about that report. That's why I left the room at the bank. To call her."

Balewa shook his head in confusion, "I don't understand. Where did you get it? And why didn't you just–?"

"Because you were about to sign your country down the road and you wouldn't have believed me." The President opened his mouth but Merlin pushed on, "There is a credenza on the right side of Renée Bérubé's desk. Inside are a series of binders on different countries, including yours. That's where I found that report."

"But how did you get it–?"

"How do you think?"

Balewa closed his mouth and glanced at Noxolo for a moment. Then he asked Merlin in a low voice, "But...how did you know about this report–?"

"I didn't," Merlin said. "I found it, if you know what I mean?"

Balewa opened his mouth.

"But none of that matters. You're focusing on the wrong thing here, Mr. President."

"What do you mean?"

"Don't you find it strange that Bérubé had this report in his files? And yet, when he and Pleasant talked to you in that bar about all of the wealth your country has, about developing the oil and gas...there was *no* mention of the riches you have in rare earths? And still nothing about it in Bérubé's office when you were about to sign those papers?"

The full impact of the statement struck Balewa and his voice was weak, "But why would they...?"

"Mr. President, do you remember when we first went into the bank for the meeting? There was a woman with a gold purse in the lineup. She had on dark sunglasses and looked at us...?"

Balewa's eyes narrowed and he nodded his head.

"And the young woman in the tight yellow dress at the closest wicket?"

"Yes, but...?"

"They were still there...in the same *exact* spot when we left. In fact, not one of the *customers* had moved in all the time we were in the meeting."

It finally dawned on Balewa, "You are right. Now that you mention it...."

"The whole bank thing is a front. When I visited Bérubé's office and found that report, I also found the second floor was entirely *empty*. Not a single stick of furniture in any of the rooms. And when I explored the main floor, there wasn't any indication of a vault either."

"But why–?"

"Because James Pleasant is an Economic Hit Man."

Balewa and Balewa exchanged glances.

Merlin could see the obvious confusion in their eyes and he explained the concept. The two listened in stunned silence. At the end, Merlin said, "When I told Lesedi about the size of the loan they were offering you, she became alarmed. She told me she had discussed the matter with an old economics professor who is part of your financial team–"

Balewa looked at Noxolo, "Professor Akintola?"

Noxolo gave him a faint nod, still trying to digest all the information..

"Your professor said the loan shouldn't be more than 5-6 percent of your Gross Domestic Product for infrastructure financing. Yet they were offering nearly 50%–"

Balewa sagged and Noxolo moved to grab one of his arms. She helped him sit down on a large sofa where he shook his head softly, "You are right. I remember him telling me the same...."

As Balewa sat woodenly, Noxolo moved across the room and grabbed a bottle of water and poured some in a glass. As she headed back to Balewa's side to give him the glass, she glanced at Merlin, "How would they even know about these rare earths if we don't?"

Merlin shrugged, "I'm not sure. But when a bank is going to give someone a house loan, they send an appraiser to evaluate the property. I'm sure they would have done the same in this case–"

Balewa's voice was weak as he took the glass from Noxolo, "Mr. Pleasant had his company send people in to gather information on our infrastructure and natural resources."

Noxolo nodded, more to herself, as she said, "Yes, I remember the Professor mentioning the extensive, up-to-date evaluations and reports they had done that he had looked over. But—"

"There you go," Merlin said. "It wouldn't take much to have extra teams of geologists sent in that you wouldn't even notice. And more than likely they started working with you because they had an idea of what they might find. Maybe they used satellite images to start with, I have no idea. But apparently, these rare-earth elements are often found together. So once they did find something, they could do a series of assays to see what they had, and to evaluate if they had concentrations high enough for economical extraction. Once they knew what you had, they simply put it in their back pocket and moved in for the kill."

Balewa winced at that comment as he stared ahead, stroking his white goatee. Then looked up at Merlin and Noxolo, his eyes filled with self recrimination, "I was so anxious to move our country ahead that I didn't take my time to think things through properly."

"Everything was designed to keep you thinking positive in every aspect," Merlin said. "Every time Pleasant talked about something he played it up, exaggerating the benefits every project would have on your country, how every aspect of the loan would improve life for your countrymen. And I wouldn't doubt those evaluations and reports were ginned up enough to make you feel you were underestimating your own potential. A few billion extra here or there can add up and put stars in your eyes. Keep in mind these men are professional con men, working on a world-wide stage. You didn't have much of a chance."

"That is kind of you to say so but...." He looked up at Noxolo with sorrow in his eyes, "If it wasn't for you, Lesedi...."

"No," Noxolo said firmly. "If it wasn't for Mr. Dragon–"

Merlin pointed a finger at her, giving her a brief smile, "Forget my name. Develop amnesia. Never mention it again." He turned and headed for the door, "In fact, both of you should forget I ever existed."

Balewa jumped up from the sofa, "But Mr. Dragon, we owe you a great deal–"

Opening the door, Merlin looked back, "The Democratic Republic of Vertrosé in now a member country of Interpol, correct?"

"Yes."

"All part of the service. And don't tell anyone where you got that report either." Closing the door behind him, Merlin headed for his room. The problem was solved. But only *one* of the problems. Because if Merlin understood how this worked, he had thwarted the Economic Hit Man. Now it was possible the situation was turned over to a *real* Hit Man. Not the kind that robbed you of your money. The kind who robbed you of your life.

Chapter 13

ALL THE WAY BACK to the airplane, Merlin wondered if he should have told Noxolo and Balewa about the potential of a hit man. No, she would be watching for any dangers to the President anyway. And she already had the known threat of Aziza Balewa being kidnapped on her plate. She couldn't afford to have her attention split unless he knew for sure–

His cell phone buzzed and rattled in the cup holder where he had set it. Merlin had already let Laurent know that Balewa had gotten his hands on the report on the deposits of rare earth in his country through a third party - which was true - that the loan had been rejected and that the President was much more aware of what his country needed and would be more cautious in the future. Pulling over to the side of the road to check on what the message it held for him, Merlin wondered if he would be ordered home or sent on a new assignment.

As his eyes ran down the text his blood ran cold.

Interpol had been able to pull on a few more threads on the two men behind the Banque Monégasque de la Finance. Davet Minard was the owner of DVM International. DVM was a Private Military Contractor registered in Gibraltar and said to employ former rebel soldiers from African nations as well as those from

South America. Already battle hardened in local civil wars, the men from these areas tended to work cheap, giving Minard a wide profit margin when he rented them out as mercenaries. For his part, Dirk VanDaele was a global arms dealer who owned Schorpioen Internationale in the Netherlands. Apparently the Netherlands was a top tax haven for many of the world's biggest arms dealers - who knew? - and VanDaele worked with them all as the middle man, taking much of the risk. His global dealings involved everything you wanted to carry out a war, ranging from small arms and light weapons (and their parts, accessories, and bullets) to machine guns, mortars, rocket-propelled grenades, flamethrowers, grenade launchers, anti-tank weapons, tanks, fighter planes and ballistic missiles. Both men were suspected of supplying the funds to finance terrorism and create instability around the world to create work and sales for their companies.

Merlin could see all the connections. Using the Banque Monégasque de la Finance they could take over the wealth of a nation. First, they funded the infrastructure projects and the money probably went back into their pockets through the companies doing all the work. Then the country goes bankrupt and they move in with the companies who take over the oil or gas fields or anything else of value. If the leader of the country won't do business with them, they assassinate that leader or back another party in a coup or civil war that they fund and supply the weapons. It didn't matter - in war or peace - they win.

Now Merlin not only had to wonder about a Hit Man stalking the President, he had to imagine a coup being backed by Minard and VanDaele or a civil war being started. Either way they could still get what they wanted from Vertrosé.

There was no indication from Interpol on what he was expected to do.

But he was The Stopper.

It was his decision.

But what *could* he do?

Chapter 14

THE BUSINESS JET dropped from the azure skies over Ténemané, the capital city of the Democratic Republic of Vertrosé. A gleaming, modern city lay along the ocean to the west while a swath of slums lay nestled against the jungle to the east. It was the yin and yang of a growing African city, the difficult past struggling to catch up with the promise of the future.

He was here because his what-to-do-next concern had been decided by a piece of information from Director Laurent. The Director had pulled some strings to get a European Investigation Order, allowing Interpol to start monitoring the men Merlin had sent them information on, and it turned out to be fortuitous.

James Pleasant had booked a flight here last night, apparently following President Balewa back home. What was Pleasant doing here? Merlin had no idea if Balewa had talked to Pleasant and Bérubé after the meeting had collapsed. Or if the two knew Balewa had the report on the rare earth deposits. Was Pleasant going to try and convince the President that it was still in his best interest to accept the loan? Or was he here to be a different kind of hit man?

As soon as the jet touched down, Merlin was up and ready. He would be arriving ahead of Pleasant but wanted to be in place to watch him once he landed.

"Do you have any idea how long you will be, sir?"

Merlin turned to see the co-pilot, Captain Faith Saab holding the back of a seat to balance herself as the plane turned towards the customs office designated for private airplanes. "Not really."

Saab nodded, "Of course. It's just that we're going to have to bring more bottled water onboard. The weather report says it's going to be well over a hundred degrees for the next week or so. It's going to be hot waiting on the tarmac, that's for sure."

"Do you want me to find a couple of studs to come on board to fan you and Captain Sherrell while I'm gone?"

Saab wrinkled her nose, "If the studs you find only perform that service, forget it."

Merlin smiled, "I'll see what else I can find."

The plane rocked slightly as it came to a full stop and the airstairs began to descend.

"Stay safe out there, sir," Saab said.

As a blast of hot African air hit Merlin and he tugged at the collar of his cotton shirt, "I intend to do that Captain. Thanks." As soon as he started down the steps he could feel the intense heat rising from the black tarmac. He had purchased the shirt and light cotton pants in a small kiosk at the Nice Côte d'Azur International Airport before they left and he was now glad he had anticipated the climate here to be brutal. Sweat began to trickle down his back underneath the holster holding his carbon fiber Beretta.

In a hurry again, Merlin used the Interpol passport to pass through customs quickly and into the terminal itself. It was a new and gleaming facility and a hubbub of activity. Merlin heard English, French, German and several languages he couldn't place as he passed through the crowds. The signs were easy to follow and he was in the waiting area for Pleasant's flight a full hour before it was scheduled to land. Grabbing a coffee from a vendor, he sat where he could watch the large screen announcing the departures and arrivals as well as the arrival gate itself. He didn't want to accidentally miss the man going through.

But as the time neared for the flight to land, Merlin suddenly realized Pleasant might spot him and recognize him from Monte Carlo. Cursing his stupidity, Merlin scrambled to find a hat. He found a lightweight, natural colored straw hat with a 14" brim that would do the job, bought it and was back in time to see passengers already coming through the arrival gate. The place was busy with people greeting loved ones and friends and it was time for more cursing under his breath and his heart beat with the fear he had missed – no, there he was. Merlin spotted the man's head thirty away and moving through the crowd. Same black slicked-back hair and the black sunglasses.

Squeezing his way through people and apologizing to everyone he jostled, Merlin did his best to catch up. It was like a salmon swimming upstream and he lost ground as the man up ahead seemed to part the crowd like the Red Sea.

And then Pleasant seemed to disappear.

Merlin pushed his way harder, ignoring the protests now as he kept his eyes moving, looking for the man with the high roller look. Spotting a down escalator off to the right, Merlin swam his way towards it, using his arms to part the crowd. He arrived at the top of the stairs in time to see Pleasant step off at the bottom and turned to the right. Taking the escalator stairs two at a time, Merlin slipped past several other riders and used the escalator's momentum to jump down the last three steps. He spotted Pleasant just going out one of the exit doors and joined the crowd heading that way. The African heat hit like a blast furnace as Merlin emerged from the terminal and his lungs protested as they sucked in diesel fumes and black exhaust smoke from the cars idling nearby along the curb of the access road.

Merlin scanned the crowd and the cars–there he was. Pleasant was just getting into the back seat of a stretch limousine parked along the curb. What surprised Merlin was this wasn't just a fancy cab ride somewhere. This was more like an official pick up of a dignitary. The driver standing on the far side of the limo was a dusky-skinned white man who was dressed in army fatigues with a woodland pattern, a green colored beret and looked hard core and menacing. The black man walking around the end of the limo wore a lightweight tan-colored suit but looked equally hardcore.

Fumbling quickly for his cell phone, Merlin was able to get it and snap a couple of pictures as the two men were getting in–

The driver caught the movement and his eyes stared hard and menacing over top of the limo.

Crap. Merlin turned and moved back inside the terminal. He swam against the main current of a crowd that was more intent on going outside and made headway difficult. Pulling the brim of the straw hat lower, he glanced over his shoulder. Crap again.

The hardcore driver was trying to get in the doors, his eyes intent on finding the person who had snapped the images.

Slowly but surely, Merlin made his way across the terminal floor and away from the doors. He glanced back once more to see the man in the beret had gotten several feet inside the door and his head was on a swivel. Moving away with larger strides as the crowd thinned out, Merlin decided fitting in would be much better than standing out like a fleeing felon. A moment later, he took a turn to the right and sat on a stool in a small coffee shop that opened onto the concourse. He casually ordered a coffee and kept his head down as he peeked under the brim.

The hard-core driver had moved twenty or thirty feet closer but he was now turning in slow circles, looking for his target. He finally gave up and headed back towards the doors and the limousine.

Merlin still had the cell phone in his hand and he called up the images. He zoomed in but neither man looked familiar. There was something familiar about the pattern in the fatigues the driver wore but he couldn't place it. Quickly typing a message and asking for the Interpol techs to try facial recognition software, Merlin sent it off while silently cursing himself. In his hurry he had failed to get the license plate of the limousine. Now he had no idea where Pleasant was going and no way to track them. The only thing The Stopper was stopping was himself.

Chapter 15

MERLIN HAD CONSIDERED staying on the plane until he knew exactly where he should stay within the city. But then he realized Sherrell and Saab would be using the bed in the suite while they waited for him. Instead, he had Saab meet him at customs and he handed her his Interpol passport. No sense getting caught with it again and blowing his cover. He was learning.

The first thing he did after that was head to the Europcar rental desk in the airport for a set of wheels. He still had over $8,000 left and he paid cash to rent a rugged SUV built in Nigeria for a week. Next, he checked into a brand new Radisson Blue hotel near the airport and grabbed a bite to eat, enjoying the breakfast buffet in the Stratus Room.

When he was finished, he paid a visit to a nearby mall where he picked up another pair of lightweight pants and two shirts that were long enough to cover the conceal holster in the small of his back. He added some underwear and socks and stuffed them all into a black duffel bag he bought. Picking up a self-sharpening travel shaver set, he returned to the hotel feeling set for a long stay, if necessary.

Returning to the Stratus Room for lunch, he sat and enjoyed the seafood buffet, furnishing it off with the floral-and-citrus-character of an Ethiopia wet-processed coffee– and then it struck him. The driver's fatigues had seemed familiar and he pulled his cell phone out and did a search on the pattern, rummaging through his memories of NATO exercises he had participated during his stint in the Canadian army– there it was. The MultiCam pattern on the man's fatigues was the Woodland pattern found on the uniforms of the KCT, the Korps Commandotroepen, the special forces unit of the Royal Netherlands Army. They also wore a Commando-green beret, which is exactly what the driver was wearing. Merlin noted one fact, the headgear was missing the brass KCT beret emblem which displayed the Fairbairn-Sykes Fighting Knife, a hand grenade and a ribbon with the unit's Nunc aut Nunquam (now or never) motto on it. Either the man was hiding his affiliation with the KCT or he was an ex-member.

He sent that tidbit of information off to Interpol, hoping it would give them a better shot at identifying the driver,

Once behind the wheel, Merlin used his cell phone and did a Google search on government buildings and the President's home. Nothing on the home popped up. But the Vertrosé National Assembly Building here in the city seemed to be the center of government activity and a possible location where a hit man or assassin would strike. His search had to start somewhere so he set the coordinates in the GPS system and put the vehicle in drive.

The National Assembly Building turned out to be a large French Colonial-style building made from honey-colored limestone. It came complete with an impressive clock tower. A wide set of stairs rose to a portico and the front entrance to the main floor The building was guarded by Vertrosé army personnel in jungle-green uniforms, black berets and carried on full display Milkor BXP submachine guns manufactured in South Africa.

Merlin lowered the window halfway down, letting in the African heat and the rumbling rattle and diesel fumes from several buses idling nearby. He rubbed the back of his hand under his chin, wondering if it was normal for army personnel to be on guard like this. In Europe or North America, it was often done when there was a terrorist threat. Was President Balewa reacting to some perceived threat? He thought back to his conversation with Noxolo and Balewa in Monte Carlo. He was sure he hadn't mentioned anything about the possibility of a real hit man or someone backing an armed rebellion in reaction to the President refusing the loan–

His cell phone buzzed and vibrated on his belt. Grabbing it quickly, expecting to receive some information, he looked at the screen. Oh, crap. He pressed the answer button with a thumb and put the phone to his ear without saying a word. He hoped he was wrong–

"*Mr.* Dragon. Can you tell me why you are in my country?"

It was Lesedi Noxolo. Merlin wondered how she knew–

"If you are wondering how I know you are here in Ténemané, you used your Interpol passport to pass through customs. Now stop pretending it is not you and answer my question."

So much for stealth. "You had me flagged?" Merlin asked.

"You are not that important. However, we do like to know when officials from other countries or members of an armed force or police force...including Interpol...enter our country."

"Paranoid much?"

"Do not mock me. Now I have asked you a question–"

"You wouldn't know if you have any members or ex-members of the Royal Netherlands Army in Ténemané, would you?"

There was a long silence. Noxolo's voice was low and intense as she finally asked, "Why are you asking?"

Merlin ran every scenario through his head. Did she know anything? Was she aware of a threat based on the refusal of the loan? Should I say something? What happens if I open up? Am I supposed to do that? Just how much do I reveal–?

"Mr. Dragon?"

When he had taken the job as The Stopper, Director Laurent had told him no one could know–

Noxolo's voice was tinged with anger, "Answer my question, Mr. Dragon. I won't ask you again."

The phone beeped in Merlin's ear. Either another call or a text message was coming through. "Call you back."

"Don't you dare–"

Merlin did. "I bet I'm going to pay for that," he said as he saw he had a message from Interpol. He called it up. His guess at the pattern on the army fatigues had been correct and had allowed Interpol to connect the driver's picture to a name. The man was on file because he was Nicolaas Kessen, a former Colonel with the KCT. Finding out the name was good. Finding out who he was and his background was bad. The fact Dirk VanDaele's global arms business was in the Netherlands meant he most likely had contacts with their military, including members of the KCT. It wasn't a stretch to believe this Kessen worked for him. Or more likely for Davet Minard's DVM International, probably supplying the kind of expertise and training a rebel army could use. A rebel army looking to overthrow a President who refused to play the game of take-a-loan-and-go-bankrupt-so-we-can-own-your-ass. Of course, it was still all speculation.

His cell phone buzzed again. A call was coming though.

If he decided to take it. A smile crossed Merlin's lips. The buzz almost felt angry. He knew Lesedi Noxolo wasn't just going to sit and wait for his return call.

Buzz.

Merlin felt the vibration in his hand and it was telling him he had a decision to make. His mind went back to Director Laurent's words when he was first recruited: Interpol had decided they a new method to deal with an increasing number of bad players around the world. Specifically, the worst of the bad players. You are that method. All of your assignments will be threats we can't deal with effectively through the federal, state or local police forces of a member country. And these threats will have to be dealt with quickly. They will need to be stopped dead. That's where you come in...do whatever it takes to remove those threats.

Making a decision, come hell or high water, Merlin would do his best to do the job as he saw fit.

He pressed the button, "Lesedi–" He pulled the phone away from his ear as a loud tirade exploded on the other end of the call. When there was a brief interlude in the explosion of anger, Merlin offered a rushed, "I'm sending you some pictures." As the harsh tone continued again, he called up the images he took at the airport and sent them to Noxolo. Putting the phone back to his ear, he regretted the move. He took his life on his hands and hung up.

Several minutes passed before a call came through again. He answered, "You got them?"

"Why do you have a picture of this man?" Noxolo asked.

Merlin thought he detected fear - no, more like alarm in her voice. "You know the guy in the uniform?"

"What? No. It is the other man. Do you have any idea who this man is?"

Chapter 16

MERLIN STRAIGHTENED UP in his seat. It appeared he had stumbled onto something that might help him complete his assignment. Or would it? "I take it this man isn't a friend of yours?"

Lesedi Noxolo emitted a derisive laugh, "An old African proverb says a close friend can become a close enemy."

Raising an eyebrow at another proverb thrown into the conversation, Merlin said, "Okay. Now can you explain that to us uneducated—"

Noxolo's voice was hard, "The man in the suit is Faraji Okafor, head of the VLA, the Vertrosé Liberation Army."

"I take it that's not good?"

This time Noxolo's quiet laugh was bitter, "Not good? Do you remember my telling you that I had received some disturbing information from the Under Secretary of the Army? That he had learned the opposition party had a plan to kidnap Aziza Balewa in order to force the President to step down and take power themselves?"

"Yes. I take it—"

"Faraji Okafor is rumored to be the one behind the plot."

"Can you—?"

"This other man was with Okafor?" Noxolo interjected. "And you say he is military? Do you know why he has come to Vertrosé and is with Okafor?"

"Lesedi–"

"Tell me what you know," Noxolo insisted, her voice rising insurgency. "And why *are* you here? You have not answered me. Is it because of Okafor–?"

"Let's just slow down for a minute–"

"There is no time to slow down. I must do my job and you must answer my questions."

"I will," Merlin said. When she began to speak again, Merlin cut her off, "You trusted me before and you need to trust me now. Do you understand?" She began talking again, insisting on getting answers to her questions. When there was a brief pause as Noxolo waited for those answers, Merlin said, "This will probably piss you off again but call me when you're ready to *talk*." He hung up.

Now he watched the Vertrosé army personnel guarding the limestone building. Would they be marching over to shoot him or take him prisoner in a few moments?

His cell phone buzzed in his hand.

He answered it without a word.

There was silence on the other end from moment and then Noxolo's tight, angry voice said, "All right. Talk."

Merlin still didn't take his eyes off the soldiers, "I need you to tell me about this Okafor."

"Why are we wasting time?"

"Just humor me." He waited a heartbeat, "Please."

There was the sound of a frustrated breath and then Noxolo spoke with words that had a bite to them, "In our struggle for freedom and independence, Adisa Balewa and Faraji Okafor fought side by side in the civil war that ensued When it was over, it was Okafor who actually supported the idea that Adisa Balewa would be the one to back when the time came for free elections. However, when that time actually came, Okafor had his own ambitions. He ran against Balewa and the battle became extremely contentious. Okafor began a very public campaign to discredit Balewa, even to the point of accusing him of war crimes."

"Was there any evidence to–?"

Noxolo spit the words out hard, "No. And I was there. Do not try to tarnish the reputation of a good man."

"I wasn't and you know it," Merlin said. "I'm just asking questions, trying to understand how it all fits together. Now, how did this Okafor become head of the VLA?" There was a long silence and Merlin wondered which way this was going to go. Was she going to continue to open up or was she–?

"There are those who fought alongside both Okafor and Balewa who decided to support Okafor." It sounded as if she shrugged a shoulder, "There were others who backed Adisa so it was understandable. Everyone is free to decide for themselves. But concerns began to arise when Okafor formed the VLA. He said it was merely a political party and there was no cause for alarm. We wanted to believe him until Okafor left the country to raise outside money to fund his next election campaign against President Balewa. That alone, the influence of money from outside our country, is not good. But the situation became much more problematic when we began to see many who fought in other civil wars on the continent, paid mercenaries, begin to arrive to bolster his Vertrosé Liberation Army. Every day the organization he formed seems to become more and more powerful as a military force. How he was able to accomplish that, how he had the contacts or where he found the money to bring these men in is difficult to understand and there have been many theories."

"I think I can help you with that."

There was more silence and you could cut the tension with a knife.

Merlin took a deep breath and plunged into deeper waters, "There are two men who are behind the Banque Monégasque de la Finance in Monte Carlo. Do you remember one of the images I sent you in Monte Carlo? One of them had that handwritten note in the upper corner; approuvé Minard."

"Yes, I remember. But–?"

"Davet Minard is one of those two men. Minard owns DVM International, a Private Military Contractor registered in Gibraltar. From what I understand, he employs former rebel soldiers from African nations as well as those from South America."

There was a catch in Noxolo's voice, "Is this Minard behind Okafor? But why?"

"Minard's partner is Dirk VanDaele. He's a global arms dealer who owns Schorpioen Internationale in the Netherlands."

Noxolo perked up, "The Netherlands? You asked about members of the Royal Netherlands Army being in Ténemané. Do you believe they are involved? But why–?"

"No. I asked you about members or ex-members. If you take a look at the man in the army fatigues, you see his beret does not have a badge or an insignia on it."

"What does that have to do with it?"

"Because he couldn't pass himself off as an acting member of the force if he wasn't," Merlin said. "In fact, that's why I hung up on you the first time–"

"Don't remind me."

A smile crept onto Merlin's lips. She wasn't going to let him forget it, no matter what. He pushed on, "The man was identified as Nicolaas Kessen, a *former* Colonel with the Korps Commandotroepen, the special forces unit of the Royal Netherlands Army. My theory is he works for Minard and VanDaele–"

"To what purpose? And why would he be here?" Be truthful with me, Mr. Dragon," Noxolo said.

The smile left Merlin's lips. He had to be all in, "Do you remember my reference to James Pleasant as an Economic Hit Man? And what it meant?"

"Yes."

"I followed James Pleasant into Ténemané. That's why I'm here."

"Pleasant is here?"

"Yes. I took those images of Okafor and this Kessen outside the airport when they picked him up in a limousine."

"They picked him up? But why...?"

"When your President turned down the loan, it appears they moved right to the final step in their plans."

"The final step?"

"Yes. As I understand it, there are a number of escalating steps they can take to get what they want. It all focuses on neutralizing or removing the politician who's refused to cooperate with taking the loan and sending his nation into bankruptcy. There is bribery–"

"Adisa Balewa is not the type of man you can bribe."

"I think they know that. And they want to move fast so there is no time to blackmail him–"

"I doubt he has many skeletons in his closet they could use."

"No, but they could set him up."

"How?"

"It doesn't matter. And they can't pressure him by kidnapping Aziza Balewa because you aren't giving them the opportunity. So...if they can't bribe the politician, pressure him by kidnapping loved ones, or trap him in a blackmail scheme, they can either rig an election or pour money into one to back their own candidate who *will* take the loan."

"We won't have elections for another three years."

"I know. I checked. Which brings us to the last step. The last resort. They remove the politician in a coup or a civil war. Minard can supply the battle-hardened soldiers, at a price of course, and Van-Daele can sell you anything you need to carry out that coup or war, from small weapons to tanks, fighter planes, and ballistic missiles. They make a ton of money and are willing to back a rival who *will* sign the loan."

"I...I must talk to the President right away."

"One other thing."

"Yes."

Merlin took another deep breath, "One other part of this last step...is to send in a *real* hit man to kill the politician."

There was stunned silence.

Chapter 17

WHEN SHE FINALLY SPOKE, Lesedi Noxolo's voice was low, almost like her mind was somewhere else. But there was no doubt the timbre was filled with tension, "We need to discuss this with the President. I will send a car for you immediately. Where are you?"

"I'm just looking at your National Assembly Building–"

"You are outside?"

"Oh, I guess so. I never considered you would be inside." Merlin could hear her push a chair back.

"I will–"

"Look," Merlin said, "What I need you to do is find where this Okafor. Once I can find him–"

"We can do it together," Noxolo insisted.

Merlin could hear her heels clicking as she walking over a marble or terrazzo floor. "It might be better if you let me take care of it."

"You are in my country, Mr. Dragon. *We* tell *you* what will be done.

Opening his mouth, Merlin became aware of a form, dressed in an interlocking pattern of green, brown, tan and black, standing outside his driver side window. Turning his head, he saw a face topped by a green colored beret. The lips were pressed in a firm line and the Dutch-accented words were as hard as the eyes that bore into him, "Don't say a word."

It was Nicolaas Kessen, the former Colonel with the KCT.

Kessen now put a battle-hardened finger to his lips in a silence gesture. His eyes flicked down to the newspaper he held near the window.

Merlin realized the newspaper was draped over a barrel and he knew exactly what it would be.

"It's silenced so the guards won't hear a thing. They will just find your body."

Just as Merlin thought. A Glock 17, a weapon used by the KCT, and a Fischer Development suppressor. It fit the gun with just one click and you didn't have to make any changes to the Glock. All that useless information passed through his head along with tactics to offset the situation. There weren't any he could think of.

"End the call," Kessen said.

Merlin spoke into the cell, "Sorry, sweetheart, I have to take the vehicle back to Europcar." He could hear Noxolo say something but it was clipped off as he ended the call.

"Good. Now hold the phone back over your shoulder and grip the steering wheel with the other. Do it now."

Complying with the instructions, Merlin saw Kessen slide toward the back door. A moment later, he heard it open and felt the vehicle sagging a touch as the man sat in the back seat.

Kessen pulled the door closed firmly. His voice was low and menacing, "It's amazing who you meet when you do a little sightseeing."

Merlin glanced into the rearview mirror and found himself looking into a pair of stone-cold eyes, "I don't understand. Do I know you?"

Kessen took the phone from Merlin's hand, "Now put your hand on the steering wheel with the other and *don't* make any moves. You do, you die. As simple as that. I'm sure the bullet will penetrate your seat and your body comfortably."

Merlin felt a push against the back of his seat. There was no doubt the bullet would penetrate everything from this range. Complying with the order, Merlin slowly moved his hand to the steering wheel, "Look. If it's money you want–"

"Shut up."

Merlin knew the cell phone wouldn't give up anything beyond the false information planted by the technicians. The internal facial recognition software wouldn't work with Kessen's face looking at it. In the rearview mirror he saw the man's eyebrows squeeze together in confusion.

Cursing softly under his breath, Kessen shook his head.

The only problem now was getting out of the vehicle alive. Even if Kessen didn't find anything, it was highly unlikely he would just walk away and leave a witness to what he had just done. The man's eyes told Merlin he would simply pull the trigger without a second thought and walk away, figuring he had made a mistake.

"I know it was you."

"I don't know what you mean," Merlin said. "I don't know you–"

Kessen jabbed the end of the suppressor barrel hard into the back of the seat, "I saw you take our picture at the airport. I know it was you."

Merlin's body jerked, "Ow. I didn't take any pictures at the airport. I just came in–"

"You're lying." Kessen shifted forward in the seat and slipped his hand over Merlin's shoulder and patted him down. He found the Horton passport in Merlin's shirt pocket and pulled it out, sliding back to look at it.

His mind whirling, Merlin tried to figure a way out of this.

Kessen voice was hard, "Who exactly are you, Mr. Horton? And why are you in Vertrosé?"

Going with his back story, Merlin hoped it would give him some time to come up with a plan, "I work for Mallard Security in Los Angeles, California. We offer personal security for celebrities and politicians–" The barrel was pressed harder into the back of the seat.

"Do you carry a weapon, Mr. Horton?"

Merlin took a chance and hedged while feeling the form of the weapon in the holster over his back pocket, "I normally do but I'm waiting for my assignment to begin. That's why I'm here doing a little sightseeing–"

Kessen was skeptical, "Someone from California is guarding a client in Vertrosé? I find that hard to believe."

"Hey, it's Hollywood, okay? Walt Disney Studios is doing some jungle movie and part of their film is being shot over here on location."

"And who is your famous client?"

"I have no idea–" The barrel was stabbed into the seat again.

"Try again."

"I have no idea, okay? I never know who they are until they arrive. A lot of these movie people are paranoid about paparazzi and stuff." He lifted his fingers from the steering wheel and waved them, "It's all secrecy, secrecy, secrecy with them. You know what I mean? Don't take my picture until I need the publicity–"

Pushing the gun barrel into the seat, Kessen said, "Keep your hands on the wheel."

Merlin wrapped his fingers back around the steering wheel, "Sorry. I'm just trying to explain myself. You know what I mean?"

There was a moment's silence and then Kessen brought the gun up, covered by the newspaper and put the barrel against the back of Merlin's head, "Drive. Got to the corner and turn left."

"Okay, but where–ow!" The barrel jabbed him hard. "Okay, okay." Merlin put the SUV in drive and turned his head to look for traffic. The barrel pressed against his cheek.

"I said drive and don't turn around."

"I was just checking for traffic. You don't want to get killed do you?" Merlin asked as he pulled into traffic. At the corner, he turned left.

Lesedi Noxolo appeared at top of the stairs under the portico of the Assembly Building. She held a phone in her hand as she descended the steps rapidly, looking for Merlin.

As he began driving away from the building, Merlin glanced into the rearview mirror and watched Noxolo looking over the cars on the street.

A moment later, she put the phone to her ear, turned and made her way back up the stairs.

Merlin had only one chance and made a decision. He did his best to keep his heart rate down, expecting a silenced shot to ring out within the next few seconds. He wondered if he would actually hear it.

Chapter 18

MERLIN PUT HIS FOOT on the brake, bringing the SUV to a stop in the street. Moving both hands from the top of the steering wheel to the center, he straightened his arms and pressed hard. The sound of the horn was tinny but kept up a continuous wail.

Kessen's free hand came up and grabbed the back of Merlin's hair, yanking his head back, "Stop it now or you're a dead man."

Merlin winced and his eyes teared up against the pain but he kept his hands firmly press down on the worn, "I figure you're going to kill me anyway. This way those army guards are coming and you won't get away after I'm dead. And even if you manage to escape, the surveillance cameras will have your picture. You'll never get out of the country–"

Kessen smashed the gun against the side of Merlin's head.

Blackness threatened to close in but Merlin fought it off, doing his best to keep his left hand against the horn as the other one dropped from the stunning blow. A veil of darkness began to fall over his eyes. A moment later, he felt himself falling to the left and then someone was there holding his shoulder. He heard a voice that sounded familiar.

"Take him out and lie him on the ground. Did we get that man?"

It was Noxolo's voice and Merlin heard her give orders, probably to the guards. He went in and out of darkness before finding himself sitting up on the old sidewalk. He felt the heat of the concrete underneath his pants. Someone shouted something and he felt a tug over his right pocket.

"It's fine. It's fine," Noxolo said.

Merlin could hear the firmness and authority in her voice. Then he realized she was kneeling in front of him, looking into his face.

"Are you all right, Mr. Dragon? Can you tell me who the man was?"

Opening his mouth, Merlin felt a croak escape, "It..." He squeezed his eyes shut and felt the world spinning for a moment.

"Mr. Dragon?"

Slowly lifting a hand, Merlin put a shaky finger to his lips, "Shhh. No one is supposed to know who I am."

There was some relief in the laughter from Noxolo, "I think it's a little too late for that, don't you?"

"Just keep in mind the woods." That was what came back to Merlin. When Director Laurent first hired him, he had told Merlin he would take him to a lonely spot in the woods and shoot him. Was that in case I didn't want the job? Or if I told someone–?

"What in the world does that mean? What woods?"

Merlin tried to clear the stupid thoughts in his head as he put it a hand to where he had been whacked. He winced from the soreness.

Noxolo took his hand away, "Let the man do his first aid."

Realizing someone was trying to check his head for cuts or maybe a crushed skull. Merlin gave her a nod. Then he said, "It was the Dutchman, Nicolaas Kessen."

"What did he want?"

Merlin shook his head softly, "I'm not sure. Probably wanted to figure out who I was and...he saw me take the pictures at the airport. Did you catch him?"

There was a moment of silence and then Noxolo said, "No. The soldiers are still looking but...."

"Okay. You can at least figure out where he went from the cameras."

"Cameras?" Noxolo was genuinely confused, "What cameras?"

Merlin looked up towards the building and immediately regretted the movement, "Ow." He looked at Noxolo, "The cameras. The surveillance cameras around the area of the assembly building."

Noxolo shook her head, "There are no surveillance cameras."

"Seriously?"

"Of course. This is not New York city or London, England. And what was that comment you made about the Euro car?"

Merlin wasn't sure what she was referring to for a minute and then it came to him, "Oh, right. No. I said Europcar. I said I had to take the SUV back to Europcar." He saw the confusion continue on Noxolo's face. "Europcar? The rental place at the airport?"

Noxolo shook her head, "I don't rent cars from the airport, Mr. Dragon."

Merlin let out a long, slow breath, "You would have figured it out eventually. And once you found out I rented the SUV there, you could get into the GPS unit and track the SUV to where I was and–" He saw Noxolo's eyebrows knit together. "No?"

"We don't have those capabilities, Mr. Dragon. Any more than we have a network of surveillance cameras. Keep in mind part of the loan the President was looking for was to help build many things, including the communications and security infrastructure in our country."

Merlin let out a harder breath, realizing how close he had come to being buried in a jungle grave that would probably never be found. A moment later, he looked at Noxolo, giving her a slight smile, "And could you stop using my name? Nobody is supposed to know I exist."

Noxolo raised an eyebrow, "If you keep that up, Mr. Dragon, I will make that come true."

Chapter 19

PRESIDENT BALEWA PACED back and forth over the hand-made Moroccan carpet in his office in the assembly building. The room was hot under the African sun and behind a desk of crimson-brown wood with bands of golden brown that dominated the room, the casement windows were open a crack to let air circulate. The window opening wasn't doing much though and Balewa mopped the perspiration from his brow from time to time as he agonized over the events that had just taken place two floors below. The added knowledge he had now heard from Lesedi Noxolo regarding the threats against him and his daughter only added to the anxiety he was feeling. "I must have Okafor arrested immediately," he said finally.

"You can't do that, Mr. President," Noxolo said.

Balewa spun on his heels, "Don't tell me what I can and cannot do. The man is threatening to kidnap my daughter." His gestures were wild and angry he strode across the carpet and moved behind the imposing desk, "And the man is trying to subvert democracy."

Noxolo's jaw clenched, "I understand that, but you have to listen."

Balewa pulled a drawer open, pulled out a bottle of aspirins and slammed the drawer shut, "I am *through* listening." He unscrewed the top, shook out a number of pills and downed them without water. He put the top back on and banged the bottle down on the desk, "I should have acted years ago." He reached for the phone on his desk, "I will call General Bamgboshe and have the army arrest Okafor–"

"The army?"

"Yes."

"And if you do that," Noxolo countered, "you will end up looking like many other African countries, eliminating your opposition only because you can. Only because you're in power–"

Slamming the phone down on the desk, Balewa's eyes blazed with anger as he jabbed a finger at her, "How can you accuse me of that? You know me–"

"And keep in mind we have no proof that we can offer the public," Noxolo countered.

Balewa looked to Merlin, who had been sitting quietly in a chair in the corner of the President's office. Moving around the desk and striding to a spot in the middle of the room, the President pointed straight Merlin as he said to Noxolo, "This man can be by my side when I talk to the country and tell them what is happening. They will listen when he tells them what he knows."

Noxolo opened her mouth to reply but instead looked at Merlin as well. She took a breath, let it out slowly and stayed silent, waiting for some type of answer.

Put on the spot, Merlin ran a hand through his hair. This was a good reason to keep your mouth shut in the first place. "I'm sorry, Mr. President, but that's not going to happen."

Balewa straightened up, an indignant look of his face, "And I'm telling you, you will. We are now a member country of Interpol and

I will call your superiors. You will be ordered to stand by my side as we tell the country of Faraji Okafor's treachery."

Merlin stood up and headed for the President's liquor cabinet. He had turned down a drink before but decided he needed a stiff belt. Well aware the other two were waiting for a reply, he calmly poured a half glass of Mampoer, an Afrikaans version of moonshine made from peaches that the President stocked and drank. He tossed the drink back, shuddering from the strength and then set the glass down, "This might sound dumb, but Interpol probably won't acknowledge my existence, much less order me to stand beside you that some press conference."

But–"

Merlin turned, "Hear me out. If it wasn't for Lesedi's competence in guarding you, *you* wouldn't know I exist either."

A light smile caressed Noxolo's lips at the complement.

"Or maybe it was just my incompetence." He winked at Noxolo.

Noxolo raised an eyebrow.

"Either way, my job for Interpol is a special one." He shook his head grimly, "You're not even supposed to know there *is* a special job inside Interpol." He held a hand up when Balewa started to protest again, "You joined Interpol for a reason. If you want the organization to work for you, you need to let me do my job. My way."

There was silence in the room for a moment.

And then Noxolo spoke up quietly, "He is right, Adisa. By letting him do his job, we protect the reputation of Vertrosé as a democratic country. We don't follow the ways of the past. We must lead the way to a brighter Africa."

Balewa considered Noxolo's words for a moment and then asked, "And what happens if Okafor succeeds in his treachery? Do

I do nothing and leave my daughter in danger, with the possibility that she becomes a pawn to wrest control of the country from my hands? I can't do that to her."

"No one is asking you to do that," Merlin said. "You two need to do whatever you can to stop Okafor and his stupid Liberation Army. *How* you do that up to you. But I can't be involved in any way, shape or form."

Noxolo shook her head in confusion, "But I thought you are willing to help–"

Merlin held up a single finger, "I am. But *not* in any public way. Keep in mind all we have is speculation and circumstantial evidence. We have nothing concrete to prove what they're up to."

Balewa and Noxolo exchanged glances, unable to refute the comment.

"Now where would I find this Okafor and his army?"

Noxolo looked genuinely pained, "We have no idea. At least for the VLA. It's deep in the jungle somewhere. As for Okafor, he has a compound on the edge of Ténemané. But...."

Merlin felt frustration course through his veins, "Of course. He's not supposed to be in the country. That's why you were surprised by the picture I sent you."

Balewa held his hands out, "That's why we need you to stand by my side and–"

Waving the thought away, Merlin said, "Can't happen." He looked at Noxolo, "You have my number. What I need you to do from here on is to feed me every single piece of information you get on where this Okafor. And you need to continue to do that until the threat is over."

Noxolo exchanged a glance with the President again and then said, "All right. We can do that. What are you going to do?"

"I think it's better if you don't know anything about what I do from here on."

"But you are in our country," the President countered, "I am responsible for what happens."

Merlin took in a deep breath, considering the situation for a moment and then said, "You make a good point, Mr. President. But I still think it's better if you don't know. It's called plausible deniability."

Balewa looked to Noxolo, wanting her to back him up.

Noxolo crossed her arms over her chest, "Perhaps he is right, Adisa. It might be better if we don't know."

Merlin saw the frustration on Balewa's face but he couldn't back off, "The truth is, Mr. President, I'm not even sure what I can do. But you have to trust me." And then another thought took precedence over the discussion, "*But...*I know something *you* need to do right now."

"And what is that, Mr, Dragon?" Noxolo asked.

"Remember what I said about the steps they can take?" Merlin made a gun with his hand and pointed across the room to the windows behind the President's desk on the left, "I would strongly suggest you secure the buildings across from this window, including the rooftops. You need to know who goes in and out of them twenty-four hours a day."

President Balewa blanched as he looked towards the double casement windows. He was the one who had opened them a crack.

"There has to be a good reason that former Colonel with the KCT was down there scouting out this building," Merlin added. "Maybe he was figuring out how to take over this building through a quick coup somehow. Or if they launch a civil war and some day down the road they march into Ténemané to take over the capital city and the seat of government. Or...he was down there for another reason. We can't assume anything and we can't take any chances."

Balewa headed across the room, "I should have been more careful–"

Noxolo moved with purpose, putting her hands on his shoulder, moving him aside, "No, Mr. President."

Turning his body, Balewa pushed back, "What are you doing–?"

A soft tinkle of glass was the only warning.

A soft grunt emerged from Noxolo's throat and she dropped stone-like, straight down to the rug.

Merlin reacted immediately and he pulled his weapon while moving across the rug. He shoved the President hard as he brought the weapon up, looking for any sign of the shooter.

President Balewa stumbled from the force of the push and tripped over Noxolo's body, hitting the floor with a grunt of his own.

Merlin spotted movement on the roof across the street. It was the top of a head moving away from the edge. It disappeared before he could pull the trigger.

Scrambling around to his knees, Balewa put his hands on her shoulder, "Lesedi? Lesedi?"

"The shooter was on the roof across the street," Merlin yelled as he headed for the door. "Alert your troops outside." He pulled the door open and froze in position. He had forgotten about the two large President's State Guards in red berets who has been standing in the hallway, set in place by Noxolo.

They were startled by his yell and sudden appearance but they had their submachine guns up and leveled at him in an instant.

Merlin raised his hands as he said back over his shoulder, "President Balewa? I think I need your help here."

From his position over Noxolo, Balewa began speaking with urgency in French to the guards, issuing instructions.

One of the guards pushed past Merlin to help with Noxolo while the other took a walkie-talkie from his belt and began running down the hallway, yelling orders in French.

Looking back into the room for a moment, Merlin saw blood slowly staining the hand-made carpet in an ever-widening circle. He realized there was little he could do. Turning, he headed after the guard.

Chapter 20

HOURS LATER, Merlin drove away from the assembly building with his mind in a whirl. He felt very much a failure to this point and wondered if this would be his last assignment. For one thing, no one was supposed to know he was The Stopper and now at least two people knew. Although he was just told one of them was on life support after taking a bullet to the chest. Then again, he was told he could make his own decisions in the field and he had decided to - no, he hadn't decided to reveal himself. He smiled grimly at the truth. Noxolo had 'revealed' him by being more competent at her job than he was. And now, because of him - he blew out a thin breath between his lips. He had to put the feelings of guilt and failure and everything else behind him and get on with actually being The Stopper. The problem was...once again he had no idea where to start.

Balewa and Noxolo had told him that Faraji Okafor had a compound on the outskirts of the city. But the President had just informed Merlin that he had sent troops there after the shooting and it was empty.

Despite dozens of army personnel scouring the building across the street, they had found no evidence of the shooter. Whoever the shooter was, he was a professional and had policed his brass, taking any shell casing with him. He doubted it was this Nicolaas Kessen, the former Colonel with the KCT. He was more likely to assign the task to someone else and not risk getting caught himself. The former KCT officer was probably with Okafor and they were plotting and planning their next move. If he found one of them, he could find the other. But if Noxolo didn't know where he was - his heart caught in his throat. He'd only known the woman a short time but he genuinely liked her. And surprisingly he felt comfortable around her, something that didn't usually happen to him. It made him more determined than ever to make Okafor and Kessen pay. But how?

Merlin pressed down on the gas pedal and pushed his way through the traffic, heading for the airport. Right now he couldn't do much here in Ténemané, or anywhere in the entire country for that matter, without a lead. Okafor's VLA was somewhere deep in the jungle but it didn't make sense trying to find them if the Vertrosé army didn't know. But it was possible to do something by pulling on a known thread in the case. In less than an hour, Merlin was back onboard the Bombardier Global 8000 and the ultra long-range business jet that was on the way to that thread.

Chapter 21

K ralendijk, Bonaire, Caribbean Netherlands
THE ONE HUNDRED AND FOUR FOOT
WINGSPAN of the jet cut through the sharp blue skies above
Bonaire, an island in the Leeward Antilles in the Caribbean Sea.
The island, along with Sint Eustatius and Saba, was a special munic-
ipality within the country of the Netherlands. After a long history
of European involvement that included Bonaire becoming a plan-
tation of the Dutch West India Company using African slaves, it
was now a top tourist destination. More specifically, it catered to
scuba divers and snorkelers who considered the surrounding coral
reefs as the one of the world's best shore diving excursion.

Four hours into the journey to the Netherlands, Merlin had received word from Interpol that customs in France indicated his target had left for this Caribbean Island where he owned a vacation
home. After a stop in Marrakesh, Morocco to refuel, Captain Sherrell and Captain Saab had pushed the aircraft hard and the twelve-
hour flight would have them landing an hour before sundown.

Despite catching some sleep in the suite in the back of the executive jet, Merlin felt the exhaustion from the worry and self-guilt
closing in. He rubbed the stubble on his chin as the plane banked
and he caught a glimpse of the pink tower and the pink-trimmed

buildings of the Flamingo International Airport off to the left. He hadn't even thought about shaving in two days despite picking up that self-sharpening travel shaver set in Ténemané. Of course the thought of Ténemané brought back the thought of Noxolo on life support - or had she succumbed? - and the feelings of guilt kicked up a notch. It was a never ending circle of self-recrimination.

The jet dropped quickly and before long he felt the bump as they touched down and heard the reverse thrusters whine in protest.

Customs was quick with his Interpol passport. He decided against using his other passport in case something in the background set up as his cover went wrong. He couldn't afford any delays. There was no telling what Okafor, Kessen and their VLA would do next or how fast it could happen. He even dreaded looking at the stacks of Antiliaans Dagblaad and the Bonaire Reporter newspapers as he passed them. He half expected headlines announcing a coup in Vertrosé but there was nothing like that. Of course the Dagblaad was in Dutch but he still felt some relief at not seeing the name of the country or the President's name. The only vehicle left at the Pays-Bas Car Rental Bonaire was a bright red Jeep Grand Cherokee Summit Eco-Diesel and he grabbed it without hesitation. Sticking out like a sore thumb was the least of his worries right now.

The GPS system took him to the left and he drove south at the speed limit along EEG Boulevard, the smooth Caribbean Sea off to his right.

Dirk VanDaele, the global arms dealer, had a walled-in, twenty-thousand-square-foot compound on the shore of Lighthouse Point with a two-story house overlooking the sea. Merlin chose VanDaele because he was more likely to be the one who recruited Kessen through his contacts and he was the start of the thread he wanted to pull on.

Passing the compound, Merlin noted the entrance was an iron gate with a security system that had an Intercom and a keypad to enter a code. Turning around and passing the compound again, he caught a glimpse of several CCTV cameras in the trees just inside the pink-painted concrete block wall. There was no doubt that an arms dealer like VanDaele was going to have a state-of-the-art surveillance system. He wondered if armed guards went with the whole package and decided he was safer to assume there had to be. Pulling the jeep to the side of the road, he drummed his fingers on the steering wheel as he pondered a way to get inside. The problem was...unless he was willing to don scuba gear and come in from the ocean side - assuming there was an opening there - getting inside undetected was a long shot. No, make that a long, long shot. In fact, getting shot to death was far more likely.

Conclusion? If Merlin couldn't get to the mountain, let's bring the mountain to Merlin. Or something like that.

Chapter 22

I T TOOK A TWENTY MINUTE Internet search before Merlin found a main ingredient that would make his plan work due to the vehicle he had rented; ammonia nitrate. At Kralendijk Garden Supplies he picked up a ten-pound bag of Overman Controlled Release Fertilizer 34-0-0 and a bottle of Spectracide Stump Remover. Ammonia nitrate or $NH4-NO3$ is a prime ingredient in fertilizer because it seals nitrogen in which is vital for plant life. It is also an ingredient for home-made bomb.

Merlin loaded the bag into the Jeep and pushed hard to get to his next stop. He arrived at Bonaire Hardware ten minutes before it closed and picked up a large plastic bucket with a screw top lid, a jug with a lid, a pair of pliers, cotton batten, gloves, masking tape, plastic bags, a box cutter, a length of household electrical wire, and a small screwdriver set. Next stop was to a gas station where he topped up the Jeep Eco-Diesel while discreetly filling the jug with diesel as well, setting it on the floor in the back. Paying for the fuel, he bought a disposable cell phone as well and was all set.

The harbor waters sparkled under the moonlight as Merlin found a secluded spot on the shore and went to work. He mixed the ammonia nitrate with the diesel fuel in the plastic bucket and then went to work on creating a home-made blasting cap. Using the pliers, he pulled the bullet from the casing, emptied the smoke-less black powder and replaced it with powder from the Stump Remover bottle. The Spectracide brand is pure $KNo3$ (potassium nitrate or saltpeter) and is used as a propellant for hobby rockets. Cutting a length of wire, Merlin stripped one end and inserted it into the cartridge with the powder, securing it with cotton batten. Using one of the screwdrivers he opened the cell phone, stripped the other end of the wire from the cartridge, set it in place across the electronics, put the phone back together and then slipped the cell phone/cartridge blasting cap inside a plastic bag. He placed that inside the plastic bucket and put the screw top lid on his AN-FO bomb.

It was nearing midnight when Merlin got back to VanDaele's compound. In a stolen car taken from two blocks away. He had used the masking tape to cover the license plate, used some horizontal and vertical strips to create a makeshift mask and now all he had to do was move swiftly and efficiently. He jammed the brakes on and slid to a stop in front of the iron gate, next to security system pad. Opening the door and then pulling the plastic bucket from the passenger seat with a grunt, Merlin set it halfway between the pad and the gate, sliding it as far back as he could. Getting back into the car, he headed back to the row of houses where he had stolen the car. Everything remained quiet so he returned the car to its spot, pulled the tape from the license and made his way back to the Jeep where he had hidden it in some low scrub bushes off the road. He grimaced as he pulled the masking tape from his face, rolled it into a sticky ball and tossed it far into the scrub brush before getting in. Leaving the lights off, he pulled back onto the shoulder, here he stopped, pulled his cell phone and dialed the disposable cell phone–

An ear-shattering boom was followed by a flash of light two blocks away in the direction compound.

The Jeep rocked as the ground underneath swayed.

Merlin's eyebrow's rose in surprise. The ANFO explosion had been bigger than expected.

It wasn't long before sirens sounded from behind Merlin and a few minutes later, several white and red-stripped Dutch Caribbean Police Force cars whizzed by, followed by a fire truck. Three minutes later, an ambulance shot by as well.

Checking behind him to make sure that was it for now, Merlin pulled onto the road and headed in the direction of the compound. When he could see the flashing lights and turmoil around the bombing site, he pulled to the side of the road and watched. He was surprised at the damage he'd done. The outer security system was a blackened, mangled heap and the iron gate was in even worse shape with only a few twisted sections evident. A large section of the compound wall on either side of where the gate had been was nothing short of a pile of rubble. Shrubs on the outside smoldered and smoked while the fire department worked to put out several trees that were burning inside the compound.

Twenty minutes later, the firemen and police working the scene at the entranceway pulled back to allow a black, Porsche Cayenne Turbo S luxury SUV to pull out from the compound. It took a left and headed for Kralendijk.

As the vehicle passed Merlin he watched carefully to see who was inside. He had a picture of VanDaele – it didn't matter. He couldn't see through the dark tint of the windows. Cursing to himself, he realized he had no choice but to follow. It had to be his man. And hopefully. he would take a room in town where he would have better access to him than the compound. At least, that was the plan.

Pulling out, Merlin followed at a distance and was relieved after a slow drive that seemed to take forever when the Porsche pulled into the entrance to the Bellafonte Luxury Oceanfront Hotel in Kralendijk.

Pulling to a stop and parking thirty feet behind the luxury SUV, Merlin watched as three hard looking men got out, buttoning their suit coats as they scanned their surroundings. A moment later, one of the men opened a back door and a middle-aged man with graying sandy hair stepped out. Bingo. It was the global arms dealer, Dirk VanDaele. Two of the men walked with VanDaele towards the doors to the hotel while the third stayed with the vehicle.

Merlin was out of his vehicle before the arms dealer disappeared inside. He wanted to make sure he would know which room the man would be in and it would be better to loiter in the lobby and watch him check in. There was no way to know if a booking had been set up beforehand with the hotel and it would go quickly. Merlin felt proud of that thinking; not taking anything for granted. He was learning. Turning his head to the left, he passed the guard beside the vehicle and headed for the entrance. Opening the large glass doors and slipping inside, he moved to the right and toward a stand that held sight-seeing brochures for tourists. He picked up a few as he kept a discreet watch over his shoulder.

It didn't take more than a few moments before the clerk handed VanDaele a room key. The arms dealer turned and said something to the two bodyguards. One of the bodyguards headed back to the front doors to the hotel while the other escorted VanDaele to a bank of elevators.

Merlin let the bodyguard disappear outside before he turned back, brochures in hand. He pretended to browse through them as he headed for the elevators as well.

He almost got there.
And then all hell broke loose.

button with the side of his clenched fist. A small bell sounded, the elevators doors opened with a low hiss and the arms dealer and this bodyguard disappeared inside. He was yelling something in Dutch but the doors closing cut off the sound.

One of the police officers spoke to the others holding him and when he gestured roughly to the glass doors at the entrance, Merlin was spun around with an equal level of roughness and hustled outside. He was surprised (and he wasn't) to see a number of patrol cars sitting in scattered positions in the entranceway outside. He was taken to the car closest to the road and shoved into the back seat. The ride was quick and he was thrown back and forth with his hands secured behind his back. The ride stopped in front of a blue and white building with the same large logo as the shoulder patches on the officers and he knew where he was. He was taken inside their headquarters in Kralendijk and hustled into an interrogation room. His handcuffs were removed from behind his back, reapplied in front and then shackled to an eye bolt in the center of the table.

A beefy officer stood guard as the rest left. It was at least an house before the door swung open again and a thin man with a dark mustache and a soul patch walked inside. He pulled out the chair on the other side of the table, set a large brown envelope on the table and then sat down. He placed his elbows on the table, coupled his fingers, placed his chin on his hands and looked across at Merlin with a serious look.

Merlin waited.

The man finally spoke, "My name is Vanderveer Breda. I am the Korpschef...the Police commissioner...for Bonaire. Can you please tell me why you bombed the entrance of Mr. VanDaele's compound?"

Shaking his head, Merlin said, "I have no idea what you're talking about, Mr...Breda, is it?"

"That's right." Breda gave him a faint smile, "We have you on the surveillance cameras for the compound. Mr. VanDaele is very security conscious and his men are on alert at all times. They gave me the video of your car going by a couple of times. You returned to plant the explosive in another car–"

"You have a picture of *me* driving?"

Breda waved his hand around his face, "Oh, no, you had some type of disguise, But you are wearing the exact same clothing as that of the perpetrator."

Merlin shrugged, "Could have been a coincidence. If that's your evidence–"

"When they saw your car sitting on the side of the road, watching the aftermath of the explosion...the same car on the surveillance that passed twice...and *then* it began to follow them to the hotel, the bodyguards alerted us."

Almost groaning, Merlin now understood why the drive from the compound to the hotel have been so slow.

Breda stroked his soul patch, "Our bomb technician has been well trained. Of course, in Bonaire he doesn't get much opportunity to practice his craft, so he was very eager to go to work on the type of explosive used in the bombing. Apparently, a homemade bomb made from nitrate fertilizer mixed with fuel oil is a common weapon of the terrorist. And...we are a very small island. Mr. De Vries of Kralendijk Garden Supplies supplied us with the recent purchases of nitrate fertilizer."

Merlin watched him reach into the envelope and pull out his bank card, laying it on the table with an audible click of the plastic.

"And a ten pound bag of Overman Controlled Release Fertilizer was purchased on this bank card in your possession." Breda's eyebrows rose, "Still a coincidence, my friend?"

"Somebody stole my card and returned it?"

Breda cracked a laugh. Then the amusement left his face as he reached inside the envelope and pulled out the passport, laying it on the table, "What I don't understand is why someone with Interpol in Canada would come to Bonaire to bomb the VanDaele compound?"

Chapter 24

Interpol's National Central Bureau office for Canada
DIRECTOR AUBREY LAURENT sat stroking his white beard as he waited for Marcel Vercher, the Acting Director at Interpol headquarters in Lyon, France. He had explained the situation regarding Davet Minard and Dirk VanDaele to Vercher and was waiting to hear what information they wanted him to send–

"Mr. Laurent?"

The hair on the back of his neck rose and his back straightened when he heard the Belgian accent, "Yes?"

"This is Mr. Peeters. I happened to be here and overheard the conversation you were having with Marcel."

Laurent knew something was up. The voice on the other end belonged to Tuur Peeters, Interpol's Secretary-General. He was a lawyer, the former General Commissioner of the Belgian Federal Police and a former member of the Belgian Federal Parliament. You never knew what hat he was going to wear in a discussion; lawyer, bureaucrat or the dreaded politician. But it was also unusual for him to be involved in these kinds of discussions; ones normally left to the Acting Director of each Bureau. "Yes, sir. I was just waiting to hear what Marcel needed me to send–"

"I had press him, of course, but Marcel has told me you have information that ties Davet Minard and Dirk VanDaele to the Banque Monégasque de la Finance. And that the bank is engaging in predatory tactics with the Democratic Republic of Vertrosé. On the instructions of these two men. Is that it in a nutshell?"

"Yes–"

"And how did you obtain this information?"

"Well...it was–"

"I take it from your hesitation that the information was obtained under less than legal circumstances. And it would never stand up in court. Correct?"

"Yes. But–"

"There are no buts in the legal world, Director. It is or it isn't. And since the connection from the bank to these two men is though a number of other companies, I would assume you have no evidence to *prove* a link? To prove they *in fact* issued these instructions to the bank in question to engage in these predatory practices *you allege*. Am I correct in my assumptions?"

Laurent felt both anger and humiliation at how the questions were being tossed across the call, "Yes, sir. You are correct. But I was hoping *someone* in power could stop these two men from putting Vertrosé in an economical vice that would strangle the citizens of a member of Interpol–"

"The President of Vertrosé is...how do you put it? He is a big boy. He can make whatever decisions he wants to make. Political decisions, financial, internal, external, it doesn't matter. It's not up to us to dictate how a member country does business."

"I understand that. But there's more. They're planning some additional measures to–"

"I don't need you to continue to explain what these men are doing," Peeters said. "Or what you believe they *plan* to do. Have you turned this information over to the proper authorities?"

"It's not that simple."

Peeters' voice rose in anger, "Actually, it is. Interpol has a motto, connecting police for a safer world. It's on our website. I can give you the link, if you like?"

"I don't need it."

"Apparently, you do. Because you seem to believe we police the world. We don't. Keep in mind Interpol enables the police forces in our 190 member countries to work together to fight international crime. *They* do the work. *They* have the responsibility in each country. Not us."

"I know. But–"

Peeters pushed on with his lecture, "Our charter was designed to keep Interpol as politically neutral as possible. We are forbidden from undertaking interventions or activities of a political, military, religious, or racial nature or involving ourselves in disputes over such matters. We only provide a range of policing expertise and capabilities in order to support...I repeat...support...three main crime programs: counter-terrorism, cybercrime, organized, and emerging crime. Now do your *job* and turn the information over to the respective authorities of the appropriate country. Do I make myself clear?"

"Yes, sir."

"Good."

The call ended.

Laurent looked at the phone in his hand. He could hear the dial tone buzzing dismissively. Setting the phone on the hook, he sat back, cursing under his breath. There were three monitors on the wall across from his desk, each tuned to a major news channel and he watched the talking heads and the scrolling news banners without anything registering. His mind was fixated on this problem. He began drumming his fingers on the desk, wondering how he could go around the bureaucrat. No, make that bureaucrat-politician. He had a hard time not cursing more. A politician acting political was one thing. But doing it as a member of Interpol and turning a blind eye–

His cell phone rang and he picked it up immediately, wondering if it was Merlin and some good news, "Laurent."

"This is Ivor."

Laurent was surprised. Ivor Knudtson was the President of Interpol. "Yes, sir. What can I do for you?"

"Marcel called me while you were talking to Peeters."

"He did?"

"Yes. Marcel Vercher is one of the few people who know about the program you are running and he alerted me to what was happening."

"Then you're aware of the problem I'm having in getting some action on this Vertrosé problem. We have good reason to believe–"

"I understand your concern, Aubrey. We all feel it. And I know the names of the men you told Marcel about. Even if Peeters went ahead and acted, these two men have a great deal of political pull. You know the phrase, Aubrey; they have friends in high places."

"That shouldn't allow them to operate with criminal intent without consequence."

"No, it shouldn't," Knudtson said. "But that's the world we live in, isn't it? Aubrey, the Executive Committee gave you the mandate to run a program that would offer us a method to *solve* these kinds of problems."

"Yes, sir, I know. And we *are* working to do what we can in the field. I was just hoping we could add some extra push to put a stop to what Minard and VanDaele are doing through their bank. And what they're planning on doing beyond that to–"

"It won't happen, Aubrey, you know that. The leaders of the major countries in Interpol either won't or can't deal with these kinds of people in the normal ways. The political donations of these two men can make or break a career if anyone opposes them. You've seen that happen often to good people, Aubrey."

Laurent's voice had a touch of bitterness to it, "I know. I was just hoping...."

"That's why the General Assembly tasked the Executive Committee to find a way to deal with these situations *outside* the political and legal spheres. That's why your secret program was put into effect. Correct?"

"Correct."

"Maybe your man isn't up to the task?"

Laurent shook his head firmly, "No. I have full confidence in him."

"Alright. But keep in mind the Executive Committee doesn't really want to know what you're doing any more than the political figureheads do. Plausible deniability and all that stuff. And also keep in mind that knowledge of the program is held in a tight circle. Figures like the Secretary-General have no idea what you're doing. He was just acting normally."

"Like a politician, you mean?"

There was mirth in Knudtson's voice, "Exactly." Then the mirth left, replaced by a serious tone," "Keep everything in-house, Aubrey. We *can't* afford to have outsiders get wind of what you're doing. That could put the program in jeopardy."

Chapter 23

MERLIN ONLY SAW A BLUR of movement from behind. And before he could react, his legs were taken out from under him and it seemed like a dozen powerful hands drove him face down onto the marble floor. The breath shot from his lungs in a painful burst. As his hands were yanked behind his back to apply handcuffs, his head was turned to the side and he caught sight of a number of men in off-white shirts, dark blue pants and a cap with a yellow hat band. And he knew exactly who they were when he saw the gold and blue badge with the central sword on the shoulder of the closest man. They were the Korps Politie Caribisch Nederland...the Dutch Caribbean Police Force. Hands began patting him down and his weapon, bank card, and passport were confiscated.

He was hauled roughly to his feet and a heated discussion in Dutch swirled around him.

Still standing over by the elevators, VanDaele barked out something and the conversation continued with it actually sounding like it quickly became a heated argument.

Merlin heard the name Interpol and that only served to add heat to whatever argument was going in.

At one point VanDaele scowled and said something as he looked at Merlin. Then he half-turned and punched the elevator

Laurent's jaw worked but deep down he knew Ivor Knudtson was right.

The call ended.

As Laurent set his cell phone down, his land line lit up and rang. He grabbed it quickly, "Yes?"

A young woman's voice sounded on the other end, "Mr. Laurent?"

"Yes."

"This is Countable Willoughby from the Ottawa Interpol Crime Unit. I just received a telephone call that I believe is of interest to you. It came from a Mr. Jan De Meern, The Kingdom Representative for Bonaire, St. Eustatius and Saba."

"Who?"

There was a light laugh from Willoughby, "I wondered the same thing and I had to look him up. Bonaire, St. Eustatius and Saba are three islands are in the Caribbean. Politically they are three special municipalities of the Netherlands, This Jan De Meern represents the government of the Netherlands on the islands."

Laurent was confused even more, "So how does something in the Caribbean interest me? If it has to do with the Netherlands, wouldn't you contact the Interpol office in The Hague? Or at least the EU regional bureau there?"

"Ordinarily, you're right. But this De Meern called up here inquiring about an individual in Interpol stationed here in Ottawa. *And* records indicate he reports only to you. Merlin Dragon?"

Laurent was thrown off guard for a moment. And then, when he went to speak, his eye caught a scrolling banner on one of the monitors across the room.

"Sir? Should I send the information to you?"

"Uh...yes. Yes. Thank you, constable."

Laurent barely heard the words on the other end as he set the phone down on the hook. Merlin Dragon and whatever situation he was in was one thing. The double-whammy was the breaking news scrolling across the monitor and the shocker it held.

Chapter 25

MERLIN LOOKED ACROSS at his Interpol passport laying on the table and wondered if his return to Canada would be the last time he used it. Of course, that could be a few years down the road after serving time in prison. Did they have a prison here on the island–?"

The door to the interrogation room swung open and a voice said something in Dutch.

An irritated expression swept across Breda's face and he looked at whoever it was. Holding his hands apart, Breda engaged in a brief argument with whoever it was and then stood up in a huff and disappeared through the open doorway.

Merlin could hear a low but definitely heated conversation outside in the hallway. Then it abruptly ended, followed by a set of angry footsteps moving away.

A moment later, a rotund black man stepped into the room, leaving the door open. Flashing a brief smile of greeting, he picked the passport and opened it. A moment later, he said, "Mr. Dragon, my name Jan De Meern. I am The Kingdom Representative for Bonaire, St. Eustatius and Saba." He glanced across at Merlin, "I have been sent here by Mr. Frits Rijna, The Island Governor of Bonaire."

Merlin didn't have a clue to any of the names and he felt silence was the best option - maybe the only option - at this point.

De Meern waited for Merlin to say something and then nodded to himself as he looked back at the passport, "The Island Governor calls on me as an intermediary in cases of disasters or matters that need the coordination of all the island governments. Or...in this case...an unusual circumstance." His gaze flicked across to Merlin, "Would you say this was an unusual circumstance, Mr. Dragon?"

"I would say there is another phrase for it, but I won't repeat it in polite company."

De Meern nodded, an amused smile on his face, "I understand perfectly." He raised an eyebrow, "Would you be willing to explain exactly what it was you were attempting to do on our beautiful island?"

Merlin clenched his jaw. Part of it was in anger at himself. The other part was simply a determination to accept responsibility for his stupidity and accept whatever came next for him. He wasn't about to compound the problem by betraying Interpol and their plans for a Stopper. Even if that Stopper was going to be someone else. He felt a twinge of guilt about the viability of the plan from here on. That was assuming he hadn't screwed things up so badly that the powers-that-be couldn't–

"Mr. Dragon?"

Pulled from his self recriminations and mental flagellations, he looked up.

De Meern was looking down at him, holding the large envelope in one hand and out something to him in the other.

Merlin realized the Kingdom Representative had placed his Interpol passport and the bank card on the desk right in front of him. And in his hand he held out the special cell phone.

"I believe you will be needing this."

Reaching out, Merlin took the cell phone and sat back, confused by what was happening.

De Meern turned his body and said something in Dutch to someone outside in the hallway. There was a comment that echoed off the walls outside and De Meern spoke more sternly.

A moment later, one of the police officers walked into the room and placed Merlin's conceal holster, holding his weapon, on the table, "Hier is je wapen, meneer."

Merlin started to move forward to pull the holster over when he realized the officer's body was on full alert as the man stepped back. In fact, his hand stayed near his own holster at his hip. Despite turning the weapon over, he was obviously still concerned - *or is this a set up?* Merlin carefully eased back in his chair.

"Is there something wrong, Mr. Dragon," De Meern asked.

Merlin was about to ask the Kingdom Representative to have the officer leave them alone when the cell phone buzzed in his hand. It startled him and he looked at it. A call was coming in. *Who would be calling now–?* It buzzed again. Marlin tapped the 'accept' call button and placed the phone against his ear, "Yes?"

"Mr. Dragon. You've created quite a stir."

Merlin blew a thin breath out between his lips. It was Director Aubrey Laurent.

"I know exactly how you feel, Mr. Dragon. This has been one day where four letter words have passed my lips far more than I can remember."

"I'm sorry. I can return everything once I get back to Ottawa–"

"And why would you do that?"

Merlin felt the confusion wash over him, "Well...considering what's happened–"

"Mr. Dragon, you're instincts have proven to be quite correct up to this point. Even if your methods are more like a sledge hammer in a China shop, you've managed to uncover factors in this case that have proven to be extremely valuable, if not troubling on so many levels. That being said...you do us no favors by alerting individuals to the fact we even have you working for us."

"I understand."

"And that *being said...I told you the decisions made in the field are yours to make. I've told my superiors that you are the man for the job and, for my part, I won't second guess you. Well, actually I can. And I might have to–"*

"Take me out in the woods and shoot me?"

There was a chuckle, "Exactly." *Laurent's voice then turned deadly serious,* "Whatever you do, Mr. Dragon, I would suggest you do it quickly. Since you left, *civil war* has broken out in Vertrosé."

"What?" Merlin slid his chair back. "Is–?"

As the legs slid rapidly back on the concrete floor, the noise caused De Meern and the officer to take a step back in alarm. The officer actually had the palm of his hand on the butt of his handgun at his belt.

Merlin realized he had almost blurted out the names of President Balewa and Lesedi Noxolo and had to cut himself off. Now he was also aware he could be shot at any moment. He held a hand up, "It's fine–"

"No it's not fine," Laurent said.

"No, I meant–"

"Then why did you say it?"

Merlin opened his mouth to explain and then decided to forget it. It didn't matter at this point.

Laurent continued on, "Whatever you did while you were in Vertrosé was effective enough to have the army on full alert. Early reports said the surprise attack by a rebel group was stopped inside Ténemané after their initial push. President Balewa was able to start an emergency address to his country but all communications were cut off only minutes after he started."

"So Balewa is alive and still in power?"

"At this point, it's any body's guess. And unless we get an announcement from the rebels that they've taken over, we have to assume one or the other."

Merlin cursed under his breath. It had to be Faraji Okafor and his Vertrosé Liberation Army.

There was silence for a moment and then Laurent spoke, his voice a mixture of bitterness and regret, "Unfortunately, Interpol is not really equipped to intervene or help in a matter like this. We don't have a standing army or anything like that. But even if we did...our charter only allows us to coordinate the efforts of local police forces."

Merlin wanted to say something but he pressed his lips together, holding back the words of bitterness and frustration.

"Mr. Dragon?"

Running a hand through his hair, Merlin couldn't help but chastised himself. It wasn't Laurent's fault. Or Interpol's fault. If he hadn't left on this stupid plan to go after VanDaele, he might have been able to use the time to stop Okafor and Kessen from triggering theirs.

The voice was more insistent, "Mr. Dragon?"

"Uh...yeah. Sorry. I was just thinking."

"I know. And I can sense your frustration. We all feel it, Mr. Dragon. We've basically been paper pushers on this side our entire careers, never allowed to actually try and effect an outcome. We thought we had a chance to do that with what you helped us uncover regarding the Banque Monégasque de la Finance in Monte Carlo. I was hoping we might get our political masters to stop what Davet Minard and Dirk VanDaele are doing,. But, unfortunately, I ended up with push back I didn't expect. These two men have a lot of connections and political clout. Maybe even inside Interpol itself."

"You're kidding?"

"I wish I was. So don't beat yourself up over mistakes. It's better to act and be wrong than not do anything at all. And those aren't just words. In many ways, this is new to all of us. This is not a movie, Mr. Dragon. This is real life with real life mistakes. All we can do...all of us...is do our best."

Merlin let out a slow breath, "I know. It's just...."

"I know. And I have no idea what you can do from here on either, Mr. Dragon. If you decide to come home, it's understandable. I guess the ball is in your court, as they say."

Merlin nodded without speaking. There was no doubt he could go home. But he felt responsible. And he *was* the Stopper. Even if he hadn't stopped much so far. He stroked his chin, thinking, "Do you know if I can land at the airport in Ténemané?"

"I don't believe so. According to those first news reports, the airport fell under rebel control before tourists, foreign diplomats, and journalists could get out in time. They all had to flee to the southern part of the city along with the tens of thousands of citizens who fled their homes as the rebels advanced."

Merlin felt the full weight of his next decision. And to complicate matters, he had put himself over 6,000 miles away from Vertrosé. It might as well have been a million.

Chapter 26

THE BOMBARDIER GLOBAL 8000 JET sliced through the night sky as Merlin watched the dark ocean heave below. They were headed back to Ténemané on the chance the airport would be retaken by the Vertrosé army in the ensuing hours. The muffled rumble of the high bypass turbofan engines filled the cabin with relaxing white noise. And the feeling of immense power the engines generated could be felt through the seats like a gentle massage. Both factors were almost soothing. Almost. Because Merlin's feelings of guilt weren't cooperating. No doubt his presence in Vertrosé and his run-in with Kessen had pushed the plans to take over the country by force. Would Balewa still be in power when the sun rose? That was assuming he was still alive. For all Merlin knew, the President had been killed, maybe even assassinated, and– Merlin set his head back on the headrest and thought back to the attempted assassination in Balewa's office in the assembly building. Something bothered him. Something about what happened in that room wasn't right. Some aspect of the event was off. But he couldn't put a finger on it–

"You should try to get some sleep, sir."

Merlin looked over and saw the pilot, Captain Charity Sherrell just coming out of the doorway to the galley at the back. She had two coffees in hand. He gave her a smile that was more like a grimace, "Yeah, I know I should. But I just can't stop a lot of thoughts rattling around in this brain of mine."

Sherrell walked over to him. She paused, concentrating a moment to keep her balance when the plane hit some turbulence, and then she extended a hand, "Then you might as well have a coffee if you're going to stay awake all night."

"No, it's fine. You take that up to Captain Saab. I can make myself one later."

"Actually, I made this one for you. I didn't think you'd roll over and go to sleep despite my suggestion. Faith came back to get her coffee ten minutes ago." Sherrell nodded, "And no you didn't notice her any more than you noticed me going by. Those must be some giant thoughts you're wrestling with."

Merlin took the coffee in hand, "More like a giant space for them to rattle around in. They're hard to catch."

Saab laughed and headed for the front, balancing herself expertly against more turbulence as she walked.

Sipping at the coffee, Merlin tried to catch those thoughts but they proved to be elusive. Half-way through his coffee, he turned his attention to another matter. Getting back into Ténemané. If the rebel group stayed in control of the airport, then what? How could he get into the country?

He watched the dark waves flip whitecaps into the air for a moment and then he had an idea. Picking up his cell phone, he did an Internet search that turned up a few possibilities. He pressed the intercom button, "Captain Sherrell, I see another airport in a city about thirty miles south of Ténemané–"

"Dellyn?"

"Yeah."

"No can do. When you asked us to head in the direction of Vertrosé and you said the airport was under rebel control, we checked all the other airports in the local area."

Merlin nodded his head. *Of course they would.*

"Unfortunately, the facilities are too short for this aircraft. Even trying to execute a short field landing would be slim, none and nope."

"Okay. I was just hoping...it doesn't matter. How close can you get me to Ténemané?"

There was silence for a moment and then Sherrell said, "There is a suitable airport to the north along the coast that *might* allow a short field landing. We can contact them to verify. But it would put you at least fifteen to sixteen hours driving time from Ténemané. And you would be on the rebel side of the city. There's no telling how long it would take you to skirt them and get to the southern part. Assuming you could."

"Right."

"Going further inland would be shorter in flying time but the roads through the jungle aren't that great and you'd be at least twice that long reaching Ténemané from that direction."

Swearing softly, Merlin let out a slow breath of frustration as he looked out at the waves below, "Okay. I guess we have no choice. The northern airport will just have to do."

"Actually, the choice we make depends on how desperate you are."

Despite talking on the intercom, Merlin turned his head toward the cockpit area, wondering if he had heard that right, "How desperate–?"

"And how ballsy."

"Could you make sense?"

"Keep in mind Captain Saab and I are Canadian Air Force pilots. Except on the weekends when we're a stripper duo." There was
a muffled laugh. "But I digress. Are you afraid of heights?"

"What are you talking about? You want me to parachute in?"

"No. You'd probably get shot trying to parachute in."

"Thanks for thinking of me."

"Look, why don't you leave the details to us and get some rest?
You're going to need it."

Chapter 27

MERLIN STOOD NEAR THE EXIT DOOR as the jet dropped lower over the water. It was just 3:00 PM but he already felt exhausted. He placed a hand against the fuselage next to the airstairs door to maintain his balance and he scratched at the two-day growth of stubble on his chin. Another aspect of the work he had never expected; an itchy growth of beard that irritated an already grumpy Stopper. But he wasn't sure if his grumpiness was a result of feeling a bit on the failure side or–

The cabin bell dinged.

Captain Saab's voice came over the intercom, *"Touchdown in three minutes. It's 108° out there so expect the tarmac to be extra hot."*

Merlin nodded to himself as he checked for his weapon under the light shirt to the back of his right hip. His cell phone was on the special belt that held his bank card and other items. Interpol passport in the back pocket on the left–

A whine sounded and the airstairs began to lower.

Merlin flattened himself as much as possible against the fuselage as the wind howled and swirled inside the cabin. The engines grew louder and a moment later the tone deepened. Merlin could feel the change under his feet as the plane slowed and the nose tilted downward.

"Two minutes"

A thunk sounded as the wheel began to lower and the hydraulics and electric motors began their noisy dance as the Global 8000 prepared to land.

"One minute."

The jet vibrated and bucked. Wind savaged the insides of the cabin. The fuselage creaked and groaned as it tried to compensate for the lowered airstairs and the internal turbulence.

Merlin edged as close to the open doorway as he could. The ocean looked to be flying past at a thousand miles an hour, a blur deep green and white

The aircraft shuddered as it turned and slowed dramatically.

A moment later, Merlin could see the roofs of several buildings and a right turn put them over the Ténemané flight tower. They were doing things backward. Normally planes came in off the ocean and took off over the ocean. They had to land toward the ocean instead of into the teeth of the armed forces guarding the tower and planes that were still on the ground.

Merlin's stomach felt like he was on a roller coaster when the jet dropped lower like a stone.

They were now only fifty feet over the blur of the black tarmac.

Tilting slightly to the right to compensate for the lowered airstairs, Sherrell took the jet in for the landing.

There was a bump and the right wheels screeched.

"Once you're on the tarmac, run at a 45-degree angle to the left. The perimeter fence is approximately one hundred yards across a grass strip."

Merlin felt a jar as the left wheels came down and a moment later, a shower of sparks erupted at the bottom of the airstairs and it slid across the tarmac. Giving it another ten seconds to reduce speed, Merlin took off through the open doorway. His feet almost went out from under him from the momentum as his foot hit the top stair but he managed to stay upright. Taking the steps two at a time, he gauged the speed and jumped running onto the tarmac. He stumbled but maintained his feet as the heat of the day hit him like a sledgehammer. Saab had been right. The black tarmac was like an open toaster oven and he was the bread - and soon to be toast if he didn't hurry. Heading in the direction she had given him, Merlin saw the ten foot, chain link fence in the distance.

Behind him, the hydraulics whined as the airstairs began to move back up in place, and the jet's engines roared as the two pilots made a tight turn at the same time.

As his feet hit the grass, Merlin glanced back.

The jet was beginning its run back down the tarmac to take off.

In the distance was a vehicle, racing in this direction.

Putting his head down, Merlin raced for the fence. As soon as he drew close, he leaped, placed his fingers through the chain link fence and began to climb. At the top, he glanced back at the tarmac again.

The Bombardier jet's nose came up and the belly missed the top of the vehicle by only a few feet.

The vehicle swerved and nearly tipped over.

Merlin could now see the vehicle was actually an armored vehicle.

A moment later, a head popped up through the roof of the vehicle. The soldier grabbed the machine gun on the roof, swiveled it around and began firing as he tried to track the jet.

But Sherrell was already climbing fast at a steep angle and heading in a turn that would take them out over the ocean.

Dropping to the grass on the other side of the fence, Merlin took off at a run, heading for the airport access road and the buildings of the city beyond.

Part A of the plan had succeeded.

He was here.

Now came part B.

Whatever that ended up being.

Chapter 28

B EFORE THE MAKE-SHIFT LANDING, Sherrell and Saab had contacted Interpol, asking for help. Interpol had reached out to several countries to supply satellite images that would allow the two pilots to create the best scenario to get Merlin on the ground and headed to an area southeast of the airport that was several blocks north of the front lines. Hopefully not an area presently crawling with rebel forces.

Merlin would be testing those plans in a few moments as he scurried across the access road. Climbing a rolling grassy, hill, Merlin paused just before the crest and checked to make sure he wasn't running into the hands of the rebel army.

But there wasn't anyone in sight, let alone rebel troops. The four lane highway that lay ahead was empty. Normally, there should be plenty of traffic but the highway was vacant of cars, trucks, buses, and even the myriad of bicycles he had seen darting like gnats between the plethora of vehicles that had filled the streets. Beyond the highway was a line of old, six to ten-story apartment buildings, a number of them just bombed-out shells.

Merlin wiped his brow with his hand. Sweat was running from every pore. The heat and humidity was higher than the first day he had arrived and was energy-sapping. He detected the scent of gasoline, diesel and black exhaust smoke, like that first day he had landed here. But there was something else. An acidic, metallic-like aroma lingered in the air...the smell of heavy weapons fire.

Merlin ran low over the crest of the hill, jumped the guard rail, scooted across all four lanes and was soon scrambling over a four foot fence and into the parking area of an apartment building. The lot was empty except for a few cars and trucks parked helter skelter like they'd been abandoned.

He kept running, moving across the parking lot to a strip of dried grass between two of the apartment buildings, Reaching the corner of the building on his right, Merlin pressed his body against the dusty brick and popped his head out, checking the street out front. It was vacant of traffic and partially filled with pieces of concrete and brick from two bombed-out buildings on the other side of the street. It looked like the fighting had passed through here quickly. More than likely the Vertrosé troops had used a few buildings to cover their retreat as the rebels advanced rapidly at the start of the civil war.

The early report Laurent had told him about was accurate. The occupants had fled their homes, moving in a panic to the south. There wasn't a single sound anywhere. No laughter of children. No conversations as friends sat talking. No television, radio or music playing of any type. Just eerie silence. No, that wasn't totally true. Over his heavy breathing, he could hear the faint sound of gunfire in the distance to his right. The rapid gunfire was followed by a series of explosions. It sounded like the front line in the battle for the country was only four or five city blocks away, as they had surmised from the satellite images.

At least he had a direction to concentrate on. Faraji Okafor, the head of the VLA, and Colonel Nicolaas Kessen, the man hired to lead Okafor's forces, should be somewhere over there. If he took them out, cut off the dual heads of the snake, maybe the civil war could be stopped. Or at least give a leadership advantage to the Vertrosé armed forces. All he had to do was sneak over there, avoid the rebel army, find their field HQ and pop Okafor and Kessen. Merlin bent his head and ran a hand through his hair. He didn't know if he had a plan or a vivid imagination. He concluded it was probably both.

Merlin turned on his heels, closed his eyes and set his head back against the building, taking a moment to catch his breath. It had seemed so easy when they came up with the plan flying back across the ocean. Get onto the country and stop the civil war. Yeah, right. So easy. Except he felt small and insignificant now that he was on the ground.

His mind went to Lesedi Noxolo, wondering how she was– it came to him in a flash. He knew what was bothering him about the assassination attempt on President Balewa.

Chapter 29

MERLIN'S THOUGHTS WENT BACK to the assassination attempt in President Balewa's office. When Merlin had mentioned the open window and the possibility of someone shooting the President, Balewa had moved across the room to close it. He was the one who had opened it earlier to let air in and he no doubt felt dumb at not realizing the danger.

At that point, Lesedi Noxolo realized the danger Balewa was in and she moved quickly across the room to move him aside. The shot came and Noxolo had taken the bullet intended for the President, saving his life.

Only that wasn't the truth of it.

The fact was...Balewa had opened the window behind and to the right of his desk before they had started talking.

No shot came.

It was possible that the shooter was still getting in position but he doubted it.

Because while they were talking over the situation, Balewa had moved around to the back of his desk to get the bottle of aspirins. He had stood there for some time by the window and even picked up the phone.

And yet, no shot came.

But *after* Balewa had come from behind the desk and crossed the room to Merlin...he then went back to close the window...and that's when it happened. Noxolo had moved with purpose...pushed Balewa to the side...he had turned and pushed her back.

Just as the shot came.

From what the paramedics had said before Merlin left, the bullet had barely missed her heart. Balewa had in fact saved Noxolo's life. *She* was the target.

Merlin shook his head as he went back over the scene. Was he wrong? Why shoot Noxolo? She handled Balewa's security but there was no doubt they were close and she was his confidant and right hand in many ways. But it was hard to believe she was so important to the President that taking her out would help Okafor in any scheme he had. Or Davet Minard and Dirk VanDaele and their economic hit man scheme through the Banque Monégasque de la Finance for that matter. There was no way he could see her as vitally crucial to Balewa's hold on power or an impediment to either scheme to take over the country literally and/or financially.

So why shoot her?

There was only one way to find out; ask her. Presuming, of course, that she's still alive.

Merlin took his cell phone in hand and called up Lesedi Noxolo's cell phone number. Tapping the call button, he put the phone to his ear as he scanned the roadway for any signs. It seemed like the line was dead and he looked at his phone. It was looking for a connection. He contemplated trying to find a land line when he heard a ringing and he put the phone to his ear again—

"Yes? Who is this?" It was a man's voice and he sounded somewhere between angry, anxious, and annoyed.

Detecting a familiar bent to the voice, Merlin said, "President Balewa?"

"Yes. Who is this?" Definitely annoyed.

About to say his name, Merlin glanced at the buildings and considered a possible open window or doorway near him with someone listening. "It's your favorite Interpol agent."

"You think this is a funny matter?"

"No, sir, I don't. I'm–"

"Where are you? You disappeared without a word." Now definitely angry. *"Are you aware a civil war has been started?"*

"Yes, sir, I'm aware. I had a job to do but I'm back in country–"

"And how are you calling this phone?"

Merlin thought that question was strange and he shrugged a shoulder, "I'm on my cell phone. I had Lesedi's number from Monte Carlo–"

"Yes, yes, but...it doesn't matter. Now that I have you, Mr. Dragon, you must talk to your people immediately. We need to have the armed backing of Interpol nations and we must have it now before–"

Merlin didn't have time to deal with this line of discussion. "Lesedi Noxolo, how is she?" he asked, fearing the worst.

That seemed to strike Balewa hard and his voice softened. *"She is in Saint Josutrutreph Hospital. I'm afraid she has not regained consciousness to my knowledge. The VLA is closing in and we are considering an evacuation of the hospital...but they are not sure if she will survive the transport."* His voice hardened again. *"Which is why you must speak to–"*

Merlin hung up. He didn't have time for the niceties of conversation.

He called up a search engine to find a map of the city. It took a few moments as the connection seemed to lag. And then a little icon popped up to show he was connected to a satellite feed. Typing in his search, a map appeared on the small screen, showing the location of the hospital. It was on the south-west edge of the airport near the front lines. Merlin looked in that direction, listening to the sounds of battle.

Time was running out.

He would have to move fast.

Turning on his heels, Merlin headed to the parking lot to see if one of the vehicles could provide a ride.

It was risky but he might already be too late.

Chapter 30

I T TOOK MERLIN nearly an hour and a half to get within a few blocks of where he estimated the hospital to be. He'd had to zigzag around streets that were filled with rubble from blown out buildings or when he'd come across a pocket of rebel troops, but he had made it. Now, as he sat idling in the battered car he'd taken from the back lot, he could hear sounds of gunfire and explosions somewhere one or two blocks to the south. The hospital should be close but he'd lost his connection to the Google map he'd been using and he could only estimate its location because a number of the city landmarks had been destroyed by the fighting. Looked at the gas gauge, he mulled over trying to drive another block over. The car was almost empty–

Movement on his right at the end of the block caught his attention.

From what he could tell, rebel troops were moving in this direction. He decided this was as far as he could go in the vehicle and he got out, leaving the door open as he scooted across the rubble filled sidewalk and into a war ravaged parking garage. His footsteps echoed off the concrete walls as he ran low for the other side of the building.

Reaching the back entrance, Merlin peered outside. The odor of wet cardboard and rotting garbage mixed with the acrid smell of battle. The back alley was narrow and the back door into the building on the other side wasn't far away but the sounds of echoing gunfire to the right sounded close.

Cautiously slipping outside, he stayed low and used a stack of cardboard boxes just to the right to hide behind. He took a moment before peering around the edge of the boxes and down the alleyway.

Rebel troops were in the street at the far end, dug in behind several battered vehicles turned on their sides. He could hear the rumble of a heavy machine gun. No, make that two. He scanned the upper windows in the buildings facing this direction, looking for a sniper.

When Merlin was sure no one was looking in this direction, he darted across the narrow alleyway to a dumpster at the back of the next building. He knelt behind the dumpster for a moment, checking to see if they'd spotted him. So far, so good. He slipped around the dumpster and moved low to the back door, pulled it open and slipped into the building that turned out to be a commercial structure with empty offices. Making his way to the front lobby, Merlin moved to the entrance way and opened the door a crack. He could hear sporadic gunfire to the right. It was much closer now and the heavy metallic-like aroma of war hung ominously in the hot, humid air.

Opening the door slightly wider, Merlin couldn't see anyone on the street. Once again, he scanned the buildings across the street for a sniper. Of course, if one was there, he would probably never know it. He didn't have much choice and Merlin scooted outside to hide behind a square, concrete city trash bin. In the direction of the gunfire, Merlin could see a number of buildings at the end of the street had chunks of brick and mortar torn from their sides. There was a lull for a moment and then the rapid fire of automatic weapons echoed off the surrounding buildings.

And then he cursed hard under his breath.

He could see a shattered 'Saint Josutrutreph Hospital' sign high on the building at the end of the block. The battle was on the doorstep of where Noxolo lay. If they hadn't gotten her out of there by now– he pushed the thought from his mind. He had his eye on a sign indicating an entrance road to the emergency room on this side of the hospital. That could be his way in – provided he could make it there without being shot.

Pulling his weapon and moving low across the street, Merlin kept close to the buildings, ready to duck for any type of shelter.

Reaching the corner of the building just before the ambulance access road, he peered around the edge. Two red beret-wearing soldiers, outfitted in light body armor, were standing near the entrance to the emergency room. They weren't standing guard so much as watching and listening in the direction of the gunfire and explosions taking place in the area of the intersection. And their attention appeared to be specifically on a park area on the opposite corner of the intersection and three makeshift bunkers of sandbags where fellow troops were taking heavy fire from rebel troops. As soon as the troops popped up and fired, they had to duck as the return fire was heavier.

Now Merlin knew why those rebel troops were moving in the direction where he had left the car. They were planning on a pincer movement, coming at the park from the angle Merlin had just come from. He glanced back at the office building and wondered how soon they would be here. Time was running out–

A piercing whistle sounded overhead and a moment later a blast in the street took Merlin off his feet. He felt himself spin in the air and then he landed hard. The wind in his lungs was expelled forcefully as he was punched by the concrete sidewalk.

It took a moment before he was able to move.

His body felt paralyzed by the blow and his ears were ringing.

He had lost his gun and he slapped weakly at the concrete sidewalk he lay on, trying to locate it.

His fingers hit cold steel and he rolled slightly, grasping the weapon.

Getting to his knees, Merlin swallowed painfully, trying to clear his ears. His noticed his pant legs had slashes in them, his right shoe looked like it had been hit by pieces of shrapnel from the exploding shell and he had rips in his right sleeve. He felt for injuries. There were none but devastating trauma had been close. The muted echoes of gunfire off the brick and concrete buildings brought his thoughts back to his task at hand and he looked around. Two-thirds of the street now consisted of a massive crater, dug by a shell of some type, but there were no rebel troops pouring into the intersection and rapidly advancing. At least not yet.

Crawling four feet back to the corner of the building, Merlin checked the entry road and the emergency entrance. The two guards were kneeling now, weapons up. They weren't firing but were watching the park area and the heavy exchange of gunfire. Like Merlin, they knew it was only a matter of time before rebel troops overran the defensive position–

Another muted sound caught his attention. He wiggled a finger in his ear and stretched his jaw, trying to get full hearing back. He closed his eyes and listened again–

His blood ran cold.

Looking to the intersection, he tried to gauge the direction the sound was coming from. It was off to the right of the intersection, where the rebel troops were. He couldn't see it but the sound told him it was there.

The faint metallic ringing of tank treads.

The rebels had a friggin' tank!

Chapter 31

THE REBELS HAD ARMOR? Merlin thought back to the Interpol report on Dirk VanDaele. The man was a global arms dealer who could supply everything from small weapons to tanks, fighter planes and ballistic missiles. Looking up, Merlin wondered if these madmen had actually supplied planes, and missiles as well to Okafor, and his VLA. Did Balewa have access to those kinds of weapons? Cursing softly and ignoring the possible disparity problem between the two forces, for now, Merlin decided the only thing he could do was to try and use the current situation. And he didn't have much time before this flank was attacked by the rebel troops coming from behind.

Slipping the weapon back into his holster, he stood up and undid three buttons on the shirt, then redid a couple in the wrong buttonholes to look disheveled. Putting a grimace on his face, Merlin bent over, grabbed his left thigh and then began to limp hurriedly towards the emergency room. He was halfway up the entrance road before the guards reacted.

They swung around and trained their assault rifles on him.

Merlin was close enough to see they held South African-made Vektor R4 weapon, capable of firing 750 rounds/minute. What he couldn't see was if they had trigger fingers.

One of them yelled, "Arrêt. Arrêt."

Putting his right hand up near his ear, Merlin made like he couldn't hear, gesturing with the other hand towards the crater in the street. Then he gestured to the emergency room doors as he kept limping and moving forward.

"Arrêt!"

He made another gesture to his left leg and foot and kept limping. He was taking a chance but–

Another whistling sound was followed by an explosion in the intersection.

The ground shook and Merlin was taken off his feet again. He landed hard again but refused to stay down as pieces of the road continued to fall around him. The rebel troops - and the tank - were moving closer and there wasn't time for personal pain to get in the way. Roiling around to his knees, he checked to see what the two soldiers were doing. They were face down, hands over their heads. Taking advantage of the situation, he ran for the emergency room entrance, skirting the soldiers and expecting bullets to rip into his back at any moment.

But it didn't happen and he pulled hard on the frosted glass door, slipping inside. He found himself in a madhouse of chaos with doctors, nurses, and patients running this way and that. No one seemed to have a particular direction in mind; it was all helter skelter panic from Merlin's point of view.

He took several steps, reached out and grabbed the arm of a nurse.

The nurse turned, anger and fear clashing in the look on her face, "Let go."

But Merlin didn't let go. He held her elbow firmly, "Sorry, I have no time for niceties." He pulled his Interpol passport, opened it with his thumb and stuck it close to her face, "I'm an Interpol agent and I'm here to find Lesedi Noxolo. She was taken in with a gunshot wound."

The nurse's eyebrows knit together and then her brow furrowed as a myriad of emotions swept through her.

Merlin spoke firmly, "President Balewa told me she was here but could be transported if things got too bad. And from the sound of gunfire and explosions outside, it apparently has." He squeezed her elbow just enough to send a message, "*Where* is she?"

Her face grimaced under the pressure of his hand and the nurse said, "She was in intensive care last time I knew. They probably would have taken her out through here if–"

"Intensive care, which floor?"

"Third–"

Merlin was off, heading for the stairs. He slammed the door back against the wall and took the steps two at a time.

Chapter 32

A T THE TOP OF THE STAIRS, Merlin took a peek through the small window in the door as he grabbed the handle to open it. The hallway was empty, which was good. Or it was bad, considering no one was running around in a panic up here. Maybe she was already gone?

Stepping through into the hallway, Merlin moved quickly, checking through open doorways on either side as he looked for someone to point him in the right direction or get some indication of where exactly the intensive care unit was. But every room was hauntingly empty. The smell in the air was a mixture of gunpowder and antiseptic, the values of life and death wrestling with one another. Bandages and gauze, some of them bloody, lay on the floor in places, evidence people had been moving with some urgency up here. He came to a cross hallway and the sign for the ICU pointed to the right. The doors were about thirty feet down the hallway and he headed for them—

"Ne bouge pas! Don't move."

Merlin felt the barrel of a gun pressed against the back of his skull as he froze in position. Someone had been in one of the side rooms and he hadn't paid enough attention. He had been in too much of a rush and he might now pay the ultimate price.

Turning his head slightly, Merlin could see it was a Vertrosé soldier in a red beret. He would be a member of State President's Guards which, he hoped, meant Lesedi Noxolo might still be here, "I can explain–"

"Shut up." A hand patted him down and his weapon was removed. The hand also found the passport. A few seconds passed before the guard reached down to a walkie talkie and spoke in a low voice to someone.

A moment later, the double doors to the ICU were flung open and a large soldier in a red beret appeared. He kicked at a door stopper on the left to keep the door open. Did the same to the one on the right, paused a moment and then marched forward with determination, looking over Merlin's ripped and torn clothing as he advanced.

The double doors stayed open behind him.

A few seconds later, two soldiers, submachine guns in hand, emerged from the ICU, one behind the other. They strode down the hallway for a few feet and then stopped, taking up a positions against each wall, weapons at the ready.

The large soldier stopped a few feet away from Merlin. His eyes were intent as he studied the intruder and then said, "I am Captain Taavi Chiamaka. You are the man who was with the President when Lesedi was shot."

It was a statement, not a question, and Merlin felt some relief, "That's right. I need to talk to her."

"That is not possible."

"You don't understand. I need to find out–"

"I'm sorry, but you won't be able to find out anything, sir. She has been in a coma since she was brought here."

The relief disappeared and Merlin felt despair replace it. He bent his head and ran a hand through his hair as a breath of frustration announced to the whole world that he had failed.

Chapter 33

THERE HAD TO BE ANOTHER WAY to stop what was happening. But what? Actually, Merlin felt a little foolish, thinking he could stop a civil war. He hadn't been able to stop much of anything–

"Sir?"

Merlin looked up. Chiamaka was looking at him. "I'm sorry," Merlin said. "You have to get Noxolo out of here–"

"Yes, sir, we know. We have the President's helicopter coming onto the roof in ten minutes. As long as we don't get shot down...."

Merlin's attention was caught by another soldier in a red beret backing out between the open ICU doors.

Chiamaka looked back at them as well, "She is coming out now."

It took a moment before Merlin realized the soldier backing out was on this end of a gurney.

The soldier on the other end gave Merlin a stern look as he emerged from between the doors. He then gave Chiamaka a questioning look.

Chiamaka nodded and gestured for them to continue.

As the gurney was wheeled down the hallway, Merlin could see Lesedi Noxolo under the covers. As they got closer he could see how chalk-white her face was and he felt a tinge of remorse at not preventing the whole episode from escalating.

A frantic doctor and two nurses burst through the open ICU doors, rushing down the hallway to catch up. One of the nurses carried a medical backpack over her shoulder.

As the medical teamed neared Captain Chiamaka, the doctor began talking rapidly in French, gesturing to the ceiling.

Merlin assumed the doc was urging Chiamaka to get her to the roof and the helicopter.

Captain Taavi Chiamaka held his hands out to calm the doctor, apparently explaining in French what was happening.

Taking the opportunity to get some needed information, Merlin pointed to Noxolo and asked the doctor, "Any idea how long she'll be in a coma?"

The doctor looked at Merlin with suspicion, not talking.

Chiamaka looked at Merlin for a moment and then spoke to the doctor, "It is all right, Doctor Jelani. This man was with the President when it happened." He looked back at Merlin, "But I don't believe the doctor can give you any time frame for her recovery. I asked previously and it will depend on how soon we can get her to adequate facilities."

Doctor Jelani spoke up, his accent more French than anything else, "He is right. This hospital has the only real equipment in the entire country to keep her in the coma necessary to allow her body to cope with the trauma. Unless we can get her to another one where we can–"

Merlin straightened up. Had he heard right? "You're *keeping* her in the coma?" He looked to Chiamaka and back to Jelani, "It's an *induced* coma?"

"Yes, of course," Jelani said. "Her body needs to–"

"Can you bring her out of it?" Merlin asked. "Right now, I mean?"

Jelani looked horrified, "No, of course not. As I said, her body–"

"Can't or won't?" Merlin looked to Chiamaka and quickly explained what had happened in Balewa's office and his theory.

Captain Chiamaka listened intently but looked skeptical at the end. "But why would someone want to shoot Lesedi Noxolo when the President was right there as you say? It must simply have been a miss and you are reading more into it than there really is."

"Maybe," Merlin conceded. "But the only way we can know for sure is to talk to her."

"And I tell you that can kill her," Doctor Jelani said sternly. He looked to Chiamaka, "And every moment we delay to get her to the airport and to another country with a hospital that can–"

"And how do you propose to get her to another country with the airport closed off?" Merlin asked.

That seemed to shake up both the Captain and the Doctor.

"Are you sure?" Chiamaka asked. He gestured to the other guard to use the walkie talkie, "Call to head quarters and see what they can tell us."

Merlin wondered how they didn't know if he knew. As he listened to the guard talking, it struck him. "You can't use the hospital telephones? Or your cell phones?"

Chiamaka shook his head, "No. The land lines in this entire area are out. And the cell phones have not been working."

Cursing softly, Merlin realized why his phone had taken some time to make a connection. Laurent had said his 'special' cell phone would automatically roll through the connections available to it, breaking passwords as necessary without him needing to do a single thing. It had probably found a satellite connection like it had done with his Internet search. Which meant all the land lines were out and the cell towers were out. Probably part of the rebel's plans to keep the defensive forces from communicating with each other and coordinating their efforts to fight back. That was also why Balewa had wondered how he had connected to Lesedi's cell. Which was all great to know but it didn't help the situation.

Doctor Jelani's voice was soft as he asked Chiamaka, "What are we going to do? We must find a way to get her to—"

"How desperate are you?" Merlin asked him. He wiggled his cell phone in the air.

Looking confused at first, Jelani then realized Merlin was suggesting blackmail to get what he wanted. The doctor spoke harshly in French to Captain Chiamaka, gesturing wildly at Merlin.

A smile that was more like a grimace hung on Chiamaka's lips as he said to Merlin, "The good doctor thinks you are an idiot."

Merlin nodded, "Yep. And he's probably right—"

"He also wants me to shoot you and take the phone."

"Oh." Merlin's shoulders slumped, sensing defeat but pushing on, "Look. I can offer a way out *if* you can provide a small fighting force. There's no guarantee—"

"I can provide the fighters," Chiamaka said swiftly. "How soon can you make it happen?"

Now feeling a bit like a callous idiot, Merlin said, "A soon as you wake Lesedi Noxolo from the coma. I need to ask her—"

Doctor Jelani understood what he wanted and began to argue with Chiamaka.

The Doctor and the Captain went back and forth, their voices getting louder and louder.

Finally, Jelani made a sound of disgust and said something to one of the nurses. She ran back to the ICU and disappeared inside.

The other nurse set the medical backpack down on the edge of the gurney and rummaged inside. She handed something to Jelani and he went to work on Noxolo, putting in a line to one of her veins.

The nurse came running back from the ICU. She held two vials in her hand and she gave one to the doctor.

Jelani quickly set up a syringe filled with an amber liquid. But before he pushed the plunger, the doctor looked at Merlin, "Are you sure you want me to do this? This could kill her. You *do* realize that?"

Merlin pushed a thin reedy breath through his lips and nodded. But he also exchanged a glance with Chiamaka, both of them wondering if this was actually going to turn out okay in the long run.

Chapter 34

DOCTOR JELANI HESITATED before he took a deep breath in to ready himself. Then with a shaky hand, he pushed the amber fluid into Noxolo's arm. With that done, he softly set the syringe, still attached to the tube, on the blankets and checked for a pulse.

It took a few tense moments before Noxolo's eyelids fluttered and she opened her eyes with a groan.

Merlin moved next to her, aware Jelani had taken the other vial in hand and was talking with the nurses in a hushed, urgent tone. The look on Noxolo's face indicated she was in pain and Merlin wondered if she would last long enough for them to put her back under. He felt like crap and realized he didn't have much time either way. He bent closer to her face, "It's Merlin Dragon. Do you know where you are?"

Her eyes semi-focused on him and her voice was rough and groggy, "Yes, in pain."

At least she had a sense of humor. And then he wondered if she really knew what was going on. "Do you know what happened?"

"Happened? What...?"

"You were shot."

Licking her lips and closing her eyes for a moment, Noxolo finally nodded faintly, "Yes. You were right. The window. They tried to kill the President–"

"No. They tried to kill you?"

Pain mixed with the confusion on her face and Noxolo shook her head faintly, "No. Not... me."

"They had several chances to kill the President," Merlin said. "Like getting those aspirins at his desk?"

Noxolo's face screwed up in pain and she was silent. Then she opened her eyes and looked at Merlin, "You are right. But why...?"

"I have no idea. But you must know something. Can you think of any reason why–?"

She closed her eyes and shook her head again.

A nearby explosion rocked the hospital.

The medical backpack tumbled off the gurney and fell to the floor.

Everyone fought to stay upright.

Doctor Jelani nearly had a heart attack when the second vial slipped from his hand. It bounced on the blankets and then headed for the floor as the gurney rolled away.

Chiamaka reached out and caught the gurney from rolling more than a foot

The nurse grabbed for the vial but it bounced from her palm before she could close her fingers.

The second nurse dropped to her knees and caught it with both hands.

Doctor Jelani took the vial in hand, relief evident on his face but determined as he moved to the gurney, "We must put her back under without delay."

Chiamaka nodded with his own relief, "Yes. And we are going to have to hurry if the helicopter is to take us–"

The doctor cursed in French when he realized the line had come free from Noxolo's arm and the syringe was broken on the floor.

The nurse still on her knees reached for the medical backpack and began rummaging through it as Jelani continued with his colorful language.

Chiamaka wiped a hand across his mouth, fully aware of how close they were to losing Noxolo. He tore his eyes from the doctor and looked to Merlin, "Can you set up the way out of the country now? We don't have much time–"

Another explosion shook the building.

Chiamaka and the soldiers held the gurney firmly this time.

Jelani now had a needle in hand and was filling it with the liquid from the second vial.

"What is happening?" Noxolo asked, her face showing fear and confusion.

Merlin realized she had no idea what had happened after she was shot. "Okafor and his cronies started a civil war," he told her. "They're trying to take the capital."

Noxolo cursed and actually tried to get up, "We must stop them."

The nurses pushed her back down, holding her in place by the shoulders.

Struggling, Noxolo said, "I must speak to the President and to General Bamgboshe. We need to–"

Captain Chiamaka moved in and put a hand on her arm, "You must not struggle, Lesedi. You will only make your injuries worse. We cannot afford to lose you as well."

"But–"

"General Bamgboshe is dead, Lesedi."

Noxolo went still and looked up at Chiamaka, "Dead? What happened?"

Captain Chiamaka took a few seconds before saying, "We found him dead at his home not long after you were shot. In fact, it would appear someone shot him early in the morning, the same day you were shot. I am sorry, Lesedi. I know you knew him well."

Nodding in shock, Lesedi Noxolo seemed to be having a hard time comprehending all that had happened. When the doctor tapped her arm with his fingers, trying to bring up the vein he would use she swatted his hand away. She looked at Chiamaka with urgency in her eyes, "Which way did Okafor have his forces attack the city? Which direction?"

Chiamaka held a hand out for the doctor to leave her alone as he looked in her eyes, "From the north. Why?"

"Not from the west?"

"No. It would have made more sense but they moved from the north to take the airport for some reason. That was foolish on their part but fortuitous for us. The President had already put us on alert and the attack from the north allowed us extra time to react and set up a line of defense." He gestured towards the sounds of muffled explosions and gunfire, "Even now you can hear how they are trying to push southward. But we have slowed them to a crawl and it's only a matter of time before we begin to push them back–"

Noxolo shook her head softly, "No, they are moving slow on purpose, limiting their losses. They are *allowing* you to fight back."

Chiamaka narrowed his eyes, shaking his head softly, "Allowing us to fight back? That doesn't make any sense. What kind of strategy is that?"

Looking up at Merlin, Noxolo said, "I think I know why Okafor had me shot. And why they killed Bamgboshe. Do you remember me telling you about our struggle for freedom and independence? How Adisa Balewa and Faraji Okafor fought side by side in the civil war that ensued?

"Yes. But what does that have to do with–?"

"Bamgboshe was the one who proved to be the brilliant strategic mind when it came to the battles. He was the one who made the difference for our side. We had a smaller, ill-equipped force and–" She grabbed Merlin's sleeve with a weak grip, "Listen to me carefully. I was with him when he devised the plan to take Ténemané and drive then-President Kayin Nabrit from power. There is a large railway yard to the north that was abandoned years ago–"

"How does that railway yard help them?" Chiamaka asked her. "You're not making sense, Lesedi."

"Do you know of the old oil terminal that is there? The trains used to take the crude oil in from the north."

Chiamaka nodded as he thought about it, "Yes, I remember my father telling me they did that until the fields to the north dried up. It supplied a lot of good jobs. But no one has used the terminal for years."

"Bamgboshe did. He used the storage tanks and the buildings to create a fuel and ammunition dump to supply our forces. You can bring in more fuel and ammunition by rail or by the seaport because you control them both in the north of the city."

Chiamaka rubbed his chin, "True. And you can also bring fresh supplies in by the airport once you have control of it. But what does that have to do with–?"

"Because *our* forces will have to bring in new supplies from the south or inland from the west. The west is faster, but even that can take one to two weeks because of the jungle and the rough roads. All the rebels have to do is put small forces in the way, harassing any resupply convoys from the west. Even if they don't stop them completely, it could delay them *another* week. I know, because that's what Bamgboshe had us doing."

Chiamaka swore as he realized the full impact of the rebel plan, "You're right. And slowly pressing our army like they are doing now will deplete our fuel and ammunition within...." He rubbed his forehead as he gave it some thought, "Let's say a week...?"

"Even two weeks cuts it too close if they can slow the resupply convoys," Noxolo said. "But we can fight back by taking out those fuel and ammunition dumps. That would put us on an even footing with them. Possibly even better."

Taking a deep breath and blowing it out in frustration, Chiamaka said, "That sounds good...*if* we had planes or rockets. But we don't. And fighting our way up there will deplete our supplies faster...."

Noxolo was taken aback by that comment and the truth struck her hard. She looked to Merlin, "I guess it's true after all. Knowing is not enough, we must apply."

Merlin raised an eyebrow, "Another African proverb?"

"No. Bruce Lee actually."

Smiling, Merlin pulled out his cell phone, "Let's make a call and get you out of here. Then we can see what we can do to prove old Bruce right."

Chapter 35

THE FIRE ENGINE WAS A BEAST TO DRIVE, at least for someone who had never driven one before. Technically a heavy duty rescue pumper with a 1,000 gallon tank, at eight-and-a-half feet wide, eleven-and-a-half feet high, and forty-feet long, the massive red vehicle was more like a force of nature as Merlin sped through the streets of Ténemané. The red and white strobe lights were flashing and he kept the up-and-down wail of the siren on at full blast as he kept the gas pedal three-quarters of the way down. Full speed wasn't needed right now. He hoped. Besides, the corners were still rough.

The plan using the fire engine - was this a real plan? - was to use it as a distraction. And hopefully not a dead one.

Merlin wiped the sweat from his brow. He'd been able to borrow a pair of heavy-duty work pants and a shirt the fire fighters said had moisture-wicking mesh vents to allow the body to self-regulate its temperature. It sounded good but it wasn't working in this heat. At least for him–

He swung to the left to avoid rubble blocking half the street and then came back to the middle.

An open-backed lorry carrying rebel troops appeared in the intersection dead ahead.

Merlin could see the surprise in the eyes of the troops as the massive vehicle headed directly for them. He spun the huge steering wheel with both hands. The rubber of the tires screeched in protest against the pavement as the fire truck veered around the corner to the left.

The lorry driver turned hard in the other direction to avoid a collision, sending the troops against the edge of the lorry and fighting to stay on.

The back wheels of the fire engine lost traction because of the fine rubble covering the street and the red beast began skidding, threatening to spin out of control.

Merlin spun the steering wheel hard in the other direction to compensate.

A loud bang reverberated off the sides of the buildings as the right wheels of the fire engine struck the curb, jumped it and slid over more debris.

Merlin spun the wheel harder.

The front wheels jumped the curb and now half of the vehicle was on the sidewalk, vibrating violently over pieces of concrete and brick.

Merlin fought to get the red beast back on the road.

His right arm flew up involuntarily to protect his face as he plowed through a street lamp and then took out a fire hydrant.

Jerking the wheel hard and getting back in the street, Merlin glanced back to see a fountain of water shooting straight into the air. Fitting. And then his heart skipped a beat when he realized how close he had come to failure...and disaster.

The fire engine's 1,000-gallon tank didn't hold water as it was supposed to. It held high-octane gasoline. And the pump house and control section, just behind the fire engine's front cab, held high-grade explosives, linked electronically to a switch in Merlin's pocket. If he had hit that lorry or the side of a building....

Merlin pushed the thought from his mind.

He pressed down on the gas pedal and pushed harder toward the airport.

Two more rebel vehicles appeared up ahead, heading in the same direction.

Would they turn around and–?

A moment later, they swung out of the way to let him pass.

Merlin allowed himself a smile. He had figured a fire engine rushing to a fire would be the perfect 'disguise' and he was right. At least to this point. People were trained to get out of the way for a fire truck rushing to a burning building. Even in war, the first instinct would be to let it pass. And all he needed was that few moments to get by the rebels and stay ahead long enough to fulfill his part of the plan.

The north side of the airport was close and Merlin looked at the skyline between a couple of half-bombed-out buildings. Through the smoke of several burning buildings, he spotted a tiny dot in the hazy sky. That should be the Bombardier Global 8000.

Captain Chiamaka was leading a small force of army personnel to the south side of the airport. The plan was to get Doctor Jelani and his nurses onboard the business jet with Lesedi Noxolo and get her to a modern facility with the proper equipment that could keep her alive.

For their part, Captains Sherrell and Saab hadn't offered an alternate plan, debated the wisdom of the plan or debated the danger. It was more a 'name the time and place and we're there' attitude. They were going to perform an extraction, similar to his insertion onto the Ténemané airport tarmac; quick, dirty and dangerous.

Now the ball was in Merlin's court to provide the necessary diversion. He became conscious of a voice with a female Aussie accent saying it was 'recalculating'. That sudden turn had put him off course. A course that had been set into the fire engine's GPS unit using satellite imagery from Interpol.

Merlin cursed. The course they had set had been taking him through the least rubble filled streets. Had he screwed himself up with that unintended turn?

He waited for the new direction to come back up. As the seconds passed he decided to take matters into his own hands. He took the next turn to the right, hoping to put himself close enough to the original course. He avoided an overturned car and shot though a stop sign before he knew it–

"Take the next turn to the left," the Aussie voice said.

"Alright, mate."

He took the next left as instructed and pressed down on the gas pedal, happy to be back on course.

Two blocks over, as he passed through an intersection, he caught a glimpse of an FV4034 Challenger 2 off to the right and his blood ran cold.

That was a British main battle tank.

Were they aware of what he was doing? If they did, all he had to do was stay ahead of the armor. Of course, from the looks of the 5 inch-or-so cannon with a muzzle velocity of 5,000 feet per second, staying ahead of a shell would be a lot harder. It was bad enough watching the disappointment on the faces of the firefighters in giving up their brand new engine recently imported from New Zealand. They had stood around in a wake-like farewell when he had driven away. Losing it now without accomplishing the mission would be like adding insult to injury.

Merlin spotted a jeep following a yellow school bus up ahead. As he drove closer, he leaned on the horn, adding to the urgency of the wailing siren and flashing lights.

Both vehicles slowed and pulled the right.

As Merlin swung to the right to pass them, he saw the wide eyes of the rebel soldiers in both vehicles.

Swinging back into the middle of the road, he glanced in the side mirrors. He didn't see them give chase but he was going to run out of good fortune before long. He glanced to the hazy sky, looking for the jet. He caught a glimpse of it between two more cratered buildings and he cursed. It was growing larger every second and he knew he was running out of time. And knowing the two Canadian air force pilots, they wouldn't hesitate to try the rescue mission without the diversion.

Merlin pressed down on the gas pedal and shot across another intersection before making a hard left as instructed, trying to maintain speed. The fire engine swung wide again and the tires mounted the curb, the front of the cab bashing aside several garbage cans and boxes that exploded, sending packing material flying in every direction. Bouncing back down onto the pavement, Merlin spotted his target on the other side of the cross street up ahead. A gas station to the north of the airport. It was going to add more fuel to the firestorm he was going to create.

Taking his foot off the gas pedal, Merlin opened the driver's side door as the vehicle began slowing. He grabbed the backpack on the seat beside him, slipped his arm through the strap and placed the pack over his right shoulder. Then he bent over and reached to the floor in front of the passenger seat and grabbed the makeshift jamming tool the fire fighters had made from a couple of short 2x4s.

The fire engine was starting to roll to a stop as Merlin stepped out onto the running board. He placed one end of the wooden tool over the gas pedal and then slid the other end down against the edge seat, jamming the gas pedal right to the floor. The engine roared and the tires squealed as the fire engine began to accelerate toward the gas station.

Merlin jumped.

And promptly banged his head against the side of the engine as the backpack's strap snared on the inside door handle.

The fire engine was racing for the gas station and Merlin's feet were being dragged over the pavement as he struggled to free himself.

This wasn't going to end well if he didn't do something.

And fast.

He had no choice.

He pulled his arm from the strap and tumbled head over heels on the pavement as the fire engine left him behind. Finally rolling over on his own and getting to his feet, Merlin felt the pain in his arms and legs from tumbling over the pavement. But he had to put that aside. He reached into his shirt pocket – and panicked. He had lost the detonator. He spun around in the street as the up-and-down wailing of the fire engine moved further away. He was going to fail – no. There it was, several feet away on the pavement. He ran for it, picked it up and headed for the open doorway in a bombed out building.

Glancing to his left, Merlin saw the fire engine roar across the street and mount the curb at full speed. It was now or never. His thumb pressed the button and he dove for the doorway.

A blinding light was followed by a concussive blast that threw him against the edge of the doorway when he was halfway through.

The pain in his side was immense and he felt his body hit the threshold as he fell–

A second explosion was followed by a brilliant flash of light and tremendous heat washed over Merlin. He felt a different pain in his legs and he groaned as he turned and looked down. His pant legs were on fire. He slapped at the flames and then pulled himself into the building where he rolled around on the rubble inside, putting out the fire.

Finally lying on his back. Merlin looked up at the broken ceiling. He had lost the backpack that contained the explosives that he was going to use for the next part of the plan. Now what?

Chapter 36

DESPITE FEELING BATTERED AND BRUISED, Merlin had to get moving. The blast should pull the rebel troops away from the airport and once they were in the vicinity of the fire they would be looking for the enemy who had caused the explosion. He moved toward the back of the building which appeared to have been a restaurant. He threaded his way through broken tables and twisted metal chairs. The heavy scent of charred wood and plaster draped everything. At the end of a long hallway, he found a door hanging at an angle on its upper hinge and he squeezed through into an alleyway. Out here the smell of garbage and urine danced with the smell of burning gasoline. He climbed through a shattered window into the next building and found himself inside an old battered apartment. He made his way through upended furniture and household items into a hallway beyond and headed to the front doors of the apartment building. The street out front was clear and he sprinted across to the other side.

The sound of an airplane caught his attention and he caught a glimpse of the Global 8000 jet in a steep climb and banking toward the ocean. He had to assume it was a successful extraction and not call them. Right now, he couldn't afford any self-recriminations to interfere if it had failed. Moving into the next building, Merlin made his way toward his next target.

After a dozen or so city blocks, the destruction was minimal. The rebels had obviously taken everyone by surprise and moved through here rapidly before the Vertrosé army had been able to re-act and slow their progress. Of course, as Noxolo had told them, the rebels were expecting that and even welcomed the slowdown, limiting their own losses while depleting the ammunition and fuel of the country's army. A clever plan and one Merlin would have never thought of.

It was sundown before Merlin reached the southern-western edge of the fifteen-acre railway yard. Emerging on the roof of a four-story building, he knelt behind the parapet on the eastern side and surveyed where he was. In the distance, he could this side of the railway yard. A set of tracks entered through a perimeter fence and split into a maze of track and switches inside the yard. He could see two sets of rebel troops carrying automatic weapons, each group sitting on a hand rail car on one of the side tracks inside the yard. And in the failing light, he could see the upper edges of the oil stor-age tanks on the north end of the railway yard that Noxolo had told him about.

His stomach growled from hunger but Merlin did his best to ignore it. He couldn't exactly stop into a nearby restaurant. And de-spite more than 90% of the buildings being empty of people, and the remaining people ignoring him, he wasn't inclined to try and raid someone's refrigerator or pantry. And it wasn't just the fact he could be taking food from someone else in the middle of a civil war, he couldn't afford to get into a fight and draw the attention of the rebel troops. Losing a few pounds wouldn't be the worst thing to happen to him anyway. He slid back from the edge and decided to move to a closer building to get a better look.

It was an hour later and the moon had risen when Merlin made his way to another rooftop. This one was on a six-story apartment building that gave him a better view of the large railway yard below.

This end of the yard was softly lit by temporary work lights placed high on several poles and he could see six massive storage tanks, each one nearly three hundred feet around and seventy feet high. There were three tanks on this side and three on the other side of two sets of side tracks. Each storage unit was stained with rust and looked derelict, as you would expect from a facility not used for its original purpose in decades. But they were clearly in use according to the activity going on around them. Merlin could see a blue diesel-electric locomotive at the head of a ribbon of black, railway tanker cars. He couldn't see how many because the far end was hidden behind the curve of the tank on this side but he could see a number of rebel soldiers working to transfer the contents of the tanker cars to the storage unit.

Merlin's blood ran cold when he spotted a dirty yellow diesel-electric locomotive on the far side of the storage tanks. It was hauling several brown boxcars and he could see at least two flatcars, each one carrying a British battle tank. The rest of the railway cars were hidden behind the storage tank. According to Noxolo, there were underground storage bunkers just beyond the storage tanks and General Bamgboshe had used the bunkers to hold ammunition for their own ragtag army. He imagined the boxcars held ammunition for this rebel army and they would no doubt be following Bamgboshe's blueprint. He ran a hand through his hair. There would probably be more ammo and more armor on flatcars that he couldn't see. He considered moving to another spot to see what else they were bringing in and then he thought; what did it matter? They could simply send the locomotive back to get more ammo and armor. Or it would be coming in on freighters through the port access he was told was on the far side. Who was going to stop them?

Which brought him back to his plan. He was supposed to get next to the tanks or the underground bunkers and use the explosives in the backpack to trigger an explosion and destroy the rebel's use of the facility. Now that he was here, even if he still had the backpack, he couldn't see any way he could have gotten close enough to do the job. Besides the ones working on the trains, there were a number of rebel soldiers standing guard around fires blazing inside old metal drums. And he could see the headlights of two vehicles that looked like armored jeeps. They were driving on the perimeter road inside the railway yard's rusted, chain-link fence, traveling in opposite directions and no doubt patrolling the area. But the soldiers and jeeps were one thing. Now that he was here, his army background told him what Nicolaas Kessen, the former Colonel with the KCT, would do. There was no doubt in Merlin's mind that the man would have snipers on the top of the old tanks.

He narrowed his eyes, trying to see any forms along the dark top of the tanks. He couldn't see anything but that didn't mean they weren't there. In fact, he had to believe they were there. And trying to cross that open ground without the benefit of a rebel uniform...he would be spotted...and dead within minutes. He considered taking a rebel soldier out and using his uniform to infiltrate the rail yard but all the rebels he had seen traveled in groups. No...he had to find some other way. The question was; what?

Chapter 37

AS HE HEADED BACK DOWN THE STAIRS, Merlin's mind sifted through the various plans he could – no, make that *might* – be able to put into effect. The problem was his options were limited. He paused in the lobby, just inside the front door, and took out his cell phone. It took a few moments before he connected to the satellite and he began an Internet search for a nearby garden center. He was considering making another fertilizer bomb like the one that had gotten him into trouble in Bonaire. If he could find an abandoned car or truck and a nearby gas station for the fuel, maybe he could make a run into the railway yard and create a chain reaction explosion. Unfortunately, there was no local source of fertilizer he could find. Then again, he was stupid to figure they would let him get close enough without filling him with 1,000 bullets. And even if he could get the fertilizer bomb next to the fuel tanks or the ammunition in the bunker, he doubted he could simply park the car and make a run for it. The plan was basically a suicide mission.

The problem was he had no other plan that even came close to the suicide mission. Slipping the cell phone back into its holder, Merlin pulled the front door open and headed outside, trying to come up with a viable plan. As he went down the three steps to the walkway, he had an idea. And immediately dismissed it. No, he wouldn't be able to steal the battle tank he saw from the fire engine–

The clicking of weapons being readied caused him to stop in his tracks.

Six large black men in green camouflage army fatigues and brown berets stood in a semi-circle in the moon-lit street ahead of him, the AK-47 assault rifles they held clearly pointed directly at him.

The big man in the center spoke in a gruff voice with a South African accent, "Reach for the sky."

Merlin slowly lifted his hands in the air.

Grinning, the big man said to the others, "I always want to say that." The smile left his face as he gestured with his head to the man his right.

The man bent at the knees, set his weapon on the pavement, and then approached Merlin by moving swiftly around and behind him, where he began to pat him down.

Merlin looked for patches or insignia but didn't see anything. These were clearly rebel troops but he hoped he could get some idea of their background and skill set.

The big man in the center lifted a walkie talkie from his belt and spoke into it, "Sweep Five to base. Sweep Five to base. We have him."

Merlin was surprised by that comment as the man searching him took his weapon and cell phone.

Static sounded through the walkie talkie and then a voice said, *"Are you sure it's him? What does he look like?"*

The big man shrugged as he looked at Merlin, "How do I know? All you white guys look alike."

The other rebel soldiers laughed.

Merlin was sure the accent on the walkie talkie told him it was Kessen on the other end of the conversation.

Angry now, the voice came back, "*What - does he look like?*"

Shrugging again, the soldier said, "I don't know. Like said, white guy...5-10 or so...170-180." He took a step and narrowed his eyes, "I don't know...maybe green eyes−"

"*Identification?*"

The man gestured with his chin to the man behind Merlin.

Shaking his head, the soldier held up the items he had found.

"No identification on him. Just a handgun and a cell phone." The man looked up at the building behind Merlin, "But you were right. We found him coming out of one of the buildings outside the railway yard's perimeter."

Merlin felt himself nearly utter a groan. Despite their brief interaction, Kessen had read him perfectly. The former KCT Colonel had set up units sweeping the area surrounding the railway yard, and specifically the buildings where someone could get an overview of what was going on. Kessen had acted professionally and Merlin had been the amateur.

"*Take him back to base. I'll deal with his interrogation myself. Over and out.*"

"The big soldier put the walkie talkie back on his belt and gave Merlin a vicious grin, "Too bad he's going to have all the fun." The smile disappeared and he gestured with his head.

Two of the soldiers slipped their weapon over their shoulder and moved in, one pulling Merlin's hands behind his back and the other applying plastic handcuffs. They then led him twenty feet down the road where he was placed in the back of an armored jeep, with a soldier guarding him on each side.

The big soldier sat in front with the driver and said simply, "Let's go."

Despite the tight fit in back, Merlin was jostled from side to side as the vehicle sped through the moonlit streets. It wasn't long before the armored jeep passed a check-point in the rusted chain-link fence and entered the railway yard. The driver drove with abandon over a pot-holed road, bumped across several sets of tracks and took a hard left.

Merlin realized they were taking him to where he had spotted the two trains being unloaded and he assumed this must be the base of operations as well. At least he knew more than before.

The armored jeep zipped past the flatcars carrying the British battle tanks and then past the line boxcars before stopping near the locomotive.

The big man got out and said, "Take him to the back."

As the door closed, Merlin figured they would be going around the back of a building they were using in the railway yard for their HQ. But he was surprised as he was thrown forward when the vehicle reversed and sped backward.

The soldiers laughed as their prisoner hit the back of the front seat and then struggled to get seated again. A moment later, one of them reached out, grabbed Merlin by the collar and pulled him back onto the seat with a harsh jerk.

But no sooner had Merlin got seated when his head was jerked back as the vehicle slid to a backward stop.

Then the soldier on his right got out, reached in and pulled Merlin to the open door, "Get out."

As soon as Merlin got his feet on the crushed stone outside the vehicle, he was surprised when the soldier grabbed his arm and pulled him to the caboose and up the short set of stairs. The interi-

or was old and painted in an ugly green color that suited a torture chamber rather than a workspace and the air smelled of sweat, cigarette smoke, and stale coffee.

Merlin half-expected Kessen to be here waiting for him. But there were only another four soldiers. Merlin was given a seat on worn, wooden bench behind a small wooden table and told not to move a muscle or he would be shot. He sat there as ordered, waiting for the Colonel to arrive to start the interrogation, but it never happened. Instead, the four soldiers guarding him sat playing cards and drinking coffee for what he estimated to be nearly four hours before something did happen.

Merlin heard a train whistle sound sharply twice. Then he heard the wave of compressing couplings banging against one another until it reached the back of the train car he was sitting in. The caboose jerked with a bang and then began moving backward. Glancing out the window, Merlin wondered if the train was being moved to a spur where he would be taken off. But no, the train just kept gathering speed. He estimated it got up to 45-50 mph and stayed at that speed, rocking him back and forth gently.

One of the guards threw down his cards, picked up a walkie talkie that he put on his belt. "I will take first watch," he said as he headed to the back of the caboose.

Merlin wondered what he was talking about but watched as the soldier climbed a few steps into the cupola. Normally used to watch and examine the train cars ahead, he watched the soldier sit and swivel the seat around to watch behind instead. That and the fact the train continued heading north, traveling backward, made Merlin wonder if these guys really knew how to run a train or get it turned around in the railway yard. Then again, it didn't matter because had learned something else. Kessen had told them to *take him back to base.* The rebel base of operations was somewhere north of the city and they were taking him there. That was information the Vertrosé army could use. Only one small problem, of course. He was a prisoner of the rebel army and heading into the lion's den.

Chapter 38

THE SUN WAS JUST PEEKING over the hills in the distance when Merlin felt the train beginning to slow. In the sharp, long shadows on the right he became aware of the caboose entering the perimeter fence of another railway yard. Armed rebel soldiers stood guard, one of them waving to the soldier sitting in the cupola as the caboose passed by.

Merlin felt the train begin a backward curving turn to the left. As it did, he saw another train, this one a line of old and battered passenger cars, sitting on a track far to the right and a number of rebel soldiers climbing on board. They were no doubt being taken to the front line for the battle to take the capital.

Several minutes passed and the train began a slow backward turn to the right. Merlin shifted slightly to look through the window on the other side and he caught sight of several buildings that looked like warehouses. And between the buildings he could make out the bulk of two large freighters sitting in a bay. This was obviously a harbor area and he had to assume this was the rear base of operations for Faraji Okafor's civil war and his attempt to overthrow his former friend. They had no doubt brought in ammunition and fuel by sea, and possibly more soldiers, and were using this depot as a staging area. He also had to assume this would also be where Kessen was. And Merlin was being taken to him for inter-rogation. Nope, not going to happen, not if he could do anything about it.

But what?

One of the soldiers grabbed an AK-47 from the floor next to the table, slung it over his shoulder and headed for the back door of the caboose, stretching his arms overhead.

The soldiers were tired from a long night and somewhat relaxed because of it.

Glancing to the right, Merlin could see another train standing two sets of tracks over and next to an open loading platform. The train was similar to the one he was on, consisting of a line of box-cars but with only a single flatcar loaded with a battle tank. Soldiers were closing one of the boxcars while others were walking to the diesel locomotive. No doubt it was another train loaded with am-mo and ready for its run to the capital. And they were going to re-load this one and send it back. Which meant he would be taken off.

Merlin saw his Beretta and cell phone were still sitting on the far side of the table where the soldiers had sat through the night.

The train brakes began to hiss and screech as the steel wheels of the train began slowing.

A plan formed in Merlin's s mind but he only had a minute or so to execute it.

He bent forward slightly, twisting his neck back and forth, pre-tending to work the kinks out.

One of the soldiers at the table looked over at him, "You were told not to move."

"I've been sitting with my hands behind my back all night," Merlin complained, putting some agony in his voice. What he was also doing was slipping his fingers into his back pocket where he had put the American Liberty nickel. As expected, the quick pat down by the soldier had been looking for large objects like a weapon or a knife and the 'coin' was missed. He pulled the coin out deftly with two fingers.

"You're just a soft American," the soldier grumbled. He got up, expressing annoyance under his breath in some African dialect, and started to move across the aisle without hurry.

"I'm Canadian, not American," Merlin countered without thinking. He reminded himself he had to stop revealing information as he felt for the heads-up side of the coin in his fingers.

"Canadian? That's makes it even worse."

The other soldier at the table cracked a half-laugh, half yawn and got up as well, grabbing an AK-47 and his cigarettes as he prepared to get off the train with the others.

Merlin had practiced a lot with the coin and he expertly slid a fingernail clockwise along the edge of the coin and the small blade of hardened stainless steel rotated out. He bent his hands at the wrist and sliced through the plastic handcuffs. He saw the legs of the third soldier begin to descend from the cupola.

Rotating the blade back in, Merlin slipped the coin into his pocket and readied himself.

The soldier bent slightly and reached out to take Merlin's right elbow, "Get up."

Gathering his feet under him as if to get up as ordered, Merlin folded the first two joints of the fingers of his left hand and threw a strike at the soldier's throat.

Gagging in agony, the soldier's hands instinctively went to his throat as he tried to pull in a breath. He staggered back a step when he couldn't, his eyes wide in panic.

Lowering his shoulder, Merlin heaved himself up and into the soldier's midsection, driving him back across the caboose floor. The other soldier was just turning in reaction and Merlin slammed the gagging soldier's body into him and pushed hard, adding to the momentum.

As the two bodies slammed against the caboose wall and tumbled to the floor, Merlin took a long step, reached across the table, grabbed the Beretta and swung it around.

The soldier by the back door was halfway around and trying to slide the AK-47's strap off his shoulder.

Merlin fired.

A blood stain formed on the soldier's chest and he fell backward, the back of his head bouncing hard off the wooden caboose floor before he settled into death.

The soldier descending from the cupola was caught off guard and reached for a side arm, his eyes wide in alarm.

Firing again, Merlin took him out with a chest shot and the man's body tumbled over the last step and he landed face down on the floor.

As the one soldier on the floor struggled to get out from the one still trying to breathe through a bruised larynx, Merlin moved quickly, flipped the Beretta around and struck each man on the temple with the gun butt.

The two men slumped to the floor, unconscious.

The brakes screeched in a final protest as the train came to a stop next to a long loading platform.

Merlin flipped the weapon back around, finger on the trigger as he went into a crouch, looking out the window on the right and then on the left.

No one reacted to the shots.

The sounds of the gunfire had been enveloped by the squeal of the train coming to a stop.

Merlin didn't have much time. In fact, it was only a matter of time before somebody boarded the caboose. Especially if they noticed the guards not getting off. Or Kessen began wondering where his prisoner was and came looking. He moved quickly, pulling one of the unconscious guards to the center of the caboose floor and stripping him of his green and brown military camouflage uniform. Tossing his own clothes to the side, Merlin redressed in the uniform, using his own his 'escape belt' and boots, added the holster, replacing the sidearm with his own Beretta, and slipped the American Liberty nickel into the back pocket of his pants.

Checking the pockets of the camouflage jacket, he found a Kinder Bueno chocolate bar and a pack of Gauloises cigarettes. Neither was relevant right now but he slipped them back into the pockets and patted the other soldiers down, wondering what else he could find. Beyond a Victorinox Swiss Army climber pocket knife with thirteen tools, he only found more French cigarettes and a variety of French francs. He slipped everything into his pockets in case they came in handy. But he couldn't afford to waste any more time in here with the bodies. On his way out the back door of the caboose, he grabbed a brown beret and an AK-47, making sure he blended in fully.

Stepping outside onto the caboose's back platform, he closed the door calmly, closing off the acrid smell of gunfire. The air outside smelled of salt water, gasoline and diesel and you could already feel the heat and humidity beginning to rise with the sun.

Merlin considered going down the steps to the right for a moment. That would move him away from the soldiers he could hear crowding around the box cars, getting ready to reload them. Then he decided against it, fearing he would look conspicuous out in the open. He turned left instead and kept his head down, wondering if he would be able to blend in with all the black soldiers he had seen to this point. But not one of the soldiers paid any attention to him as he descended the steps. And he could see why. Most of the men he could see *were* black but there were also a small number of Hispanic, Latino and Caucasian soldiers. The Interpol report had said Davet Minard's company employed former rebel soldiers from African nations as well as those from South America. But he imagined a number of these men were probably standard mercenaries as well, soldiers for hire. He spotted two soldiers wearing Commando-green berets They appeared to be supervising the overall operation, their instructions going through a number of subordinates. No doubt these two were from Kessen's former Special Forces unit in the Royal Netherlands Army. It would make sense using men you knew. Especially ones who would add structure to a group battle-hardened in jungle warfare but lacking in the standard military discipline Kessen would need to make their plan work.

Pausing on the bottom step, Merlin heard orders being given and the box cars doors began sliding open. No one appeared to be interested in the caboose. All attention was on the other cars. Setting foot on the concrete loading platform, Merlin found himself in a bee-hive of activity. There were stacks of various ammunition boxes, cases of rations and personal items as well as medical supplies and the soldiers went to work loading them on the train. Farther down the platform, forklifts were carrying larger boxes and repair parts for the maintenance support of their front line equipment. Essentially, everything needed to run a war.

Slipping the strap of the AK-47 over his shoulder, Merlin began to walk slowly toward the buildings and the dock beyond, forming a tentative plan to find a motorboat or some other craft he could steal and head back to Ténemané. He had to let the Vertrosé army know of this staging base and ultimately to find some way to take out the makeshift railway yard depot they had created back in the capital–

He spotted some cardboard boxes and a new plan formed.

Chapter 39

THE LETTERING ON THE SIDES of the cardboard box told Merlin what they contained; Charge Demolition M112 With Taggant (1-1/4 LBS COMP C-4) MB-98D114-003C.

Merlin was standing dead still in the middle of the activity, mulling over what he could do with several 1.25-pound blocks of C-4 plastic explosive. He had an idea, but getting them first was the real problem.

Transferring the strap of the AK-47 to his left shoulder, he began walking toward the boxes as casual as possible. He discreetly patted his pockets, trying to remember where he had put the pocketknife. He found it in a top pocket, slipped it out and opened one of the small blades. Palming the pocketknife in his right hand, Merlin moved to the boxes in the middle of the activity, picked up two of them, one stacked on top of the other, and headed for the nearest open boxcar. Soldiers were putting ammunition cases on the boxcar floor as other soldiers inside were taking them and stacking them against the end wall. Fortunately for Merlin, it was early and the soldiers were still wiping sleep from their eyes and they paid little attention to him. He was just another worker.

Merlin set the two boxes down and watched the soldiers from the corner of his eye as he casually slit the packing tape holding the top flaps closed. Merlin then placed the Swiss Army knife, blade still open, back in his pocket as he slipped his other hand underneath the open flap. Contrary to popular belief that C-4 is formed into large bricks, it's actually cast in rectangular blocks that are long and thin, approximately 2 inches by 1.5 inches and 11 inches long, and that factor allowed Merlin to wrap the fingers of his left hand around several of the charges covered by semi-translucent plastic.

Hesitating a fraction of a second to make sure he wasn't being watched, he pulled them out and tucked them into his left pocket. With the olive-colored C-4 material being pliable, he bent the rectangular blocks slightly to hide them in the pocket.

Slipping his hand inside the box again, he pulled out several more, transferred them to his right hand and his right pocket, putting a slight bow in these blocks as well– a hand fell on his shoulder and a Dutch-accented voice spoke.

"Wij zijn hier niet om spinnen te neuken."

Merlin's heart rate shot up as he looked to see a large soldier standing beside him, a smile on his face.

Merlin had no idea what was said but he imagined the soldier must have assumed he was a countryman. In the brief flash of looking at each other, there was no indication he knew what Merlin had taken from the box. Knowing the army - any army - Merlin felt the comment was some Dutch expression that had any number of vulgarities attached to it and the implication was to move faster or work harder. At least, he *hoped* that's what it was. As his hand moved discreetly back to the pocket with the open bladed knife, Merlin gave him a half-smile and a nod as he held his breath.

The soldier squeezed Merlin's shoulder, turned, and headed back to the line of boxes.

Merlin blew out a breath of relief and quickly placed the bottom box on top of the first, effectively hiding the fact he had slit it open. Then he glanced over his shoulder.

The big soldier was yelling and gesturing to several other soldiers to move faster.

Sliding the boxes to the left against the inside wall, Merlin turned around and walked briskly back into the activity. He bent over another set of boxes, placed his hands on the sides as if he was going to pick them up, and checked again for the big soldier.

The big man was moving back to the boxcars, talking loudly over the noise of the loading effort, and gesturing out some instructions to the workers inside.

Moving away from the boxes and losing himself in the mass of workers, Merlin began looking for another item that he knew had to be here. It took some time, making him wonder if he had missed what he was looking for. Maybe they had already loaded them– bingo! He spotted what he was looking for in six stacks of four boxes each; Australian-made Instantaneous Electric Detonators. But this was going to be a little dicier. A trio of soldiers stood next to them. One soldier, who looked to be in charge, was looking at something on a clipboard as he talked to the other two–

Two blasts of a train whistle told Merlin the other train was leaving and he cursed under his breath.

That other train was part of his plan.

But with only the C-4 in his pocket, trying to get over there and climb onboard now would leave him short-handed of a vital component for his plan to have any chance of working.

He would have to work fast. But fast could mean mistakes and a fatal ending.

Pulling the Swiss Army Jack knife from his pocket again, he palmed it as he headed for the boxes. Just as he was passing them, he pretended he had forgotten something and turned to go back, kicking hard enough with his toe at the bottom box of one stack to topple it.

The trio of soldiers was startled by the thudding of the falling boxes and one of them swore at Merlin.

Merlin shook his head and made a sound of disgust at his clumsiness.

The soldier with the clipboard spoke sternly with a South African accent, "Idioot!"

Holding his hands up, partly in an apology and partly to hide his face, Merlin dropped to one knee, slid a box back in place and then picked up another, stacking it on the first. When he saw from the corner of his eye that the trio of soldiers went back to their discussion, Merlin quickly slit the tape on the third box, pocketed the knife again and slipped his hand inside the box. Watching the trio from the corner of his eye, Merlin wrapped his fingers around four electric detonators and pulled them out. The metal tube and two wires of each cap were small enough to fit in his hand and he slipped them into his pocket quickly. Not wanting to push his luck any further, he then went to work placing the box on the other two and used the last box to cover the slit as he stood up.

Backing away from the stacks, Merlin blended into the other workers, skirted the trio of soldiers and headed for the front of the train. He spotted someone's military grab bag and snared it on the way past, slipping the padded strap over his other shoulder.

Reaching the front, he glanced back quickly to make sure he wasn't being watched. Then he took a quick step and jumped from the platform to the tracks in front of the diesel locomotive. The crushed gravel crunched under his boots as he quickly moved across the other tracks and toward the train that was slowly moving forward. He kept his eyes on the caboose, making sure no one was in the cupola who could watch him approach. Reaching the train, he glanced back to make sure no one was watching him from that side either. But they were too busy with their work, and, so far, no one appeared to be interested in the caboose with the bodies. That couldn't last forever and Merlin moved faster.

As this caboose came closer, Merlin watched to see if anyone was on stairs or the front platform. But it was clear. He grabbed the railing and pulled himself up onto the step, crouching as he climbed to the platform and peeked inside through the small window in the door.

There were four soldiers inside. They were setting their weapons on one of the tables or lighting up cigarettes, obviously getting ready for the journey to Ténemané. Even out here he could smell fresh coffee brewing.

Sliding to a sitting position with his back to the caboose wall, Merlin set the AK-47 propped against the wall and then slipped the grab bag off his shoulder, checking it. It held a first aid kit, rations, a flashlight, several packs of cigarettes and two magazine pouches holding six magazines each that would fit his weapon. Someone would be pissed but he was happy.

He added the eight rectangular blocks C-4 and the four blasting caps from his pockets and set the bag down on the platform beside him. Then he pulled his Beretta and settled back, trying to relax as he waited for the train to pass through the perimeter fence. Once it started, he held his breath, wondering if the guards he had seen coming in would spot him going out.

But they weren't paying any attention and he was beyond their view in a few seconds.

Pulling out the Kinder Bueno chocolate bar, Merlin began eating breakfast and watching for the time to make his next move.

Chapter 40

TWENTY MINUTES INTO THE TRAIN RIDE, Merlin heard the heavy chugging of the diesel locomotive deepen over the deafening clacking of the rails. He could also feel the train begin an uphill climb and that was his signal. This was the spot he was waiting for. Rolling around to his knees, he slowly rose and looked through the small window. All four soldiers were sitting and smoking, drinking coffee, and playing cards. That meant no one was in the cupola, watching over the train.

Setting the strap of the AK-47 over his left shoulder, he added the grab bag over his right shoulder to keep his hands free. Then he climbed over the railing and carefully down to the draft sill and coupler between the caboose and the boxcar.

The train swayed back and forth, the metallic clanking of the sill and coupler ringing ominously and Merlin grabbed the railing behind him tighter. One false step and he would be under the heavy metal wheels.

For a moment, he imagined himself lying across the tracks in three pieces and then pushed it from his mind. This was going to be difficult enough without the distraction of dying a horrible death.

Concentrating on balancing himself, Merlin took a step to the other side of draft sill and coupler and grabbed onto the side railing of the boxcar's ladder. He had another queasy moment when he realized how rusted the ladder was. The possibility of a horrible death flashed through his mind again. If the ladder gave way– he chastised himself. Concentrate, Dragon. Bending slowly at the knees, Merlin let his right hand slide down the ladder as he reached down to the coupler with his left. It took him a moment to unhook it but a deep clunk finally sounded and the caboose detached from the box car and began to fall away.

Gripping the side of the ladder tightly, Merlin carefully swung his body around and began climbing. The rusted metal rungs vibrated under his boots but remained intact and he reached the upper edge of the boxcar and pulled himself on top. Lying flat, he turned and looked back at the receding caboose. No one stood on the back platform and he assumed the soldiers still didn't know they were unhooked. But it wouldn't take long before they came to a rolling stop and alerted someone on this train.

Turning back around in the stomach, Merlin carefully rose, setting his feet shoulder width apart. The heavy noise from the steel wheels over the rails was deafening and the vibrations and wind made standing difficult. But once he was balanced, he began walking forward with his eyes looking intently down at the roof of the boxcar; afraid he would slip and go tumbling over the edge. Glancing up as he neared the end of the boxcar, he cursed. The diesel locomotive looked a long ways away. Hopping to the next boxcar, he continued his forward trek. After ten boxcars, he had mastered the technique and was looking down at the flatcar carrying the British battle tank.

Sweat drained from every pore in the hot and muggy weather and he had to wipe the perspiration from his hands several times as he climbed down. And once down, he had to brush rusty ladder flakes from his hands before he could move on. The fleeting thought of a rusty ladder breaking away had to be pushed to the back of his mind again and he turned his attention to his next scary task...the slow walk around the edge of the battle tank and along the side beam of the swaying flatcar. He had considered climbing over but the metal was hot from the scorching sun and he was afraid he would be spotted from the caboose of the engine. It was a tight fit and he kept feeling his wet, gritty hands were ready to lose their grip with every step. But he managed the twenty-seven feet of battle tank without falling off. Finally reaching the front of the armor, he stepped back onto the floor of the flatcar–

A blur of movement in his peripheral vision caused him to flinch. Something missed the back of his head, struck a glancing blow off his shoulder and knocked the AK-47 to the side. He grabbed for the AK-47 as it was slipping off his shoulder but it tangled around his elbow. He decided in a flash to throw himself into a forward roll. But the military grab bag over his other shoulder interfered with the roll and it was aborted. Merlin found himself on his back, looking up, with both arms entangled by a strap. He caught sight of a rebel soldier on the front of the tank under the cannon where he had been hiding.

The soldier's eyes were wide in anticipation as he let out a battle cry, leaped and tried to land on Merlin with both feet.

Merlin rolled to his left, pulling his arm from the bag's strap, discarded one impediment– he promptly swore as his momentum sent the bag tumbling to the edge of the car where it went over. But his concern at losing the bag and its contents of C-4 and fuses was replaced immediately by a cold stab of fear.

The rebel soldier straddled Merlin's legs, one one foot on the strap for the AK-47 that was wrapped around Merlin's elbow to prevent him from using it. Sunlight glinted off steel as the rebel shifted something nimbly from one hand to the other.

Merlin had seen what the soldier held once before. It was a facón, a twenty-inch long fighting knife used by the gaucho of the South American pampas. And from the soldier's swarthy complexion and features, Merlin assumed the man was Brazilian and probably had a lot of practice with the weapon in some of the more lawless favelas in his country. Which meant Merlin was in trouble unless he found some way to fight back. And the only thing he could do was fight dirty with the only opening he had. The man's spread legs. Merlin sat up and fired a punch straight up into the man's genitals.

The stunned soldier doubled over in agony and took a step back, dropping the knife.

The point of the knife hit with a hard ping on the metal floor between Merlin's legs and he blanched, realizing he had almost castrated himself. He pulled a leg out from between the man's legs and straightened it, driving his boot into the soldier. The man's hands were crossed over his stomach area and Merlin heard the crunch of hand bones.

The man screamed in agony.

Merlin rolled and came up, grabbing the material of soldier's uniform and throwing him toward the edge of the rail car.

The soldier's eyes opened, but half of the agony was replaced by rage and he reached out and grabbed the strap of the AK-47 still wrapped around Merlin's elbow.

The barrel of the weapon struck Merlin on the side of the head as the man's momentum carried him to the edge of the car and over.

Merlin felt the breath knocked from his lungs as he hit face down on the flatcar's floor. His shoulder screamed in pain as the man's body weight was over the flatcar and only the strap of the AK-47 held him from dropping to the gravel along the track.

The soldier was dangling over the edge of the car, screaming in anger and pain as his feet dragged and bounced over the gravel and the end of the railway ties

Merlin was pinned face down as the man held onto the strap by one hand. He struggled to get free and then his heart rate rose through the roof when he realized what the soldier was doing.

Yelling and putting all his effort into pulling himself up by the strap, the soldier's eyes expressed rage.

But he wasn't just trying to get back on board.

Merlin realized the soldier's fingers on the free hand had slipped onto the trigger of the AK-47.

And the business end of the barrel was aimed at the top of Merlin's head.

Merlin ducked his head to the side.

The soldier pulled the trigger and the weapon roared.

Feeling the heat from the barrel as 600 rounds per minute shot through it, Merlin kept from panicking and reached around, feeling for the facón. He found it and brought it around his head, desperately trying to free himself from the grip somehow.

Screaming in pain as the knife sliced across his fingers, the rebel soldier reacted by taking his hand from the strap. His eyes shot open in panic when he realized what he had done. He grabbed for something but a moment later he screamed and dropped from sight.

The scream abruptly stopped as the speeding train moved on.

Chapter 41

MERLIN LAY FACE DOWN FOR A MOMENT, his body shaking as the adrenalin from the fight continued rushing through his veins. He looked at the facón in his hand and the thin ribbon of blood on the edge of the twenty-inch blade. That could easily have been his. He slowly got to his knees, cursing softly. Time for a new plan– he cocked his head as he spotted a one inch stretch of green and brown camouflage material on the edge of the flat car to the left. He shrugged the strap of the AK-47 off and crawled on his hands and knees to the material, the facón in his hand ringing dully on the metal floor of the flatcar. His spirits rose when he realized the strap of the grab bag had snagged over the two-inch protrusion of one of the steel support beams running underneath the floor of the flatcar. He carefully put his hands on the strap to hold it in place as the flatcar vibrated over the rails. Then he slid his hand forward and wrapped his fingers around the strap, lifting the grab bag and crawling back with it to the floor in front of a tank tread. He set the facón down, reached out and pulled the AK-47 over by the strap before sitting back against the tread.

His heart was still racing and his breathing was raspy as he sat for a few moments, gathering himself. But that's all he could afford, a few moments of rest. There was every possibility that the soldiers in the caboose he had detached had alerted whoever was in the diesel locomotive that someone had cut them loose. And the rebel soldier he just sent over the edge was only one of a number he might meet on the way up there. He got to one knee, slipped the knife inside the grab bag and slung it over his shoulder. Then he checked the AK-47 to make sure it was still working and not totally empty after all those bullets the rebel soldier had fired over his head. Satisfied it was good to go; he slipped the weapon over his other shoulder and headed for the ladder on the next boxcar. As he neared the top, he peered over the edge. There was no one waiting for him. Clambering on top, Merlin balanced himself and then made his way across the final series of boxcars between himself and the diesel locomotive.

Reaching the back of the dirty blue locomotive, Merlin slipped the AK-47 over his shoulder and crept low across the roof on the left side, doing his best to avoid the smelly, black plume of diesel exhaust. The power of the locomotive could be felt through the vibrating steel as he moved forward. A set of double train horns was ten feet ahead and the whistle blew as the train approached an intersection and Merlin nearly went deaf. Sticking his fingers in his ears and wiggling his jaw, Merlin did his best to clear them. He was more prepared for the second blast but it was still rough on his ears.

Two-thirds of the way to the front, Merlin lay on his stomach and inched his way to the left edge.

The tracks curved to the right and the steel wheels screeched against the sides of the rails as the locomotive followed the bend.

Merlin held on with his left, pulled his Beretta and slowly peered over the edge. A small open window was just below, with a foot wide platform just below the window. To the right of the window, the cab jutted out and through another small closed window, he could see a white rebel soldier sitting in a seat, his hands on the throttle. The soldier turned and looked back.

Merlin pulled his head back and waited a few seconds before he peeked over again. He could hear a muted conversation which meant there was at least one other person inside the cab. He had no way of knowing how many but decided there was only one way to find out. Turning on his stomach, he worked to place the strap of the grab bag around the twin horns and did the same with the AK-47, making sure the barrel was just under the bag's strap and the butt end extending toward the edge of the roof. With that done, he pulled the facón from the bag and then crawled back to the edge, facón in one hand and Beretta in the other. Turning on his side, he threw the facón to the front of the locomotive. It banged and clanged on the roof before disappearing over the end and clanging again on the small snub nose in front of the cab.

Slipping feet first over the edge, Merlin landed on the small platform. He held the frame of the open window with one hand to keep from falling off and stuck the Beretta through the opening

Two black soldiers were on the far side of the cab. One of them had an AK-47 in hand and was looking through the front window, trying to figure out what had happened.

The other soldier was standing at a door on that side that faced the front, looking to see what had caused the noise as well. His weapon was propped against the seat and he had a set of binoculars in his hands.

Merlin went for the one holding the weapon. He pulled the trigger, the Beretta barked and he took the soldier out with a shot to the back of the head.

The other soldier turned at the sound of the shot, dropped the binoculars and reached for his weapon.

Pulling the trigger twice more, Merlin took him down with two slugs to the chest.

Merlin then made a move to get inside the cab – and swore. He realized he had no way to do that. There *was* a second door, but it was also facing the front of the locomotive like the other one. He swung the weapon toward the other window and the engineer soldier, who was now looking around in surprise. Merlin yelled over the noise, "Don't do anything stupid. Understand?"

The soldier lifted his hands overhead and nodded.

Merlin tried to figure out what to do next and he came to just one conclusion. "Stop the train," he yelled.

"What?"

"Stop - the - train."

The engineer nodded, turned and set to work.

Merlin glanced back along the speeding train. Now all he had to do was hope a set of soldiers hadn't set out to catch the train and were just around the corner.

Chapter 42

AS THE TRAIN CAME TO A STOP, the engine rumbling in idle, Merlin glanced back once more to see if anyone was coming before yelling at the soldier engineer, "Okay, good. Leave it running, put your hands up and don't do anything stupid. Get out and down to the ground."

The man lifted his hands, nodding as he said something and then leaned over to his right, reaching down for something,

Merlin's heart skipped a beat and he yelled, "I said nothing stupid."

The man quickly reached high again with his hands, "I'm not. I'm not." He got off his seat and headed to the cab's door in front.

Merlin watched the man climb to the gravel bed along the track and then told him to, "Lie face down." Once the man complied, Merlin put the handgun back into the holster, reached up to the butt end of the AK-47 and lifted the grab bag off the horns. Squatting on the narrow platform, Merlin dropped the bag to the ground.

The man flinched when he heard the bag hit the ground.

Merlin jumped to the ground, stumbling a bit from the force and then turned the AK-47 to the prone soldier, "Get up."

The soldier got to his feet, hands up and turned to Merlin, his South African accent heavy, "Yeah, you can have the whole train, all right. It's all yours–"

"Shut up. How many are chasing the train? And how far behind are they?"

Shrugging, the rebel soldier said, "I don't know what you mean."

Deliberately lifting the AK-47 to his shoulder to make sure there was no misunderstanding, Merlin said, "In that case, I'll just take the train. And since I don't need you...."

The soldier put his hands out in front in panic, "Jirre! No, no, no. Look. They aren't coming from behind. Well, they are. But those guys who were on the caboose are too far behind to catch you unless you stay here for too long. But...."

"But what?"

"I'm...I'm supposed to stop at a small station about two miles ahead. They have a force there to search the train...."

Merlin lowered the weapon to his waist but kept it trained on the soldier, "Okay." He took a step back and glanced at the long line of rail cars, "I saw forklifts putting large crates inside these front cars. What's in there?"

The soldier looked very much like he didn't want to answer and then gestured to the boxcars, "I'm not sure about all of them...but...the second one has M2A3 and M3A1 in it–"

"Cutting charges?"

"Yeah. And some Bangalore torpedoes," he added as an afterthought

Merlin looked to the boxcar. Cutting charges were used for a number of purposes, including clearing roads of concrete blocks set in place to keep the enemy from advancing or removing automobiles or other equipment damaged in battle that blocked a street. A Bangalore torpedo is an explosive charge placed within one or several connected tubes. It is used by combat engineers to clear obstacles or cut paths through wire obstacles and heavy undergrowth from a distance. Merlin had a different purpose in mind for the contents but he still needed some items. He looked at the South African, "How did they contact you to let you know you about the caboose and that you needed to stop up ahead?"

The South African thought about it for a moment and then patted the pocket of his jacket, "Oh, right. One of the other guys...Hansie...he had a cell phone and they called him. He passed it over to me so the Colonel himself could tell me what to do–"

"Kessen?"

"Yeah. You know him?"

"Let's just say we had a brief conversation that didn't leave either one of us too happy."

"Yeah. Well, he is some pissed. Asked if we'd spotted a white guy on the train–"

"Good to know." Merlin gestured with his fingers to pass over the cell phone.

The South African dug into his pocket and tossed it over.

Merlin caught the cell phone and slipped it into his pocket before gesturing with the AK-47, "Okay. Let's go and open up the second boxcar."

The soldier looked half-agitated and half-concerned, "Ag, man! You don't need me to take care of that. I would suggest you move on with the train before they come–"

"Open - the - door. And don't make me ask again."

The South African made a sound of disgust and then his boots crunched over the gravel on the edge of the tracks as he headed for the second boxcar.

Merlin took a step back to let him pass safely and then reached down and snagged the strap of the grab bag, throwing it over her shoulder. His own boots crunched over the gravel as he followed the soldier.

Reaching the boxcar, the South African flipped the handle and the boxcar's door rumbled as he pushed it open. Then the man stepped back and gestured to the exposed crates inside, "There you go. Now can I leave?"

"No. Lie flat on the ground over here. Do it now."

As the man lay prone on the gravel, Merlin shouldered the AK-47, opened the grab bag, and went to work preparing the C-4 blocks and the blasting caps into a charge that would create quite a bit of havoc. Merlin used the jack knife's screwdriver to take the back off Hansie's cell phone, used the blade to strip the covering from the ends of the wires on the blasting caps and set them in place across the electronics, turning the phone into a detonator. He memorized the phone number and then placed Hansie's cell inside the grab bag with the charges. Placing the bag against the crates, he closed the boxcar door and slipped the weapon off his shoulder. "Okay, up," he said to the South African

The man rose to his feet, wiping gravel dust from his hands and uniform as he grumbled, "Now what?"

"Is there a dead man switch on the locomotive?"

The South African paused in his cleaning efforts and his brows knit together, "Why would you need to know that?"

"Because I don't need you driving the locomotive and pretending something goes wrong when we try and go through that small station where your buddies are waiting. That's why."

Letting out a breath of frustration, the South African said, "In this model, the deadman is actually a pedal on the floor. And it's a real pain. The old timers showed me how to make a metal shoe heavy enough to slip over top and I had one made. You can keep an eye on me, hey?"

Merlin nodded to himself, remembering how the man had reached down for something

The South African held his hands out in a beseeching manner, "But look, brah. There's gonna be a real Barnie when you don't slow down at that station and I don't want to be on board when they start firing, especially in the front seat where they can get a bead on me. They don't pay me enough to die and you don't really need me. It's been ten years since I ran one of these and I labeled everything. The throttle control has eight notches, plus idle. Notch 1 is the slowest speed, and notch 8 is the highest speed. To get the train moving, all you have to do is release the brakes, I got them marked, and you put the throttle into Notch 1. That's it."

To Merlin, *not* having to keep a watch on this mercenary, no matter if he agreed to cooperate or not, was the better situation. He had no idea what hand-to-hand combat skills he had and being in close quarters in the cab of the locomotive without knowing wasn't smart. Plus, he would be preoccupied with the rebel soldiers trying to stop the train. He waved the AK-47 toward the edge of the jungle some fifty yards away, "If I see you trying to get back on the train—"

The South African took off at a run.

Climbing aboard, Merlin found everything marked as said. And he found the heavy metal shoe that fit over the pedal on the floor in front of the driver's seat. Everything looked good to go, but a house cleaning was in order before anything else could go on. Moving the two dead bodies to the door on the far side of the cab, he dropped them to the gravel beside the tracks. Using rags he found in the back corner, he did his best to mop up some of the blood but there was more than they could absorb. Giving up, he tossed the rags down to the side of the tracks, went back to the metal shoe, slipped it on, sat down in the seat and put the throttle to Notch 1. The diesel engine rumbled and the locomotive began to move.

Chapter 43

T HE LOCOMOTIVE WAS CHUGGING HARD at full speed as the train neared the station where the South African engineer was supposed to stop. The heat and humidity had intensified and the heavy copper smell of the blood still on the floor filled the cab. With the dead man switch neutralized, Merlin was able to open the door in front of the driver's chair and lie prone on the floor, AK-47 in hand. The sound of the clacking rails was loud and the wind whipped at his hair as he set his elbows down to form a tripod and aimed the weapon, ready for the...what did the South African say? *There's gonna be a real Barnie when you don't slow down at that station*. Whatever the *Barnie* was, he was ready.

Or was he?

Either the South African he let go had warned Kessen's men ahead somehow (maybe the soldiers chasing the train had caught up) or they were just taking precautions. But the fact a black Humvee was parked across the tracks told Merlin they were determined to stop the train, one way or the other. It was now a do or die situation in getting back to Ténemané. He slipped a hand to the cell phone on his belt, briefly considering the extreme measure of taking everyone he could see with him. But the memory of one of those brilliant smile from Jigs (and the fact he still owed Jaimee

Hartman a date for taking care of Jigs - or was that two dates? - he couldn't remember)...it didn't matter. People were counting on him. He readjusted his elbows tripod and aimed towards the men he could see behind the Humvee. Then he changed his mind. There were a number of rebel soldiers kneeling on the small platform, weapons trained at the onrushing train. They would have a better shot at him. He adjusted his aim, gauged the distance, and opened fire. The heavy pounding of the weapon echoed loudly and added uncomfortably to the deafening sounds in the cab of the locomotive.

It appeared the rebels were only half-expecting someone to be shooting from the train because, once a number of them fell, the others scattered for cover inside the small, weather-beaten station.

The battered and blue locomotive, the throttle at notch eight, pulled the line of rail cars toward the Humvee with fierce determination.

And just like the South African, these mercenaries weren't willing to die for whatever pay they were getting. They scattered away from the Humvee and the steel ribbons that reverberated with a warning.

Slamming the door shut, Merlin rolled to his right, tucking his head under.

The diesel locomotive exploded through the Humvee. Wheels and seats, window glass, metal gears and steering wheel ripped apart, shattered and burst in every direction or was crushed to oblivion under the angry wheels of the train.

A secondary sound of metal tearing and exploding wrapped itself around Merlin. He flinched when he was struck by something hard. Pieces of metal banged and bounced off the walls inside the cab, rebounding and collided with more shrapnel thrown inside by the force of fast-moving locomotive meeting parked Humvee.

A moment later, as the train hurtled away from the station and the wreckage strewn across a hundred yards, Merlin felt a stab of fear. Despite the swirling roar of the wind inside the cab, that hurtling locomotive under him felt like it was actually slowing. He rolled, pushing away pieces of rubber, glass, and metal– and swore. He knew instantly what the problem was. The metal shoe over the deadman pedal was gone. The train *was* slowing. And what's more...he couldn't see the metal shoe under the rubble thrown inside from the interaction of speeding train and exploding vehicle.

He swung around to his knees and swore again as pointed metal pieced jabbed him. He looked around and located the AK-47, using the butt end to feverishly push aside sharp metal and glass as he began looking for the shoe.

He could feel the speed dropping fast.

Merlin considered making a run for it and blowing up the train from a distance once the rebels got here– he swore under his breath again. Jigs would tell him to man up and look harder.

He moved faster, pushing and kicking aside debris– there it was.

Grabbing the heavy shoe he moved back to the pedal and used his fingers to move small pieces of twisted metal from underneath it–

He pulled his hand back in pain when a sharp end stuck him like a pin. Reflexively putting his finger in his mouth, Merlin swore under his breath and then shook his hand, throwing blood across the cab as he chastising himself. There was no time for pain as he felt the train slowing to a near stop. In fact, there would be a lot more pain if they caught him.

Setting the AK-47 down, Merlin squatted and fit the heavy shoe over the pedal. Then he reached up and cranked the throttle back to eight. The wheels spun and screeched on the rails as full power was applied. The locomotive jerked and Merlin fell back into the debris There was a bang as the coupler between the locomotive and the next car protested the sudden weight applied to it. The banging sounded all the way down to the last car.

As the train began accelerating again, Merlin got to his feet, picked up the AK-47 and moved to the window, looking back towards the station. There was nobody chasing yet although he could see men scrambling for vehicles behind the station. He was grateful as the scene began receding in the distance as the train picked up speed. He brushed debris off the seat and sat down, slumping back and trying to slow his heart rate. That wasn't easy because next up down the line was his next task - the railway yard in Ténemané.

Chapter 44

T HE DIESEL LOCOMOTIVE IDLED in an old industrial area of Ténemané north of the airport as Merlin used the binoculars to reconnoiter the railway yard up ahead. The day was blazing hot and sweat trickled down his back as he brought the situation into focus. He could see the movement of rebel soldiers beyond the entrance in the perimeter fence but there wasn't anything across the tracks this time. Then again, he had gotten the train up to 95 mph, traveling the distance back here in half the time it took them to take him to the other yard. He looked further down the railway yard and saw the tracks near the storage tanks and the underground bunkers were clear. They had figured he was going to drive the train back and crash it into either one. They were only—something caught his attention. He pulled the focus back and then swore under his breath. Off to the left, inside the railway yard, was a British battle tank heading this way to the entrance.

There was no time to play around. If they got that tank across the tracks, it was doubtful the locomotive could plow through it like the Humvee at the small station. Merlin let the binoculars drop to his chest, still held by the strap around his neck, and he jumped back to the controls. Immediately cranking the throttle to position eight, he held on as the train bucked and the wheels spun with a metallic scream, trying to gain traction. Maintaining his balance and grabbing the AK-47 he had left on the seat, Merlin moved to the open doorway and out onto the small platform. Stepping between the two round safety bars, Merlin took a step and jumped–the strap of the weapon snagged on the edge off the safety bar and his body was turned and slammed back against the bar with his knees banging against the platform edge. Groaning in pain, Merlin struggled to get a foothold as the locomotive accelerated. Wrapping a hand around one of the bars, he got a foot on the edge of the platform and then lifted his body to get the strap free. With the speed increasing, there was no time to turn and Merlin pushed off to get clear of the line of steel wheels. His back slammed hard onto the gravel bed and he tumbled several times head over heels, the binoculars smashing him in the face.

Coming to rest on his side, Merlin groaned in pain and he chastised himself for moving too fast. There had been time to get off and he should have been more careful. He wanted to lay still for a moment but the increasing clacking of the wheels over the rails told him he had to keep moving. Getting to his knees, he winced as the gravel bit through his pants as he looked for the AK-47. He saw it, picked it up, and realized the magazine was bent from the fall. The weapon was useless and he tossed it aside. Rising to his feet, he dug into his pocket for his cell phone and checked it. He was relieved to find it all right. Watching the train moving past him, he put the phone back in his pocket, lifted the binoculars and looked down the line– crap! He realized he could see the entrance but his target inside the railway yard was hidden by a small rise now that he was on the ground. He turned gingerly, taking a look around. Off to the side of the track bed, about one hundred feet away, sat of an old wooden signal tower with a set of wooden steps on the far side.

The tower looked like it had been dragged over there, probably no longer in use. Merlin took off at a run that actually turned into half-run and half-limp. The jump had jammed his knee and he rubbed at it as he hobbled to the wooden stairs and began climbing. The old light tower was rickety and he felt the boards creak with dryness under his boots. But he couldn't worry about going through, he had to get to the top of the ten-foot tower and make sure he timed everything just right. Once on the upper platform, he lifted the binoculars and took a look. The train was still accelerating but it had to be at least going seventy by now. He swung the binoculars to the left and felt some relief. There was no way the battle tank could get to the tracks in time before the train barreled through the entrance–

He realized the turret on the battle tank was rotating. He squeezed the binoculars tight. The cannon was moving in the direction of the onrushing locomotive. Would they really risk trying to just hit the train and not destroy the track as well? He hadn't expected that.

The upper half of a soldier popped up in the hatch, binoculars in hand. After a quick look, focusing the binoculars on the locomotive, the soldier pointed in the direction of the train while yelling urgently to someone inside the battle tank.

A moment later, a ball of fire erupted from the muzzle of the cannon and the tank recoiled hard.

Merlin lowered the binoculars in shock. They had actually fired a shell at the train.

Two seconds later, the guts of a building off to the right exploded as the shell struck.

They had obviously missed. Feeling some relief as the train barreled into the train yard, Merlin wondered if they would try to track it. He focused on the battle tank again–and felt the cold stab of fear.

The soldier in the hatch was looking through his own binoculars again. But he wasn't looking at the train. He was actually focused on Merlin. And he was pointing directly at his position on the old wooden platform.

Another shock of fear bolted through Merlin.

The turret had been rotating and the cannon was mere inches away from having him in the tank's cross-hairs.

Merlin dropped the binoculars to his chest, turned and made a run down the rickety stairs.

The old tower swayed under his rapidly moving weight.

He was off balance and stumbled as his feet hit the ground.

Arms flailing, Merlin struggled to stay upright.

After a couple of frantic steps, he managed to dig his left heel in and push off, running hard to the right.

The battle tank boomed again.

There was a whistling sound that grew louder.

A couple of seconds later, Merlin felt himself tumbling head over heels as the shell exploded behind him. He landed hard on his back felt and it felt like an angry mule had kicked him. His ears were ringing with a steady, irritating, high pitch sound.

Merlin groaned as he rolled to a knee, his body aching everywhere. But he couldn't afford to just lay there until he felt better. Another shell would do more than just make him ache. And he didn't have any time left either. The train would probably be reaching the target any minute. He began another limping, hobbling run as he reached for his cell phone. Dialing the number for Hansie's cell phone, he pressed send– and cursed long and hard as he watched it stick in send-mode and the little icon spun in a stupid little circle as it searched for a connection. *C'mom, c,mon.*

He was near a line of buildings now and he heard the faint roar of vehicles racing in his direction. If they caught him before– he heard a ringing sound through the phone– an explosion in the distance told him he had triggered the C-4 in the boxcar. And that explosion was followed by another...and another.

The ground shook under his feet as an even bigger explosion sounded and just before he ran between two buildings he caught a glimpse of a massive fireball and thick, black smoke over the railway yard. It had worked. He had started a chain reaction explosion in the ammunition dump.

The sounds of vehicles approaching grew louder.

Now all Merlin had to do was stay alive.

Chapter 45

STOPPING AT THE FRONT EDGE of an old building consisting of faded brown brick and gray, weathered wood, Merlin sank to a knee and peered around the corner. The dusty and rubble-filled street was empty and he hobbled across, skirting a ten foot crater made by a mortar shell, and into the long grass between an old gas station and some kind of warehouse. The air and the ground under him reeked of gasoline. Placing his back against the concrete blocks of the gas station, Merlin rubbed his sore knee while peering around the corner to see if anyone had watched him crossing to here.

At the end of the street, a large jeep filled with rebel soldiers, took the turn on two screeching wheels and barreled down the street.

Merlin's hand moved to his Beretta. They all had AK-47s and he was outgunned but–

The jeep took a sharp left, nearly throwing off a couple of soldiers, and shot into a gravel parking lot, disappearing behind the building. They were headed to where he had been a few moments before.

Another vehicle came around the corner. This one was a black SUV and it shot down the street, passed the parking lot and then slowed, obviously watching for him as the first vehicle checked the area around the tracks. The sounds of other vehicles weren't far behind these two.

Massaging his knee for another moment, Merlin realized he didn't have time to let it recuperate. He had to move on before the slowly moving SUV reached this building. Turning, he placed his hand against the concrete blocks, using the wall like a crutch to keep his weight off the knee as he hobbled his way through the unkempt grass to the back of the building.

Reaching the far end of the gas station, Merlin looked back to see if the SUV was at a spot on the street where they could see him. He was okay so far. Then he peered around the corner. The back of the station was another stretch of gravel and there were a few old cars sitting with their trunks against a high, dilapidated back fence. The smell of gasoline here was decorated with the scent of motor oil and greases.

Merlin headed for the cars and the fence, cursing that he would have to climb with a bum knee. Gravel crunched under his boots in a limping pattern of sound as he decided to check the cars first to see if he could use one of them. The first two appeared to be dead hulks. And then he saw a set of keys dangling from the ignition of an old Cortina Perana made by Basil Green Motors in Edenvale, Gauteng near Johannesburg, South Africa. He opened the door and then glanced to the gas station and the glimpse of road he could see beyond and he thought better of the makeshift plan. The only escape route was into the teeth of those vehicles.

Cursing again, he abandoned the idea and gingerly climbed onto the trunk of the Perana instead. But even from there he had to grit his teeth against the pain, jump and catch the top edge of the fence. Now his back joined in with the protests from the arms and shoulders as he pulled himself up. Despite the agony, he managed to scale the fence and drop to the other side. A groan escaped his throat as his knee buckled–

An explosion of automatic gunfire erupted.

Merlin instinctively ducked his head. Chunks and splinters of the fence rained down on him.

Voices shouted and vehicles revved their engines.

Crap. They had spotted him. Merlin took off at a limping run. He was in the back yard that was littered with junk. Old car parts, gears, dirty wire rope and other unidentifiable pieces of metal were scattered haphazardly, making for a winding, difficult path away from the battered fence.

Straight ahead was an old house of weather-beaten boards and Merlin headed for the back-door, thinking of hiding. But an old, sagging garage of corrugated steel sheets sat off to the right edge of the house and Merlin spotted a bicycle leaning against the left wall. He made a beeline for it only to realize it had no chain as soon as he moved it. He looked around to see if it was lying on the nearby ground and then, glancing back, he let the useless bicycle tumble to the ground when he spotted a brown beret at the top of the fence.

They were closing in from behind.

Darting to the front of the garage, he kept moving down the gravel driveway that led to the street sixty feet ahead. There was five-foot tall, chain link fence on the right, another driveway and then another house of sun baked boards. There were a number of cardboard boxes stacked haphazardly on the gravel driveway as well as some old wooden chairs and other household items. Someone had obviously cleared out when the civil war had started and they had left items behind in their panic. Or they just didn't have the room in some vehicle. Either way, that didn't matter–

The sounds of a vehicle sounded far to the right along that street, echoing off the walls of the houses.

Merlin cursed. He considered hiding or making a stand in the house on the left. Then he considered the one to the right on the other side of a wire fence. That might throw them off but he would have to climb–

On the other side of the fence he spotted the front of a bicycle wheel with double spokes that was propped against the far side of the stacked cardboard boxes in the gravel driveway. He didn't waste any time clambering over the fence, ignoring the pain. Darting to the other side of the boxes he hoped to find a working bicycle– he didn't. It was a homemade minibike, consisting of bent pipes, welded into a makeshift frame and sporting a 6.5 hp gasoline motor. The twelve-inch wheels looked like they had come off a go kart. The term Frankenstein minibike came to mind but beggars can't be choosers, he told himself. The real question was; would it work? Lifting the minibike upright, he found it had gasoline in the small tank. That was a positive.

Shouts sounded behind the house.

Merlin straddled the frame and looked for how to start it. It had a pull start and he grabbed the T-handle and pulled. Nothing. He pulled again. Still nothing. Grabbing firmly once more, he yanked it hard...and a high pitched buzz echoed off the houses.

That was another positive. Now...could he ride it? He had only ridden a bicycle but how hard could this be? He would know soon enough. The motor was hooked up to a throttle on the handle bars and he twisted it. The buzzing increased. Good so far. Letting off on the gas, he engaged the clutch and then twisted the gas just enough to get it rolling. He placed his feet on the welded foot pegs and his knees stuck out like wings to the side as he wobbled along the gravel, trying to get a sense of balance–

An open jeep carrying six soldiers appeared in the street.

There was no time left.

Merlin twisted the throttle savagely.

The back wheels spun violently, spitting out loose gravel in a rooster tail.

A moment later, the back wheel caught traction and Merlin hung on as the homemade minibike did a min-wheelie and shot directly toward the Jeep in the street.

One of the soldiers spotted him coming, his eyes wide.

Merlin let off on the gas, the front wheel came down and Merlin yanked the Franken-bike into a right turn.

The soldier was bringing his AK-47 up to fire.

Fighting to keep the minibike upright as the back tires slid around towards the Jeep, Merlin twisted the throttle hard.

The engine buzzed loudly.

The soldier pulled the trigger.

But Merlin was already ten feet down the street as the weapon erupted.

He still ducked his head involuntarily at the sound and nearly lost control as his weight shifted.

Letting off on the throttle, Merlin spread his legs wide, the soles of his boots dragging along the street as he tried to control the wobble. Pain shot up his leg from a protesting knee but he ignored it. Bullets would be far more painful. Finally regaining control, he put his feet back on the foot pegs and applied the gas again. The gasoline engine buzzed loudly and it wasn't long before he estimated he had accelerated to nearly 60 mph. He was on a mini crotch rocket and it was half-thrill and half-terror at the thought of losing control and ripping the clothing and half the skin from his body.

Behind him, the Jeep's wheels screeched as it tried to make a U-turn. The severity of the attempted turn threw off the aim of the soldiers and their weapons discharged in every direction.

Bullets whistled past Merlin's ear and he ducked. The minibike wobbled again but this time he was ready and his muscles tightened as he fought to maintain control. A bend in the street came up and he concentrated on leaning left, his pant leg dragging against the road as he cut the corner hard putting some distance between him and the jeep. He managed to stay upright despite the heavy lean and when the road swung back to the right, he let off on the gas and leaned the minibike in the other direction, the other pant leg brushing the road. Coming out of the S-turn in the street, he brought the minibike back level and twisted the throttle.

The engine buzzed loudly.

But Merlin barely heard it.

At the far end of the street was the British battle tank, the rebel soldier in the turret looking and pointing directly at Merlin.

The tank's barrel was lowering and coming to bear on the minibike.

Chapter 46

MERLIN LEANED HARD TO THE RIGHT, the material of his pant leg vibrating as it was jammed against the road.

The tank's 120 mm rifled cannon boomed and the tank jerked in recoil.

Merlin heard the whistle of the shell passing overhead.

A house exploded somewhere behind him.

The rebel soldier had his hands on the tank's 7.62 mm cupola machine gun. Swiveling the weapon and trying to track the minibike, he pulled the trigger.

The heavy staccato of the weapon pounded like a jack hammer in the air as bullets ripped a line of holes across the road in the direction of the minibike.

Merlin took the minibike onto the ragged front yard of a house. The Franken-bike vibrated violently across the uneven ground as he drove hard to avoid the deadly hail of gunfire.

The soldier kept the hammer down, tracking the minibike, yelling in frustration as he was just a tad behind the homemade vehicle.

Leaning to the left, Merlin brought the minibike back to the road. He hoped getting closer to the tank would make it harder for the solider to bring the machine gun down to bear on him. It seemed to be working but a heartbeat later he felt fear.

The battle tank's engine roared and the treads ground the roadway to hamburger as it began a turn toward him.

The soldier lifted his end of the machine gun up and the business end down, still pressing the trigger and desperately trying to cut the minibike - and Merlin - to pieces.

But Merlin was too close to the tank and, as he passed, he lifted a hand and gave the soldier a one-finger-salute.

Banging his hand repeatedly on the hot metal of the turret, the soldier yelled to his men inside to get the tank turned around.

Once he was beyond the battle tank, Merlin swung the minibike to the middle of the road and glanced back. He could see the tank was halfway around, the treads still grinding up the road. The soldier on top was swinging the machine gun around in his direction, yelling in anger and frustration as he did.

Merlin doubted the tank could get much more than 40 mph out of its engines and he should be able to stay ahead easily. But beyond the tank, he could see the Jeep with the other soldiers heading his way in pursuit as well. From the age of their battered vehicle he estimated they could get 65 to 70 mph out of it. Which meant they would catch him eventually. His lead was only temporary.

He turned his attention to finding a successful escape route. An intersection came up and Merlin slowed as little as possible and took the corner to the right. Glancing back, he saw the jeep had swung wide to avoid the turning tank and that had slowed them as well. He twisted the throttle and accelerated back to his top speed. The road curved to the left and on the right he saw the chain link fence of the railway yard and the fire and black smoke beyond. It was only now that he realized the storage tanks on this side of the tracks were still intact and he cursed. He had removed the forward ammunition supply but they still had plenty of fuel for their vehicles. How much of a victory he had achieved was debatable. Then again, it was going to take time for the rebel soldiers to bring in more boxcars loaded with ammunition. And from the sound of the repeated explosions he had heard, he'd taken out at least a dozen or more train loads they had stockpiled. Hopefully, at least, he had given the Vertrosé Army a temporary advantage, one that could turn the tide in the Civil War.

But right now he had more important concerns. Avoiding capture and staying alive. His mind whirled through his options and found few. He was on a minibike, one that he barely fit on, and he was being chased by soldiers in jeeps. And a tank. Don't forget the tank. If it got a bead on him at long range....

Merlin felt something vibrating against his chest and he looked it down. The binoculars were still hanging from the strap around in his neck. He touched his chest with one hand underneath the binoculars. The thing had been banging against his sternum since he ran from that platform. The adrenaline rushing through his veins had kept him from feeling the weight, but right now it felt like he was going to have a bruise that would last for months. And then something else caught his attention.

An entrance to the railway yard was up ahead. Fifty feet or so inside the fence were two army jeeps, four soldiers in each one. They were rushing for the entranceway and no doubt the road he was on.

A road to the left was ahead but he wouldn't make it before they spotted him.

Merlin quickly scanned the buildings on the left, looking for a way off the road. But every battered house seemed to have a rusted iron fence or a weather-beaten, painted block wall standing six feet high and acting as a blockade. Didn't these people trust anyone?

Finally, an opening appeared in a wall up ahead and Merlin angled the minibike toward it. He made the turn into the front yard of a dilapidated house just as the first jeep was turning in this direction. All he had to do was get around this house to the back yard and– he realized it wasn't going to happen. The sides of the house were packed tightly against the neighboring walls on either side. And on the other side of each wall was the neighboring house. Merlin cursed. These people used every friggin' inch of space. There was no way to get to the back yard, if there was one.

Dismounting the minibike in a hurry, Merlin turned it off and pushed it to the front door. Which he found locked. Raising a boot...his knee gave out and only his hands on the handlebars kept him upright. He had forgotten about the knee. Riding the minibike had allowed it to rest and recuperate somewhat but it was still not enough. Bracing himself this time, he cautiously raised a boot and then kicked. The knee protested but the sound of dry, splintering wood was welcome. The door banged back against something soft sounding and rebounded to close again. But Merlin put his foot up again to catch the door, pushed it back in and wheeled the minibike inside the house. Laying the minibike down on the worn wooden floor, Merlin turned, grabbed the door and looked to the road.

No jeeps or tanks.

Closing the door, he struggled to drag a large and worn easy chair in front of it. Then he piled a few other pieces of furniture on the chair. This way, if they checked and couldn't open the door, they would assume it was locked and he hadn't come inside– he cursed himself. He had taken the time to move the furniture in front of a door he had just kicked in. The splintered wood— forget it.

Angry at himself for wasting time, he looked around, wondering what he should do next. The rest of the furniture was well worn, the wall paper was faded, the whole place smelled musty and the scattered clothing told him the occupants had left in a hurry. A narrow hallway led to the rest of the house. He lifted the minibike off the floor and wheeled it through the tight hallway. He passed a couple of bedrooms, took a tight right turn at a bathroom and found himself at the back door. He took the minibike outside into the yard, closed the door behind him and stopped. Across the sparse grass was a ten-foot fence that cut him off from the back yard of the next house.

The faint, metallic sounds of clanking tank treads bounced off the walls.

Merlin silently cursed. He wasn't ready to abandon the minibike just yet but he had to keep moving away from the road. And this house. Once the two groups met in the street out front, they would start checking the houses for him. The minibike wasn't that heavy but with his bum knee right now he doubted he could get over the wall with it.

Laying the minibike down, Merlin moved back inside the house and took an old TV off a battered, three foot high cabinet. His knee protested as he dragged the heavy cabinet outside and across the grass, but he managed to get it set against the wall.

This sounds of the clanking tank treads were closer, possibly just a few houses away now.

Retrieving the minibike, he got it up onto the table and then was able to hoist it to the top of the wall. He balanced it for a moment and then the weight of the minibike at the awkward angle caused it to slip from his hands and over to the other side. He cursed when he heard it hitting, hard sun baked ground on the other side. Pulling himself up, Merlin straddled the wall and slipped over to the other side, his knee barking agony as he dropped to the hard earth beside the minibike. The binoculars banged into his already sore chest as well and he slapped at them in annoyance. Turning his attention to the minibike, he found everything looked to be okay and he lifted it upright, wheeling it to the back of the next house. Merlin found the door mercifully unlocked and he moved inside quickly.

This place smelled of old wood and kerosene. Reaching the front, he found a sparse living area on the left and a spartan kitchen area on the right. The sound of a vehicle in the street out front caught his attention. Was he heading into a trap? Moving to a curtain-less window in the kitchen, he peeked outside.

He didn't see anything on the street beyond the wire fence in front of his house.

The clanking of the tank treads seemed to be moving away as well.

But a moment later, a jeep with four rebel soldiers slowly cruised along the street out front. The soldiers had their AK-47s propped up on their hips as their eyes scanned the houses on both sides of the street.

When the jeep disappeared down the street, Merlin felt some relief. He leaned the minibike against a battered counter and sat down in one of two chairs at a worn, wooden table. Pushing his fingers through his hair, he wondered what he should do next. The side of his forehead felt sore and he touched it gingerly. His fingers felt a slight swell as well as a jagged cut that left blood on his finger tips. Wiping them against his pants, he also noticed blood on his wrist, dripping from under his shirt sleeve. He checked his arm and then realized he had a jagged tear in the material on his shoulder. Looking under the shirt, he realized a bullet had grazed the skin, leaving a bloody groove. He winced as he touched it. The adrenalin from the chase had kept him from feeling it but a burn was now starting.

Merlin looked around, wondering if he could find some bandages. A quick search in the drawers turned up nothing. He had passed a small bathroom and wondered if there would be something in there. He checked out the window first to make sure the troops weren't close. He couldn't afford to be caught off guard if they were doing a house to house search. The street was quiet and he turned, moving quickly to check the bathroom. But he came up with nothing, not even aspirin, and he slammed the small cabinet door shut and hustled back to the kitchen, checking out front again. Still no sign of the rebel troops.

Merlin turned to sit down for a moment again when he spotted a roll of tuck tape on the counter. He picked it up, ripped off a piece and placed it over the cut on his forehead. Then he put two pieces in an X over the shoulder wound. It was better than nothing.

Next, the duck-tape doc's stomach growled and Merlin realized he hadn't eaten in some time. Lifting the binoculars from around his neck, he set them on the table. Moving to the cupboards, he took a quick look, finding nothing more than a couple of cans of tomatoes. It wasn't long before he found a can opener and he leaned against the counter, watching the road while digging in with his fingers. Tomatoes and tomato juice from a can seemed like a gourmet meal. He finished off the second can, sitting at the table while trying to formulate some plan.

Chapter 47

MERLIN AWOKE WITH A START. A metallic sound echoed in his skull but he couldn't see anything. Why couldn't he see–? He calmed himself when he realized he couldn't see because it was dark. The sun had set and only the moonlight streaming in through the window lit up a small square patch of wooden floor boards in the kitchen. He rubbed the back of his neck and stirred on the chair. He had fallen asleep from exhaustion– the metallic sound echoed across the floor boards and he went on alert. Reaching for his Beretta– it wasn't there. Why not? He reached out and his hand touched it on the table beside the binoculars. Letting out a low breath, he calmed himself again. He had set the gun on the table when he was eating and the metallic sound was from the empty can of tomatoes he had set beside it. Knocking it off the table had woken him up. Get a hold of yourself, Dragon.

He had no idea how long he had slept, but he still felt exhausted. But that was it, wasn't it? Trying to stay ahead of the rebel soldiers, the lack of food and sleep was going to do him in. Sooner or later he would fall asleep at the wrong time or suffer in a fight because he was weak from lack of food. He had to get moving.

Stretching his leg out gingerly, he rubbed his knee. It felt much better but his body felt like he had ridden a roller coaster upside down. He touched a finger tip to the duck tape on his forehead. The swelling ached as did his shoulder but it shouldn't slow him down.

Pulling out his cell phone to see what time it was, Merlin realized it had run out of juice and was nothing more than a small doorstop right now. He cursed himself silently. He should have tried contacting President Balewa before he had fallen asleep. Putting the cell phone away, he holstered the Beretta and picked up the binoculars, slipping the strap around his neck again. He grimaced when the binoculars touched his chest in the spot where he felt bruised after his run from death. Suck it up, Dragon, time to get to work.

There was no power and Merlin had to feel his way in the darkness through the house and into the back yard. He found the night air to be warm and muggy, and it carried the scent of burning wood over that of battle. His body protested in agony as he scaled the back wall and dropped to the ground on the other side. Moved diagonally across the yard to the left wall at the back corner of the house, he rested for a moment. Then he worked to pull himself onto the wall and from there he climbed onto the flat, sloped roof of the house. Crawling to the front, he lay in his stomach. The sounds of battle sounded far off to the left, south of the airport, and the occasional flash of an explosion told him heavy fighting was going on.

He turned his attention to the railway yard, where fires continued to burn inside where the ammunition dumps had been. Orange flames licked the black smoke that rolled into the moonlit sky. A massive crater, framed by twisted railway tracks was more evidence of his handiwork.

Using the binoculars, he scanned the activity in the flickering light. A locomotive with a long line of boxcars behind it sat on the far track and rebel soldiers were busy unloading the cargo. No doubt they had brought more ammunition in. But at least he had slowed their ability to fight. He had put a wrinkle in their plans, but there was no telling how long before they overcame it. He noted a battle tank was sitting across the tracks near the entrance on the right. They weren't going to allow another explosive laden train to be driven into the oil tank area.

He swung the binoculars to the area around the oil tanks, wondering if there was some other way he could take them out. But the armed presence had been toughened and they now had an armored Humvee, with a soldier manning a heavy machine gun on the roof, sitting watch. He wouldn't have a chance to get anywhere near enough to do any real damage.

A group of soldiers, who appeared to be engaged in intensive discussions, caught his attention. He moved the focus in and out, wondering if he could actually pick up a few words by reading their lips– surprise, surprise. The man in the center of the discussion was Colonel Nicolaas Kessen. Merlin was sure of it. No doubt he was trying to iron out Merlin's *wrinkle,* regain the advantage, and move the civil war forward to success.

Not if he could help it. Merlin decided to do something stupid. Or at least try to.

He checked the entranceway to the railway yard just down the road. It looked like they were four rebel soldiers guarding the entrance. A Jeep was parked sideways across the opening, manned by another soldier sitting in the driver seat, armed with an AK-47 like the others. He held his casually across his lap.

Merlin watched as a cargo truck with a canvas soft top approached the entrance. Three of the rebel soldiers stood with their weapons on their hip as the fourth talked to the driver. Then they stood aside and waved the truck in as the Jeep pulled ahead to allow entrance. Once the truck drove into the railway yard, the Jeep moveed back into position to block the entrance.

Sliding back on his belly to keep his profile from being seen, Merlin dropped back to the ground and moved back across the back wall to the house where he retrieved the minibike.

The potholed road out front was lit only by the moonlight and once Merlin had the homemade minibike started, he kept his speed down to stay as quiet as possible. Plus, he couldn't afford to go head over heels into a shell hole and possibly damage his transportation before he was finished with it. He moved a block beyond the guarded checkpoint where he abandoned his ride and walked the block over to the roadway running along the railway yard.

He checked the Beretta and then slipped it into the back of his waistband. Wincing from the pain, he removed the duct tape on his forehead so he wouldn't look like a total idiot. Taking a deep breath to ready himself, Merlin then left the shadows and walked down the center of the road toward the entrance.

The rebel soldiers on guard caught sight of him approaching and they immediately went on alert.

Merlin was sure only the fact he was dressed like them, minus the brown beret, kept them from shooting him.

Unless, of course, they were just waiting for him to get close enough so they didn't waste bullets.

Merlin raised a hand in greeting as he neared the soldiers, "G'Day, mate. How's it going?" Then under his breath, Merlin chastised himself, "I had to use an Australian accent? What the hell is with that? And G'Day? It's friggin' night–"

One of the soldiers challenged him, "What's the password?"

Merlin's eyebrows knit together. He hadn't thought of that. He threw his hands up in frustration as he kept walking, "How the hell do I know?" He gestured back over his shoulder and then tapped the binoculars a couple of times with his other hand, "I've been out there trying to get some Intel when they started chasing me. I had to hold up in a bombed out building." He gestured down at his tattered uniform, "Look at me. I've been–"

"What's the password?" The soldier challenged louder.

Merlin's mind whirled and then he said, "ABBA."

"Abba?"

Merlin shrugged, "That's what it was when I went out a couple of days ago. I don't know. I think the great warrior Kessen is a closet ABBA fan. Had the posters on his wall and the whole thing."

The soldiers looked at each other and laughed.

Taking advantage of the temporary lull in attention to duty, Merlin pulled the Beretta and crouched in a firing stance, aiming at the four soldiers standing on the gravel. He squeezing off seven shots. Enough bullets found vital spots to drop them.

The fifth soldier in the Jeep had been startled by the shooting and he was just now bringing his weapon to bear on Merlin.

Firing twice more, Merlin caught the fifth man once in the head and once in the neck.

A burst of fire from the soldier's AK-47 ripped through the night air.

Merlin ducked instinctively.

Slumping ahead, the AK-47 stopped firing but the soldier's body pressed on the Jeep's horn and a long loud beeper erupted.

Moving quickly beyond the dead soldiers to the Jeep, Merlin yanked the man away from the horn and pulled him sideways, letting him drop to the dirt. He took a quick look into the railway yard and waited, listening. With all the activity going on, no one appeared to be alarmed enough by all the shots to be heading this way in force. Merlin assumed the gunfire had just blended into the battle in the distance. But he had to get to work fast before another truck passed through this checkpoint or there was a new set of guards headed to relieve this crew.

Merlin tucked the Beretta into his waistband and quickly pulled all of the bodies to the darkness inside the wire fence. He patted down each dead man, finding a cell. But when he tried to use it, it couldn't make a connection. He tossed it and then took a brown beret from one of them to complete his uniform again.

Merlin turned and headed for the entrance. But he stopped after several feet and went back to the dead bodies, where he snagged a brown beret to complete his uniform. He then jogged back to the entrance, where he threw all but two of the AK-47s to the ground over beside the bodies.

Putting one weapon in the back and the other on the passenger seat, next to a walkie-talkie, Merlin climbed into the driver's seat, cranked the wheel hard and floored it into the railway yard.

Chapter 48

MERLIN SLOWED THE JEEP about one hundred yards away from the first group of soldiers working inside the railway yard. He wanted to blend in as much as possible and speeding recklessly would only attract unwanted attention. He slowed to a crawl as he crossed several sets of tracks and then turned to drive along the wide gravel strip between the next set of tracks so he could survey the activity around the boxcars. The soldiers were loading crates and boxes from the boxcars into the backs of a dozen 2½-ton 6x6 off-road cargo trucks with canvas soft tops, like the one he had watched go through the checkpoint.

Parking the Jeep, Merlin watched the unloading and loading going on. The pungent, sweet smell of exploded ammunition and military shells hung heavy on the hot night air, mixed with the scent of charred and burning wood. The soft roar of flames and the crackle of wood punctuated the orders shouted and the thud of heavy crates loaded into the trucks. From here, he could see it was crates of ammunition and explosives they were loading. He also spotted boxes labeled 'Ration de Combat Individuelle Rechauffable'. Those were French field rations. No doubt they were moving all these supplies from the train to the front lines of the battle. He had slowed them down but would it be enough to tilt the battle in favor of the Vertrosé army? He doubted it.

He took his attention from the loading efforts and looked around. Far off to the left were the storage tanks. He had hoped to take them out as well with the train he sent rocketing into the railway yard, but he had failed. He glanced at the loading operation, thinking for a moment, and then shook his head. Getting enough explosives from here to there was definitely undo-able. No doubt he would be caught and shot in a heartbeat. Then again, maybe not. Through the activity of the workers, he spotted Colonel Kessen again. And just like when he saw the man from the roof, he was in intense discussions with a group of men. If Merlin was caught trying to grab a case of explosives, no doubt Kessen would make sure he died a slower death than a dozen bullets to the head.

Rubbing the back of his neck, Merlin considered the situation. It didn't look like he could do much more damage to their supplies. Or find some other way to slow or stop their attacks. Or could he? Laurent's basic words that first day he became The Stopper came back to him. *All of your assignments will be threats we can't deal with effectively any other way. Those threats will have to be dealt with quickly...they will need to be stopped* dead. *That's where you come in.*

Merlin sat up straighter. Maybe he hadn't stopped them quickly...but what about dead? What about the tactical brains behind Okafor's civil war...Kessen himself? He might never get this close to the man again. But being this close *and* in the middle of the rebel army was still a problem. He glanced at the AK-47. No...he couldn't simply shoot the Colonel and walk away. That was a suicide mission. Then again.... The walkie-talkie beside the weapon caught his attention. That was obviously the way the rebel army was communicating with each other and their central command. But that didn't help him at all. Or did it? He picked up the walkie-talkie and a plan slowly began forming.

He still had the pocket knife and under the flickering light, he used it to take the back off the walkie-talkie. He looked at it closely, examining the circuit board. He pulled a few components up, following the wiring from one connection to the other. Satisfied his plan might work *if* he could get another walkie-talkie, Merlin carefully set the still open walkie-talkie down on the passenger seat. Then he got out and walked casually towards the activity, acting like he belonged.

Reaching the area where the crates and boxes were being stacked before loading onto the trucks, Merlin look for what he needed. Sweat began trickling down his back and he wondered if it was because of the heat or nervousness. He decided it didn't matter as he spotted what he needed, stacked boxes of the C-4 plastic explosives. And beyond that were the boxes of electric blasting caps. The problem, though, was simple. How could he take a box of each, pretending he was like one of the other soldiers loading the trucks, and *not* load them on a truck without looking suspicious?

Without an immediate answer, Merlin kept on walking, looking for a better opportunity. The problem was...there wasn't any. He cursed under his breath. His plan would have to be modified...no...make that abandoned.

Up ahead was an area with a number of make-shift picnic tables and a set of soldiers sat around eating the French field rations. As he drew closer he could smell North African lamb stew and Basque duck and vegetable soup, just two of the varieties available in the packs. Some of the packs had small bottles of wine as well; a real treat in this heat if it was cold– Merlin saw something else. Because of the heat and humidity, a number of the men had taken off their berets and shirts. And that included a muscular soldier who sat facing forward, his bare back against the table as he ate. He was important for one reason - his shirt lay on the table. And lying on his shirt was a Commando-green beret.

Merlin quickly unbuttoned and took his beret off, doing his best to look like one of them. He approached the table casually, giving a nod to another soldier as he reached down for a ration pack from an open carton. He lifted his leg over the seat and sat just behind his target, laying his beret down in the middle of the table just this side of the Commando-green beret, and he went to work on opening his rations.

The men talked softly as they ate, their words drowned out by the loading and unloading activity.

Merlin scratched his head as he glanced around him. When he was sure no one was paying any attention to him, he moved his small bottle of wine to just near his beret, watched from the corner of his eye as his fingers reached out and pulled the other beret over, effectively switching the two. Calmly palming the beret, Merlin pulled it to his open shirt and tucked it under his arm. It was time to go. He quickly got up, lifting his leg up over the seat.

Another soldier at the next table looked at him.

Merlin reached over and grabbed his bottle of wine, making as if he couldn't trust to leave it behind until he got back to his seat.

The soldier gave a smirk as if he understood and went back to his own meal.

Moving away from the tables, Merlin slipped the Commando-green beret on and buttoned his shirt as he moved back toward the items he needed. He stood more erect and in command as he closed in on the boxes of C-4 plastic explosives.

No one paid any attention to him. He was just another rebel soldier and Merlin took advantage of that. His heart was pounding as he simply walked into the midst of the soldiers working around the boxes. And since there was no way he could just slit a box this time and pocket some of the bundles like before, he just picked up two boxes of C-4.

There were only a few glances in his direction as the work continued.

Turning and moving toward the electric blasting caps, Merlin kept as calm as possible, even though his heart was tapping out a heavy rhythm against his chest. Reaching the stacks of boxes, Merlin set the two boxes of C-4 down on a stack, slid his hands down and under a single box of fuses and lifting all three up again. He watched the workers from the corner of his eye as he turned and walked away. But instead of heading in the direction of the trucks they were loading, he casually headed for the jeep. No one stopped him. No one gave him more than a curious look. It had been easy. Maybe too easy– he cursed under his breath.

Four rebel soldiers were standing at the side of the jeep, discussing something.

Merlin slowed his pace for a moment, considering heading back to the piles of crates and boxes and discarding the C-4 and fuses–

One of the soldiers turned his head and saw Merlin. He tapped one of the other soldiers on the shoulder, said something, and they all turned to look at Merlin.

There was no turning back now.

For all intents and purposes, this was the moment of truth.

Chapter 49

THE TALL, BURLY SOLDIER on the other side of the jeep strode around the back end and toward Merlin, his fists clenched. The other three soldiers looked amused at whatever mayhem they thought was about to take place. Merlin heard a 'watch Buhari' comment as one of them slapped the shoulder of a comrade with the back of his hand. From their brown berets, their casual stance and the way they handled their weapons, Merlin assumed all four men were some of Faraji Okafor's local force, battle hardened but not highly disciplined soldiers or mercenaries. Could he use that?

In the flickering light from the fires, Merlin sized up the striding soldier as the alpha male of this makeshift pack and he decided he had only one chance. That was to channel a former Sergeant from his BMQ days...Basic Military Qualification Training boot camp.

The burly soldier called Buhari showed his teeth as he neared Merlin, "What exactly do you think–?"

Merlin set his voice into a replica of his old drill-sergeant, barking out, "What exactly are you men doing here?" He brushed past the burly soldier with disdain and set the boxes on the driver's seat,

"Shouldn't you be working to offload the cargo like the rest? We're fighting a war. Or haven't you heard?"

Buhari was taken aback for a moment and he closed his mouth. Then he tried to assert his authority again, moving beside Merlin and jutting his chin out, "The question is; what are *you* doing parked here–?"

Merlin turned his head and lifted his face closer to the big man, "Why? Is this a no-parking zone? Because I don't see a damn sign anywhere."

The big man opened his mouth again–

Taking a step to the side, as if dismissing his authority, Merlin pointed beyond the workers to the circle of men talking, "If you want to know what I'm doing *or* want to question his orders, why don't you go talk to the Colonel? He's right over there."

The three soldiers looked to where Merlin was pointing. One of them straightened up when he saw Kessen in the distance.

Buhari turned his head to look as well.

Looking over at Buhari, the three soldiers looked to be less enthusiastic now.

But Buhari dismissed their concerns with a sneer and turned on Merlin again. He tried to regain the advantage again, pointing to the passenger seat, "*Why* is your walkie talkie all apart–?"

Merlin put his hands on his hips, "Are you the walkie talkie police or the parking police? Cause I'm getting confused. Which is it?"

The three men looked at each other as the big man seemed unsure on how to answer.

Taking an assertive step forward, Merlin gave the big man a firm look, "Maybe it's all apart because another big lug like you didn't know how to use it? And now I'm the one who has to try and fix it. Unless *you* want to take up the job?"

Buhari glanced at the walkie talkie, his eyebrows knitting together.

Merlin could see the mixture of confusion and concern written on the faces of all four men. The problem was he needed more than that. He needed them gone. And when one of them glanced to the Commando-green beret he was wearing, he launched into a spiel, "Look. I don't have time for this. Kessen wants me to run a covert infiltration into sector G7 to take out their RF booster amplifiers and blind their defensive command structure. If you want to talk to the Colonel about it, go ahead, be my guest. But I'm not willing to have him chew out my ass because I didn't get my work done. Now why don't you meter maids leave a damn ticket on the windshield and let me get to work?" He turned to the jeep and began shifted one of the boxes over to the passenger seat.

There was silence from the four soldiers and then Buhari muttered something under his breath.

Merlin turned his head, barking at him, "What was that?"

Buhari held his hands up in surrender, his face showing anger at his humiliation in front of the others, but he took a step away.

Merlin turned dismissively and set back to work on moving the boxes. A second later, he heard their boots begin to crunch on the gravel as they walked away. A realization popped into his head - he needed something else - he turned his head, calling out sharply, "Hey?"

The four men stopped and turned to look back.

Snapping his fingers several times, he said, "I need another walkie talkie while you're talking to the Colonel." When they just stood there, he snapped his fingers several times again, "Let's go. Fork one over."

One of the soldiers grumbled as he looked at the others but he pulled his walkie talkie from his belt and tossed it to Merlin.

Merlin grumbled a "thanks" in return and turned his attention back to the boxes. But his ears were listening to the sounds of crunching footsteps moving away from him. After a few moments, he glanced over his shoulder to make sure they were moving away. They were. But for how long? And would they eventually go to Kessen after thinking or talking it over? He couldn't trust to blind chance or a lack of military training and discipline any longer. Jumping into the jeep, he started driving away, slowly at first, so as not to draw attention. Moments later, he pressed down on the gas, moving away at a faster clip from the flickering lights of the bunker fires and into the inky blackness at the edge of the railway yard.

But once he felt safe to stop, he cursed under his breath again. He would have to work on the walkie talkie like someone reading braille. But he had no choice and he set to work, feeling more than seeing as he traced the wires attached to the circuit board with his fingers. He had to trust he would do it right. Using the pocket knife, he began making a detonator using the walkie talkie and the fuses he had stolen. Everything felt right once he had that task done but he still worried as he set to work on the C-4, wiring block after block together. Every so often he glanced at the fires and the activity around the box cars. No one came to look at where he had been. But that could change at any moment, so he worked briskly but carefully, preparing his answer to Kessen smashing the side of his head with the gun outside the National Assembly Building.

Once he was done, Merlin ran a walkie talkie through a number of channels, looking for one they weren't using. He couldn't afford to have the fuses triggered before he was ready–

A crack of light to the East between caught his attention and Merlin's heart rate shot up.

The sun was about to rise.

He was out of time.

Choosing a channel that appeared to be free from chatter, Merlin set the two walkie talkies to the same frequency. Then he hurriedly put two of the boxes of prepared explosives on the floor in front of the passenger seat. The last box of prepared explosives, the one containing the wired walkie talkie, was placed on the passenger seat and he was ready.

Chapter 50

MERLIN TOOK THE JEEP IN A U-TURN, bumping over a set of tracks and back, and then drove slowly back to the activity. As he approached the spot where he had bluffed the four rebel soldiers, he slowed down, checking to make sure they weren't looking for him. Everything looked good. Making a left-hand turn over several sets of tracks, Merlin then turned at an angle over another set and put the left wheels of the jeep over the rails. The vehicle would now be guided directly to the area where Kessen was talking with a group of his men next to the tracks–

A loud voice began cursing and yelling in the area of the tables. Kessen looked over, as did the others in his group.

A bare-chested soldier was calling out for the man who had taken his beret, cursing him out and threatening bodily harm if his property wasn't returned.

Two of the rebel soldiers in Kessen's group said something to him and then headed for the commotion.

Merlin's jaw clenched and he felt adrenalin surge through his veins.

Kessen himself seemed to be looking around.

Merlin had no doubt, once Kessen was told someone had taken a Commando-green beret, he would put two and two together.

Time was running out.

A moment later, Kessen went back to discussing something with the remaining men

This was it.

Merlin knew wouldn't get another chance. He pressed down on the gas. The adrenalin rush caused him to press too hard and he gunned the jeep's engine. The vehicle growled and lurched.

A few men looked over.

Lifting his foot, Merlin, waited a second to make sure the men went back to work. Then he held his breath, controlling his foot better and pressed down slower this time.

The jeep moved forward. And in a moment, the wheels began bumping up and down on the railroad ties, making a thump, thump, thump sound.

Merlin swore softly. He knew the noise would eventually attract attention, even over the activity.

But he kept going, increasing the speed.

Just a little more.

A few seconds later, he decided he was close enough. It was time to execute the final part of the plan.

Grabbing the final box of prepared explosives containing the walkie talkie, Merlin let off on the gas. Then he slid to the edge of the seat, leaving the jeep in gear. As the vehicle slowed, Merlin jumped out and quickly pushed the box down in front of the driver's seat.

The weight pressed down on the gas pedal and the jeep picked up speed again.

Merlin had to jog to keep up, nearly stumbling over the ties in the flickering light as his right hand extended to grip the steering wheel. He had to make sure the wheels were as straight as possible, so the vehicle wouldn't wedge the wheels against the rail– but he couldn't keep up...he had to let it go.

Stumbling to his knees, he grimaced as the edge of a railway tie banged into a kneecap. Cursing at the pain, he got to his feet and massaged the knee as he stepped over to the gravel on the edge of the tracks. But there was no time to waste and he took off in a limping jog.

His mind calculated the blast radius and told him to push harder. Pain shot up his leg as he did and Merlin did everything he could to ignore it as he counted off the yardage in his head

Finally, he turned, pulled the walkie talkie from his belt and watched as his handwork bumped the last yards to the target.

A number of rebel soldiers jumped back from the tracks as the jeep rolled past them.

Kessen and the others in the group turned at the bumpity-bump-bump sound.

When they saw the jeep coming straight for the area where they were talking, they looked at each other, wondering what was happening. A second later, they stepped back from the tracks to give the jeep enough room to pass.

Lifting a hand, Kessen pointed at the runaway vehicle as he barked an order to the group of soldiers just standing around, watching it roll.

Merlin pressed the talk button on his walkie talkie, "Hello, Kessen. Remember me?"

Kessen must have heard the voice through the speaker because he froze and looked at the jeep.

"Goodbye, asshole–"

The explosion knocked Merlin on his own ass and he groaned as his already sore body hit the gravel.

A moment later, he lifted his head and moaned softly, watching jeep and body parts falling back to earth in the midst of rolling smoke.

Chapter 51

MERLIN SHIFTED HIS LEG away from the center console of the stolen Jeep with a wince. The sun was already blazing hot and the metal was uncomfortable against his bare skin. In the confusion inside the railway yard after the explosion, he had commandeered a jeep and left behind the chaos and torn bodies from his handiwork. Leaving the yard the way he had gone in, he drove through the rubble-filled streets to the West and then drove to the South, toward the front lines of the war for Ténemané.

Now he sat one block away from where he could see Vertrosé troops behind a barricade in the street. The sounds of battle a few blocks to his right echoed off the damaged buildings. He had no doubt weapons would be trained on him and he had stripped down to his shorts, tossing the uniform and Commando-green beret to the rubble-filled road. He wasn't going to gamble on being mistaken for the enemy. His Beretta and other items were sitting on the passenger seat. Wiping the sweat from his brow, Merlin put the Jeep in gear and let it roll forward slowly, right hand on the steering wheel and the other high in the air.

Half a block away from the troops, the click click click of weapons being readied and brought to bear echoed off the battle beaten walls of the nearby buildings.

Merlin stopped short of the barricade that consisted of an overturned car, chunks of building and barbed wire. He put the Jeep in park and slowly raised his other hand, calling out, "Tell your commander my name is Merlin Dragon and I have information for President Adisa Balewa." The only sound for a few moments was the sounds of battle a block or two over. He called out his statement louder, wondering if he would have to drive close.

A soldier finally yelled back to him, "Get out of the jeep and stand in the street where we can see you."

Merlin grumbled, "I'm not sure you're going to like what you see but okay." He complied, doing his best to keep his bare skin away from the hot metal as he swiveled on the seat and put one foot over the edge. He kept his hands over his head as he stood up and stepped away from the Jeep.

There was laughter and comments as the soldiers looked at the nearly naked man standing in the street in nothing more than undershorts and boots.

Waiting for a few moments, Merlin called out again, "Guys, this is kind of hot out here and I'm frying. Please tell your commander—"

"Walk this way. Keep your hands up."

Merlin gestured with his head, "I have stuff in the jeep that I don't want to leave behind—"

"Do it *now.*"

"Okey-dokey." Walking forward slowly, Merlin approached the barricade.

Several soldiers moved to an area where they pulled aside a section of barbed wire that would only allow a single man to enter.

As he stepped through, Merlin's elbows were taken firmly by a soldier on each side. He heard more comments and jokes about his lack of the attire.

A wolf whistle split the air.

Merlin looked over to see two female soldiers smiling and looking him over. Under the hot sun, his skin glistened from perspiration like baby oil on a body builder and he muttered to himself, "All I need is some Jello to roll around in." But all he could do was stand there and wait.

A barrel of a soldier approached from one of the bombed out buildings. His eyebrows were raised as he looked Merlin over. He stopped a few feet away, "You are Mr. Dragon?"

"That's right."

"I am Captain Okuro." He held out the walkie talkie, "The President is on the other end."

Merlin put his hand around the walkie talkie to take it but was surprised when the soldier held firm.

Okuro looked at Merlin hard, "Do not think you can fool us. Do you understand me?"

Nodding once, Merlin said, "Understood." When the soldier let go, Merlin pressed the push-to-talk button as he lifted the walkie talkie to talk, "Mr. President?"

"Yes. This is Mr. Dragon? We thought you were dead."

"Not quite. Noxolo was right. They were using the old oil tanks for fuel storage and the underground storage to put ammunition and stuff like your General Bamgboshe had in your drive to take Ténemané. Problem was, I was taken prisoner by the rebels and couldn't let you know."

The President sounded disappointed to hear confirmation they were using that plan, "I see. That means we will have difficulty holding out."

"Not necessarily. I was able to escape, take over a train load of supplies and drive it back into the railway yard, exploding some C-4 inside one of the boxcars near that ammunition bunker."

"We saw and heard the explosion at the railway yard. That was your doing?"

"Yeah, I was able to take out the ammo depot–"

Okuro stepped forward, his eyes wide in surprise, "They have lost those ordnance supplies in the railway yard?"

Merlin nodded at him, "Yeah. I wasn't able to take out the fuel storage but–"

Snapping his fingers at one of the other soldiers, Okuro gestured for the man's walkie talkie as he said to Merlin, "Tell the President I will contact Major Janie to make a push against the rebels before they can regain the advantage."

Merlin relayed the message as Okuro moved away a few feet, talking urgently into the walkie talkie.

"That is good," Balewa said. "Perhaps we can turn the tide against Faraji Okafor and his forces now."

"One other thing," Merlin said. "When they took me prisoner, they took me by train north to another rail yard. One with a seaport–"

"Addosie?"

"I have no idea. All I know is I stayed awake until we got there and I don't recall going through another yard with port facilities."

"Then it must be Addosie. France offered a nearby destroyer to aid us. We thought Okafor and his forces had supplies coming in though our port here once they drove into the northern part of the city. We

asked the destroyer to patrol the harbor and cut off any ships coming in. But they never encountered any. Now we know why. I can ask the French to sail north and cut off the supply line in Addosie."

"That makes sense," Merlin said. "One other thing. Our friend, Colonel Kessen...?"

"The one helping Okafor with his military strategy?"

"One and the same."

"What about him?"

Okuro was listening and he looked at Merlin, gesturing with his walkie talkie, "I have the Major now. Tell us where this Kessen is and we can make a push on his position–"

Merlin pressed the push-to-talk button and told both men, "I'm not sure where Kessen is right now but I can tell you he's fallen to pieces."

"Fallen to pieces?"

"Yeah. I blew him up with a jeep full of C-4."

There was deep laughter of relief from both men.

Merlin grew serious and he pressed the push-to-talk button, almost afraid to ask, "How is Noxolo? And my plane and crew...?"

You could hear the President take a deep breath, "Your crew received injuries but I am assured they are in good condition."

Feeling some relief at the news of Sherrell and Saab, Merlin still felt some fear at Balewa not mentioning Noxolo with them. That couldn't be good. He waited fearfully for an answer

The President took a moment before he said, "As for Lesedi...I am not sure at this moment. I did hear from Captain Chiamaka after you arranged to have her flown out. She is in Johannesburg, South Africa and Doctor Jelani had said she was still in danger. Unfortunately, with most communications cut off and the civil war going badly, I have not had a chance to find out much more I'm afraid."

Merlin felt disappointment, "I understand." He took a deep breath himself and let it out slowly, "Okay, Mr. President. Right now I need to find some clothes and get dressed."

"Get dressed?"

"Yeah. I removed my uniform so your troops wouldn't shoot me. I'm just wearing my shorts and boots–"

Another loud wolf whistle echoed off the surrounding buildings.

Merlin looked around at the two female soldiers– no, make that four grinning female soldiers now.

There was laughter from Balewa, "Thank you for putting on a show for my armed forces, Mr. Dragon. It is very much appreciated."

Shaking his head, Merlin said, "Yeah, well...my agent Jigs will send you the bill."

Chapter 52

THREE DAYS LATER, after his army retook the airport, President Adisa Balewa provided Merlin with a small plane to take him to Johannesburg, South Africa. The ride was like a roller coaster as they passed through a storm and he was glad to arrive in one piece, missing the Bombardier Global 8000 more than he ever though he would.

The drive in the taxi was slow in the stop and go traffic, the air was hot and humid and he was sweaty and tired by the time he finally entered the doors of Johannesburg Hospital. Lesedi Noxolo was here in the Johannesburg Hospital Trauma Unit, the only Level I Trauma unit of its kind in South Africa, and capable of handling everything from minor injuries to major polytrauma.

Merlin took the elevator to the third floor, standing at the back of a number of other visitors and hospital staff, all of them silent and serious looking. When all of them got off on the 3rd floor, he understood why they all acted so somber. The hallway and waiting areas were hushed and quiet as other members of the public talked among themselves or to doctors or even priests and ministers. This unit wasn't where you came to visit recovering patients. Or ones talking about their progress or time frame for going home. This was the place where you worried if there *would* be a recovery or a loved one going home ever.

"Sir?"

Merlin turned his head to see Captain Chiamaka standing there, somber but with his hand out in greeting.

When Merlin gripped his hand, Chiamaka gave him a nod, "Thank you again for your help. I was glad to hear you had survived."

"Me, too. How is...?"

"Much the same, I'm afraid." Chiamaka gestured to a hallway, "I will take you to where she is. This is Trauma Ward 377, the in-patient ward. We must go to 376, the trauma intensive care unit."

Merlin nodded and he let Chiamaka lead the way. This didn't sound good at all. Despite taking out the ordnance bunkers and Kessen, and the Vertrosé army pushing the rebels back, many people had lost their lives. And even worse, he still hadn't stopped Davet Minard and Dirk VanDaele from trying again. Or maybe pulling their crap on another innocent country. All of that, coupled with Noxolo still in intensive care, meant there was more failure in his mission than there was success.

Entering a quiet space with only the sounds of machines pumping and hissing, Chiamaka took Merlin to one of eight intensive glass-walled care cubicles. The patients in each cubicle were hidden behind a curtain at the foot of the bed.

Doctor Jelani was there, talking quietly to a doctor and a nurse who left as Chiamaka and Merlin approached. Jelani shook hands with Merlin, his voice hushed, "Thank you, Mr. Dragon, for your help. It is very much appreciated."

"You're welcome. How is she exactly?"

Jelani shook his head somberly without a word. Then he gestured to the open doorway, "It might be a god idea for you to go in and pay your respects. She is semi-conscious at the moment. I would take the opportunity while you can."

Merlin steeled himself as he walked softly into the cubicle. As he came around the curtain to the side of the bed, he saw a paler, more vulnerable-looking woman than the one had traded barbs with from the first day they 'met' at the casino in Monte Carlo. The blankets were pulled up under her chin but her arms were on top of them, intravenous lines hooked up to both wrists. Merlin bent over, talking softly, "Hey, Noxolo, how are you doing?"

There was no answer for a moment and then the dark eyelids fluttered and her eyes opened slowly. Noxolo looked up toward the ceiling and blinked slowly a few times as if she was trying to focus. A moment later, she turned her head slightly toward Merlin. The lips moved.

"Pardon?"

Noxolo swallowed and then the lips moved again

Leaning closer to her face, Merlin asked softly, "Can you say that again–?"

Reaching up, Lesedi Noxolo wrapped both arms around his neck and pulled him down, kissing him fully on the mouth. She laughed softly and said, "I said I am grateful for your help, Mr. Dragon. Does that show it?"

Merlin felt some strength in her arms as he tried to pull back in surprise. She was stronger than he thought she would be under the circumstances.

Noxolo lifted her head slightly and said with some mirth in her voice, "And if you pull all those curtains for some privacy, I can show you just how grateful I can be."

Merlin wasn't sure what to say, "I'm...I'm not sure that's necessary–"

Her weak grin was mischievous, "You are in an intensive care unit, Mr. Dragon. I am sure you will survive the ordeal. And if you don't, I will make sure you go out happy."

Confusion showed on Merlin's face, "Uh...the way they were talking...."

Letting him go, Noxolo laughed softly again, "Yes, I asked them to play like that for me."

Merlin heard low laughter from Chiamaka and Jelani on the other side of the curtain at the end of the bed.

Noxolo turned serious and reached out, taking his hand in hers, "But thank you, my friend. You saved my life. And from what I have heard, you have saved my country."

Merlin squeezed her hand back gently, "Thanks but there are still a lot of people who lost their lives."

"Yes. But it is the nature of our profession. We strive to protect and occasionally lose some. Is that not true?"

Merlin nodded softly at her comment but still felt like a failure in some ways.

Doctor Jelani appeared beside Merlin. He gave Noxolo a gentle but firm look, "And now that you have had your fun, I must insist that you rest. Doctor's orders."

Noxolo gave him a sleepy nod in return, "Understood." She looked up at Merlin, her eyes already starting to close, "Perhaps we can meet again in Monte Carlo and I help you with that bet of yours."

Merlin opened his mouth to answer but he could tell she was already asleep. He patted her hand, "Maybe someday we can."

Chapter 53

MERLIN CLIMBED THE AIRSTAIRS and entered the Bombardier Global 8000 to find Captain Charity Sherrell and Captain Faith Saab standing in the back, waiting for him. He still wore the Vertose Army uniform and he tossed the beret to one of the seats.

For her part, Sherrell had a bandage on her neck, the result of a bullet grazing her during the extraction of Lesedi Noxolo. Saab Looked perfectly normal but Merlin had been told of other non-evident injuries with both Sherrell and Saab. They had suffered serious injuries to an arm and a thigh respectively from .45 caliber bullets penetrating the cockpit cabin when they had been taking off. Those were serious injuries and they had barely been missed by .50 caliber slugs from the heavy machine gun fire that had raked the plane. Those would have blown off an arm, if not a leg.

And then once they had gotten the plane out over the ocean, things had gone from bad to worse and the flight to South Africa had been perilous. All those bullet holes in the plane's skin had caused depressurization of the plane and they had to stay low, even flying through a storm they hit within ten minutes, instead of climbing over top of it as airlines usually do in their flights. That meant the doctor and the Captain couldn't tend to their wounds immediately because they were too busy keeping Noxolo from rolling all over the place. In addition, the efficiency of the aircraft was affected by the bullet holes and there had been damage to the controls by the gunfire as well. Through all of that, they struggled in pain, losing blood and keeping each other from blacking out.

Through the entire ordeal, the two Canadian military officers had performed heroically and unselfishly. Even now Merlin noticed they were concerned more about him, wondering how things had gone and if he was all right.

But Merlin refrained from any comments or explanations, kept a stoic face and gestured to Sherrell's bandage, "I hope that injury and the others you suffered won't hamper your duties?"

The two officers glanced at each other and Sherrell said, "No, sir. They won't–"

"Good. Because we need to get going. We have fuel and the plane is cleared to fly?"

Saab raised an eyebrow, "Yes, sir. We reached out to Interpol Pretoria and they put us in contact with the South African Air Force. Their capabilities have been limited because of local economics but they sent over some great flight mechanics, welders and–"

"So we're good to go, then?"

"Yes, sir. Uh...what...what about the woman we flew here" We haven't heard–"

Merlin waved away her question, "We'll probably hear about her later." He rubbed his hands together, "Now, can we head for home? I'm tired of all this heat and humidity." He snapped his fingers, "Oh, right, the Vertrosé Army has retaken the Ténemané airport and we need to stop there on our way back. Okay? Good. Let me know when we're at cruising altitude so I can take a shower."

With that said Merlin sat down in one of the four plush seats and began buckling in for takeoff.

Sherrell and Saab stood looking at him for a moment, confusion on their faces over his cold dismissal of them. After a glance at each other, the two officers turned and headed to the cockpit.

Merlin sat with his head back, eyes closed and resting. The takeoff was smooth and ten minutes later he heard a voice over the intercom.

"We're at cruising altitude, sir."

That was it. Short and sweet and Merlin allowed himself a brief smile.

The shower he in the back was his first in a number of days and was both refreshing and soothing for his own battered, bruised and wounded body. Then he treated himself to a couple of sandwiches and several hot coffees from the small galley as he sat quietly throughout the flight north along the African coastline.

Touchdown in Ténemané was equally smooth and he pressed the intercom button, "Please taxi to the red building on the right and lower the airstairs."

Six minutes later, the engines whined to a lower tone and the sound of the hydraulics whispered through the cabin as the airstairs lowered. The heavy heat of the day washed inside the plane as Merlin pressed the intercom again, "Please come to the back when you've shut down."

Standing up, Merlin heard footsteps climbing the stairs.

And then footsteps sounded from the front of the plane and the two pilots appeared. "You wanted us back here, sir?" Saab asked.

"Yes. Stand over there, please."

The two officers did as told, confusion and questions mingling on their features.

President Adisa Balewa entered the plane, his smile lighting up, "Mr. Dragon, so good to see you again." He pumped Merlin's hand vigorously.

"Nice to see you as well, Mr. President."

Two officious looking men entered the plane, one of them carrying a large briefcase.

Balewa looked to the men, "We are ready?" When one gave a nod in return, Balewa turned his attention to Sherrell and Saab, "And these are the two pilots?"

"Yes, sir," Merlin said. "This is Captain Charity Sherrell and Captain Faith Saab." He looked at the two, "And this is President Adisa Balewa, President of The Democratic Republic of Vertrosé."

The two women immediately came to attention.

Balewa moved forward eagerly, gave a brief salute, and then pumped their hands with enthusiasm, "I am honored to meet both of you. You did my country a great service by bringing Mr. Dragon in to help us." He put his hands on his chest, "And then flying back in to rescue Lesedi Noxolo and flying her to South Africa was not only a great service but something I am *personally* grateful for."

"Just doing our jobs, sir," Sherrell replied.

"Yes, I imagine you were. Still...." Balewa glanced to Merlin, "I know what Mr. Dragon does is of a secretive nature." He looked at the two officers, "And much of what you do will be hidden from your friends, family, and countrymen as well. We understand that. But we still wish to have you know how grateful we are and recognize you for what you have done."

Sherrell and Saab shared a sideways glance, still unsure of what was happening.

Balewa smiled at their reaction, turned his upper body and held a hand out.

The man with the briefcase stepped forward, lifted the case sideways and the sound of it being opened echoed inside the plane. The second man stepped forward, pulled an item from the case and handed it to the President.

Balewa stepped forward with a medal in his hands, a gold cross with a red and white ribbon, and he pinned it on Sherrell's chest, "This is our Croix de la Valeur Militaire, The Democratic Republic of Vertrosé's Cross for Military Valor." He held his hand out for a second medal and pinned that one on Saab, "Both of you have exhibited the valor this medal represents."

Sherrell and Saab both looked down at their medals and then shared another sideways glance.

Balewa held his hand out again.

The man passed over another medal, this one a silver cross with a red and black striped ribbon.

Pinning it on Saab this time, Balewa said, "And this is out Croix du combattant. The Combatant's Cross recognizes those who fought in combat for The Democratic Republic of Vertrosé." He held his hand out for another medal and pinned that one on Sherrell, "I thank you for your service, Captain."

Sherrell opened her mouth slightly to say something but was still without words as she instead looked at the medal pinned on Saab's uniform and shared a bewildered look with her.

Balewa stood taller as he looked from Sherrell to Saab, "Now...as for the woman you flew to South Africa...Lesedi Noxolo. She will survive, thanks to both of you and your bravery in the face of enemy fire." He bent his head in a nod, "She is also a dear friend of mine, a very valuable countryman and again I thank you from the bottom of my heart." He held a finger up, "But Lesedi also reminded me that as a former French colony, we have the privilege of awarding something very special. I have checked with the French government and they agree." He turned and held a hand out.

The man gave him a medal that had a white, five-point star, backed by a green wreath, and attached to a red ribbon.

Balewa pinned it on Sherrell, "This is the French Legion of Honor. This is the highest French order of merit for military and civil merits *and* an order of distinction first established by Napoleon Bonaparte in 1802. " He kissed her on both cheeks, pinned another on Saab and kissed her twice as well before stepping back.

Turning, Balewa shook hands with Merlin, "And thank *you* for everything you have done, Mr. Dragon. You will be pleased to know we have been talking with the World Bank *and* the United Nations to get a loan without certain strings attached. We have an opportunity for a bright future, thanks to you."

Merlin opened his mouth to push away the accolades and then just said, "Thank you. I hope everything works out for you and your country."

Balewa then strode to the airstairs and the three men left the plane.

The two women were still standing quiet and stunned, looking down at the medals, touching them lightly. When they looked up, they saw Merlin grinning broadly. Sherrell narrowed her eyes, "You knew they were going to do this, didn't you?"

"Guilty as charged. That's why I kind of cut you short back in Johannesburg–"

Saab raised her eyebrows, "Kind of?"

Merlin shrugged, "What can I say? I was afraid I'd give it away. But those medals look great pinned on your chest."

Sherrell put her hands on her hips, "Which means you've been looking at our chests. Right?"

Opening his mouth, no words came and Merlin gestured with a hand to the awards.

"He's so easily played, isn't he?" Saab said to Sherrell.

A big grin split Sherrell's face, "Yep." And she moved forward, embracing Merlin, slapping him on the back a couple of times, "Soldier to soldier, we're glad you're safe."

"Yeah," Saab agreed as she moved in when Sherrell released him. After the hug and back slaps, Saab stepped back beside Sherrell and stood at attention, lifting her hand in salute, "Now...are we going home...sir?"

Merlin gave her a quick salute in return and a smile, "Yes, Captain, let's head for home before another war breaks out."

The two officers turned and headed for the cockpit.

Dropping himself into a seat, Merlin looked out the window for a moment. All he could do was hope these people could make a real future for themselves now. He buckled in as the engines started and the aircraft turned and headed for the runway.

In a few moments, as the Bombardier rose into the blue skies over Ténemané, the African heat shimmered in the air as if it was waving goodbye.

Chapter 54

The Stonecliffe Arms Apartments, Ottawa

MERLIN KNOCKED LIGHTLY on Jaimee Hartman's door. It was nearing 11:00 PM and he wasn't sure if she was still awake. He had slipped into his own apartment and changed from the Vertrosé army uniform into a pair of slacks and a cotton shirt before he came to get Jigs. There was no sense in getting involved in awkward question.

The door swung open and Jaimee appeared in the doorway. Her blue eyes lit up, "Oh. Hi, Merlin–" The smile left her face and she put her hand on Merlin's jaw, turning his head slightly, "What in the world happened to you–?"

Merlin winced from a bruise on his jaw he didn't know he had, "Ow."

"Oh, I'm sorry." Jaimee pulled her hand back but the concern remained in her eyes, "Were you in a fight?"

Lightly massaging the side if his jaw, Merlin wasn't sure what to say, "Uh...well...."

Holding both hands up, Jaimee said, "I'm sorry. I know certain things and questions are off limits. Your job is your job and...." She turned her head and called out, "Jigs? There's someone here to see you. Jiggsy?"

The blue, wooly Chartreux came bounding from somewhere, speeding up when he saw Merlin.

Bending to catch the leaping cat, Merlin let out a low groan from the effort. The cat buried himself in his arms and Merlin actually staggered back a step as he tried to keep the weight from pressing into his sore body.

Jaimee crossed her arms, "I certainly hope she was worth it."

"She was worth it? What do you mean...?"

Moving her finger up and down in a gesture at his body soreness, Jaimee said, "The woman who left you feeling that way."

Merlin's eyebrows knit together, "The woman? There wasn't any woman. Well, there was but not like that."

"Uh, huh."

"Honest–"

Jaimee winked at him and her face lit up.

Merlin let out a breath between his lips, nodding, "You're teasing. Of course. What can't I see that?"

"Cause you're a sweetie-pie, that's why." Jaimee moved forward and kissed him lightly on the lips. "And you owed me that as well."

His brow furrowing, Merlin said, "That's what you said when I left."

Jaimee crossed her arms and shrugged, "So I just collected on the interest on the debt. You have an objection to that?"

"No, I guess not–"

Leaning in, Jaimee kissed him again, "There. I gave it back."

Merlin shook his head, a sheepish grin on his face, "I better go before I get too deeply in debt."

"Why? What do you think could happen?"

"Uh...never mind. I have a feeling I'm...never mind."

Jaimee held up three fingers, "You now owe me three diners *and* the musical at the National Arts Center."

Merlin nodded, "Noted. I'll call you tomorrow and we can set a date." He turned and took a step down the hallway.

Jaimee leaned forward and said, "Okay. And if you need a massage while you're in bed tonight, call me." Then she giggled.

Shaking his head, Merlin continued on toward his apartment.

"Oh, wait. Merlin?"

"Pardon?" Turning back, he saw her door was still open but she wasn't in the doorway. He heard her voice calling out to him from inside her apartment and he walked back.

Jaimee appeared in the doorway again, holding a brown box about a foot square and four inches deep as she pushed a strand of black hair from her forehead, "There was a courier at your door a couple of hours ago. He was really pounding and I offered to sign for it. I hope that was okay?"

"Of course." Merlin shifted Jigs in his arms to look at the package, "Who is it from?"

Shaking her head, Jaimee said, "I have no idea. It has your address but not your name. The man *did* say it was for you but there isn't any return address or a name or any logo anywhere on the package."

"He knew it was for me but it's not labeled that way?"

"Isn't that what I said?"

"Uh, yeah...it's just...strange. Government or military packages usually have markings—"

"It's a plain package," Jaimee said, a mischievous look on her face, "It isn't filled with dirty pictures from the woman who wore you out, is it?"

Merlin shook his head, an amused smile on his lips, "No, it's not–"

"So there *was* a woman."

"No. And stop it."

Jaimee giggled

Merlin shifted Jigs again and the cat yawned. Squeezing him with affection, Merlin was tired and he said, "Don't worry, we'll get you home in a minute." He looked at Jaimie and gestured with his chin to the package, "Can you open it?"

Shrugging, Jaimee said, "Sure. Just a sec." She disappeared inside for a moment and came back, slitting the tape on the edges of the box with a silver letter opener. Palming the opener, she then flipped open the lid, looked in– and blinked.

Merlin moved his head to see past the top that was in the way of him seeing what she was looking at, "What is it?"

Looking up at him, Jaimee blinked again with no words. Then she looked back in the box, reached in and lifted something toward her eyes.

"Jaimee?"

She held it up, her voice hushed, "This is the French Legion of Honor medal." Her eyes lowered as she looked in the box, "And there are two other medals in here...."

Merlin closed his eyes. He had turned down the medals because he was supposed to be an unknown quantity and he didn't want *any* kind of record about him anywhere. But he had allowed Sherrell and Saab to receive theirs because they had put their lives on the line without a single thought for their own safety. He grimaced as he opened his eyes, "Can you–?"

Jaimee held a hand up, put the medal back inside, closed the box and lifted Merlin's elbow so she could slip the box under his arm, "I understand. Mums the word."

Merlin used his elbow to press the box against his side and hold it in place. He wasn't sure what to say.

Moving in and grabbing the lapels of his shirt, Jaimee pressed her warm lips against his and held them there for a long moment. When she broke off the passionate kiss, she looked into this eyes, "That's for whatever you did. And we won't talk about it again." She stepped back into the doorway and pushed another strand of hair behind an ear, "Now you take Jigs home to his own bed. And let me know when you need a baby sitter again. Okay?"

Merlin nodded, his face flushed from the kiss and his voice quiet, "Yeah. Thanks for taking care of him." He turned and headed down the hallway. He turned when she called his name softly again.

Jaimee was leaning out the open doorway, "Keep in mind that massage. And if you play your cards right, you'll get everything one of those massage parlors over in Vanier will give you. If you know what I mean?" Her soft laughter was cut off by the closing door.

Merlin stood there for a moment, thinking. Then he turned and began walking back to his apartment. He gave the Chartreux a tight hug, "You know Jigs, I can put my life on the line as The Stopper...but I'm still afraid to make a mistake with a woman. Go figure."

Jigs purred softly.

Did you love *Economic Hitman*? Then you should read *Box Set: Rory Mack Steele Thrillers Books 1-12* by Eugene Lloyd MacRae!

Now in a single box set - 855,000 words - the first twelve action-packed thrillers in the Rory Mack Steele series. Like fast-paced thrillers? Then you'll love to go along with Private Detective Rory Mack Steele and his sister Skye Steele in a set of adventures that will keep you turning the pages.

Read more at eugenelloydmacrae.com.

Also by Eugene Lloyd MacRae

A Rory Mack Steele Novel
Betrayal
Storm
Hunted
Stealing a Country
Fire Plague
Jewel
The Echelon Mind
The Chinese President
Knights of The Golden Circle
Cruise
Mask
The Overstolz Code
Box Set: Rory Mack Steele Thrillers Books 1-12

The Stopper Files
Iron Pipeline
Economic Hitman

Watch for more at eugenelloydmacrae.com.

www.ingramcontent.com/pod-product-compliance
Lightning Source LLC
Chambersburg PA
CBHW020441270626
47155CB00022B/836